ANCHORED

Anne-Marie Jewel

To
Bryan & Dani
aka
"Coach"
love y'all

Acknowledgments

This project has been years in the making and I cannot express enough gratitude to friends and family who have been a part of this journey with me.

God~ I love You. Thank You. Let's do this!

Ed and Janis Russo~ Your love for God and for one another is inspiring. I cannot express my gratitude for sharing your story of long faith and healing and allowing me to adapt it to fit these characters and the story. Thank you for all the bits contained within these pages that breath your messages. Thank you for being real, your transparency and honesty, and loving every person who walks through your doors with unconditional love, acceptance, and forgiveness. You both have impacted our family immeasurably, and we are so beyond grateful God planted us in the WC at Life Church. Love you both very much!

Bryan and Darci D'Onofrio, Greg Bales, and the entire drama team~ Your encouragement and endless support have given me the confidence I so desperately needed to step out into this new adventure. I'm so grateful for the time we shared together; the laughs, the prayers, the tears. Those years molded me, and I will be forever grateful that God directed me to a group of weirdos who accepted me with open arms (especially at a time when I was vulnerable and afraid of rejection.)

Heather Schneider~ My dear sweet friend, thank you for going on this journey with me! Thank you for your enthusiasm and love for these characters. This was such a fun experience to walk through with you. Can't wait for the next one!

Lisa Healy~ Wow! Who would have thought we would be here when I dropped Pey off on her first day of 1st grade! Thank you so much for all of your help! You're the best editor and a literary genius, and I'm so glad God directed me to you.

Christian Balderas and ALTR Worship~ I have no words, mostly because yours are always better. I'm just so beyond happy for you all and I feel like God really must love us more (even tho I know He doesn't play favorites) for planting you as our house worship leaders. Love you all so much and thank you for allowing me to put a piece of your heart into this.

Life Church~ My "red earth of Tara" and my best friends within ~ I get to do life with the best of the best.

Suzanne Conyers~ Your input and help with the design of the cover means the world to me! I love working with you and I look forward to some more opportunities down the road!

My David ~ My love, my rock, the stability I need to keep me grounded. Your support (now and over the past 20 years together) means the world to me. Thank you for always having my six, you know I've got yours. You're my best friend, the love of my life, and the best dad to our kids that I could have ever asked for. Your encouragement and faith in me completing this kept me going. Thank you for believing in me. I love you the mostest of all. You're the best.

ONE

Sweat ran down Alex Murphy's forehead and streamed down his nose before it came to a rest at the tip, gradually becoming so heavy it dropped onto his soaked jersey. His team, sluggish from heat and exertion, found relief under the shade of the tent on the sidelines. Alex took a sip from his water bottle and rallied the players together. "Hey guys, we're killing it out there. Listen, we just need one goal to tie this thing up and it's still anyone's game. But we also need to keep them from scoring. We're going to keep three in the back; Carrie, you good with moving to right mid?" Carrie was quite new to the game of soccer and had no clue what position Alex was referring to, but being his biggest fan and cheerleader, she nodded her head in agreement as she delicately dabbed sweat off her face with a towel. Determined to best the opposing team, Alex continued to review a defensive formation with his fatigued players.

On the opposite bench, the other team was strategizing how to land a game-securing goal. "I don't have to remind anyone here this is a championship game," coach Joshua Levingston said. He was determined to beat Alex, his biggest rival this season. "Everyone on this team deserves to be here after an insanely incredible season, and we can't give up now. We're up by one goal, but it will just take one from them to tie it. We need another point and this game is ours."

Renae Rivera squinted to see Joshua, her hand above her eyes to block out the sun. The clouds were motionless today, providing little relief to the players. Occasionally, her focus would shift from her team to the opposite bench, her eyes fixed on Alex. Recognizing that his star player was distracted by the presence of her ex-husband, Joshua called her out. "Renae, you good?"

Renae's attention shifted back to her team. "Yeah, score and shut them down. Let's win this thing!"

The sides huddled up and chanted their team cheers together one last time. The referees tossed their water bottles to the side and slowly jogged to their places. "Good luck, man." Joshua shook his close friend Alex's hand as they headed back on the field for their final twenty minutes of play.

"Thanks. You too. But I think you have the advantage on your team this season." Alex nodded his head in Renae's direction. Renae had more experience playing the game than all of Alex's players combined. And she was good.

The game pressed on and possession shifted between teams frequently. Shots were taken and blocked or missed, fouls were called, and both teams were losing energy. With two minutes left on the clock, pressure was rising, and players and spectators were shouting. Joshua controlled the ball on his side of the field and was quickly overcome by three players, leaving Renae open on the left. Seeing that this was his best chance of scoring, Joshua booted the ball to his teammate, who ran full speed towards the goal. Carrie, seeing an opportunity to impress Alex, sprinted to catch Renae. The players charged behind as the goalie backed up to save an attempted shot. Renae's vision was solely focused on the goal. She neared the box and prepared to shoot when suddenly a foot met her ankle and she fell forward over the ball and onto the sharp blades of plastic turf. Her chest felt hollow as she tried to catch her breath. A whistle sounded as she saw a blur of yellow and black walk towards her. As she stood up, tiny pieces of rubber from the turf stuck to the sides of her hot, red cheeks and knees. Tension escalated quickly, both on and off the field while Renae's nose began to itch out of irritability. Unaware of who tripped her, she adjusted her sock and shin guard. Joshua approached and tried to block her view as the referee raised a yellow card in front of a shocked Carrie, but he wasn't successful in hiding the perpetrator. Renae shook her head in frustration as Joshua tried to refocus her attention on the game. Of course it would be Carrie. Renae knew Carrie had eyes for Alex, and she would do anything to impress him and destroy Renae. At least that's how Renae perceived things.

Carrie looked to Alex and apologized for not knowing any rule about 'intentionally tripping players.' Alex placed his hand on Carrie's shoulder, assuring her it was okay. Renae could feel her entire body flush with rage.

"Make a wall!" Alex instructed to his players. "She can hit this!" Renae glared at her ex-husband as she placed the ball in front of her for a penalty kick. Her anger rose as she thought of how kind and sensitive his reaction was towards Carrie when she maliciously and illegally took her out. The more she looked at him, the more irrational she became. She looked to her best friend, Joshua, who could clearly read her mind. He shook his head and mouthed "no" to her. Her breaths slow and heavy, Renae resigned herself to retribution. With Alex and his team still preparing for her shot, she drew back her strongest foot and planted it to the ball. Alex fell to the ground, the wind knocked out of him.

Now, if there's one thing a southern girl learns growing up, it's where to hit a boy where it hurts. And Renae Rivera was a southern girl with impeccable aim.

As she looked down at her ex-husband doubled over in pain, a small smile swept across her face. The referee, exhausted from the heat, fouls and tension, repeatedly blew his whistle in Renae's face, his arm extended with a yellow card.

"Why are you giving me a yellow card? I heard your whistle! It's not my fault he wasn't ready!"

"You heard no such thing! That was malicious, intentional and uncalled for!"

"You're uncalled for," Renae said to his face.

The referee fumbled in his pocket and drew a red card. "Off the field!"

Renae glanced at her ex-husband trying to hide his pain. Carrie was already by his side. The referee blew his whistle again. "Off!" he commanded.

Renae turned around and passed Joshua, who was standing directly behind her. "Happy now? You threw away that shot," he scolded.

"There's like a minute left!" she shouted. "Just play defense! You won the game! You won your championship, be happy! I'm happy! I'm so happy I'd give you a hug, but you kinda look like you're a little mad at me right now...so, I'm just gonna grab Maddy and wait for the whistle."

Joshua shook his head and turned to check on his old friend as Renae exited the field to find her mother and daughter. She quickly found her pink-faced and sweaty six-year-old who was dressed in both teams' colors, her curly hair in a single ponytail, holding the hand of an older version of Renae. "What? Why are you looking at me like that?" Renae asked her mother as she grabbed the hand of her little girl.

"I'm not saying a word," replied her mother. Ruth Rivera was a short and civilized woman raised in the South. Her thin red lips curled in disapproval as she dropped into her bright pink camping chair, folded her arms, and looked straight ahead to the activities on the field.

"Mommy, is Daddy going to die?"

"No, baby, he's going to be fine. See, Uncle Josh is helping him up. He just needs an ice pack. He's fine."

"He may not ever be able to have kids again!" yelled Ruth to the girls beside her.

Madeline hugged her mother's waist and spoke with as much sincerity as a 6-year-old could muster. "Mommy, I know that was an accident and it was a bad call." Renae looked down at her daughter, who was staring back with her innocent brown eyes. Maddy looked up to Renae and only thought the best of her, even in her worst moments.

Even though Renae and Alex were no longer together, he was Maddy's father, and this sweet little girl loved both parents unconditionally. Renae began to feel a slight twinge of guilt. They heard the final whistle blow and the fans of Joshua's team erupted in cheers over their victory. Renae stalled before rejoining her teammates for a series of post-game photos and the trophy ceremony. She didn't want to be forced to shake hands with Alex or Carrie.

The referees gathered their equipment and exited the field, relieved their day on the pitch was finished. "Man, I really hate reffing these church leagues. They're the worst."

"Congratulations, Coach." Renae jumped on Joshua's back and they headed across the long stretch of green fields to pick up their trophies. Joshua was no longer mad at his best friend, especially since he knew she had a huge part in his team winning the championship. He turned to her and wrapped his arm around her as Alex and his team followed behind them. Alex had physically recovered, but the sight of Renae and Joshua together hurt him even more. No matter how many times Joshua insisted they were still just friends, Alex interpreted their recent behavior otherwise. His somber spirit lifted quickly as soon as his team surrounded him, celebrating their second-place victory. They had fought hard to get to there, and they were all thankful for the leadership of their coach.

After the team photos were over, Renae headed to her car with Ruth and Maddy. Joshua lingered behind with players who wanted individual pictures taken with him and the trophy. Overheated, the ladies waited in the car for their remaining passenger to finish. Since Maddy didn't get a chance to see her father after the game, Renae told her they could wait for Alex as well. When they settled the details of their divorce, Alex and Renae pledged to be supportive of one another when it came to their relationship with their daughter. They both agreed they each had a significant role in her life as parents, and neither of them wanted to ruin that for their little one. Renae watched from her rearview mirror as Alex and Joshua walked towards the parking lot with their respective trophies in tow, their teams scattered behind.

"I hope some of the poor sportsmanship around here doesn't keep you from playing next season," Joshua remarked to Alex. "You put together a really good team with some great players."

"Yeah, thanks for organizing all this and inviting me to coach; it was a lot of fun," Alex replied. "We'll definitely join you again next year if you're still doing it. Probably won't invite a couple of the players back, but we'll see. What about you? You inviting the Beast to be back on your team?"

"She's the reason I'm holding this trophy."

"Yeah, well, she's a free agent. If you didn't invite her, I might have. Maybe she could take out her vindictiveness on someone else. What the hell set her off?"

"Your 5'2" cheerleader. The trip. You and she. Together."

Alex threw his head back in disbelief. "Believe me, nothing going on there."

"I'm staying out of it. You coming to the party tonight?"

A stone cold Renae walked up to the boys as Madeline threw her arms around her daddy. "I'll take the trophy to the car, will you grab Maddy?" Renae quietly asked Joshua. Her body position strategically closed off Alex so she wouldn't be forced to look at him nor face him. Joshua nodded as he handed off his prize to Renae, who was eager to retreat.

"Hey baby girl," Alex dropped everything to pick up his daughter and hold her tight. "Yeah, I plan on it," he replied to Joshua's question about the party.

"Daddy, I think Mommy is sorry she hit you and you can't have babies anymore. It was an accident."

"I know it was. Besides, who needs more babies when I have my hands full with you?!" He squeezed his little girl tight and tickled her sides. She squealed and laughed in delight.

"You're all sweaty, Daddy! Can you come have ice cream with us?"

"Who says we're stopping for ice cream?" Joshua poked at his favorite wiggle worm's back, making her squirm and laugh so loud she caught the attention of bystanders nearby.

"Mommy...said...we could...have...ice cream!" Madeline cried out between giggles.

An attractive woman standing nearby approached the two men. Joshua's interest was piqued. "You know, I have mixed feelings about children growing up with two dads, but you two seem to be doing a great job with her. She's absolutely precious and I can see how much you both truly love her. God bless you and your little family." Joshua's face felt hot as he watched the beautiful stranger walk away.

"Wait, did she think we're together?! I'm not with him!"

"Honey, grab our things, would you?" Alex playfully yelled to Joshua while Alex carried Madeline to her mother's car. "Sweetheart, I'm going to skip out on ice cream today, but how about we get some next weekend."

"Pinky promise." Madeline agreed and she wrapped her pinky finger around her daddy's.

Renae sat in her grey sports sedan with the air conditioning on full blast, wearing an oversized sweatshirt she found in the trunk. She saw her ex-husband's legs in the rearview mirror and rolled her eyes. "Mom, can you put Maddy in her car seat? Alex is bringing her over and I really don't feel like seeing him right now."

"No, what you don't feel like doing is confronting the feelings you have for the person you attacked out there on that field," her mother retorted as she opened the door to greet her former son-in-law.

"What?!" Renae rolled her eyes as her mother closed the door. She didn't have any feelings for Alex. Okay, so she still found him handsome. Extremely handsome. And he wasn't in bad shape for being a middle-aged dad. Lately he treated her with respect and was an absolute gentleman, even through the divorce. And the way he treated their daughter, well, he was Maddy's hero. Renae hated that she viewed him this way. But so what if she did; it didn't mean she had feelings for him. There was a reason why she left him. She put on her sunglasses, turned up the volume on her car stereo and slouched in her seat until her passengers were ready.

"Hey, Mom," Alex greeted his former mother-in-law with a hug and a kiss on the cheek.

"Hey, hon. You could use a shower." She lovingly tapped Alex's cheek. "My little girl didn't hurt you too badly, did she?"

"Physically or emotionally?" Ruth moaned in disapproval. "No, my ego may be a little bruised, but it's nothing I can't get over. And I'm feeling 110% better now that I get to see you."

"Well, we miss having you around. Come see us sometime, okay. We'll send Sourpuss to her room and the four of us can have a nice dinner."

"Sounds like a plan. You just let me know when and I'll be there. And between you and me" he leaned over to whisper in Ruth's ear, "I kind of would like Sourpuss to stay." Ruth gave him a smile and shook her head. She would never understand how her daughter let Alex go, but their affairs were none of her business, as her daughter constantly reminded her.

"See you tonight, man," Joshua called to Alex as he shut the trunk to the car and headed to the passenger side of Renae's car.

Alex gave his daughter one last kiss on her rosy cheek and squeezed her tightly. His heart broke at the thought of not seeing her again until the following week. Divorce was hard. Not seeing your precious child each day made it twice as hard. Once he saw she was buckled safely into her booster, he closed the door, waved, picked up his bag and trophy, and made his way across the parking lot to his own car.

Renae watched in the rearview mirror as Alex walked away. *Focus, Renae*, she internally challenged herself. When she saw her passengers were ready, Renae pulled out of the parking lot, determined to stop looking back.

* * *

One of the benefits of living in this rural town in Florida was the art showcased across the sky each evening. Tonight, the canvas was covered in hues of blue and pink, creating a soft vision of cotton candy as the sun began to set. Renae dug through her purse in the passenger seat to find her sunglasses while she navigated through the neighborhood to reach Joshua's house. Hours had passed since the team took the league championship, and a few teams made plans to celebrate the close of the season with appetizers and dinner at a local restaurant. Renae pulled into the driveway of Joshua's slender but cozy two-story stucco house, and headed to the door. Joshua greeted Renae with a hug and a beagle at his heels. It was always hard to tell who was more excited to see her, Joshua or the beagle.

"Come on in, I just need to get my shoes on."

Renae met Joshua Levingston when they were ten. They both had moved into a new town during grade school and didn't know anyone, but they discovered their friendship on the soccer field and had been inseparable ever since. They experienced happiness and heartbreak together: graduations, weddings, miscarriages, births, deaths, and divorce. Through the years, over miles near and far, they were always there for each other. This season was no exception. Renae was just so thankful their homes were in the same zip-code again since he moved back into town after his wife passed away. His was the shoulder she cried on, the ear she vented to, and the heart who hurt with her during and after the divorce. His were also the arms and the voice that lifted her up when she fell.

Renae followed Joshua down the small entryway hallway, pausing at the corner table which featured a 4x6 photo of Joshua, his wife Angie, and Milo their beagle. Angie's head was tossed back as the sun caught the golden hues of her blonde hair. The joy on her face reflected the love in her heart. Joshua was staring at his bride, his hand on her belly. His love for her was evident by the way he looked at her. Milo was sitting attentively for the camera. His black hair had accumulated some white in it since Renae took this photo on a weekend trip with Alex and her friends. This picture marked a point in their lives when they were much happier, and life was less complicated. It was taken before a major turning point in all their lives.

"Where did you find this picture?"

"It was tucked away in a book Angie had. I was about to donate some things I didn't need and I found it in a box," Joshua replied as he stood from the bench next to the table, shoes on and ready to go.

"That was a good trip," Renae reflected. "Milo, look how tiny you were!" Milo jumped at Renae, his white-tipped tail wagging eagerly.

"Yeah, I thought it would look better framed than hiding in a box." Joshua looked over Renae's shoulder to peek at the picture.

"It's beautiful; it should be out. Besides, this place is becoming one big showroom of a mancave. I could seriously put this in Man Cave Digest. And it's so clean!"

"I just hired a new housekeeper. There's no way I could keep up with this on my own. So, you ready to go?" Joshua ushered Renae towards the front door and held it open for her. Milo watched as his master walked through the door and shut it behind him. He sat down and whimpered. Milo loved his master and hated being alone.

"That's a cute outfit, by the way, is it new?" Joshua noted as he slid into the passenger seat of Renae's car. There were few people Renae could ride as a passenger with, and Joshua was not one of them.

"Kind of, I just needed an occasion to wear it," replied Renae.

"It looks great, and I'm glad you're showing off your arms."

"Oh, shut up, whatever," Renae shot back.

She had chosen a navy and white striped wide-leg jumpsuit and paired it with a white, sleeveless denim vest, exposing her tan arms. Her tan was the only thing she liked about her arms. She always felt they were too big. Joshua was so supportive whenever she pointed out her insecurities.

"I'm a guy, the closest thing you have to a man in your life, and if I have a positive opinion about the way you look, I'm going to tell you," he responded.

Renae smiled. She liked his compliments. "Well, you look extremely handsome, so I guess we're going to look like quite the couple tonight." Joshua and Renae liked to make a monthly habit of dressing up and going out together. Neither of them was interested in finding romance, which made them completely compatible in their shared single status.

Joshua hesitated to speak for much of the short-distanced trip. He was deep in thought about how to approach the fact Alex would be there as well as Renae's potential reaction. He truly loved the laid-back, fun-loving side of her. Her quiet and irritated side worried him.

"So, you know we're not the only team that's going to be there, right?" he began.

Renae nodded her head. "Yeah, I know."

"That includes Alex's team." He turned to observe Renae's reaction. She came to a stop at the red light and put her hands in her lap, the sound of her bangles hitting each other breaking the momentary silence.

"They're together, aren't they? Alex and Carrie."

Joshua tried to cut her off, but she kept talking, looking straight ahead. "You're telling me so I'm not surprised or hurt when I see them together, aren't you?"

"No, Renae, they're-"

"You don't think I'm over him, and since he's moved on *and* he'll be there with Carrie, you're afraid I'm going to flip out, aren't you?!"

"Renae, no, stop, listen-"

"I'm a big girl, Joshua, I can handle the two of them together. Alex and I are over, he can date whomever the hell he wants, even if she is a prissy little-"

Joshua interrupted her. "They're *not* dating! They're not together! I just wanted you to know since you had such a knee-jerk reaction to seeing them play a soccer game together and almost crippled the guy!" Renae remained silent as she pulled into the parking lot and found an open space beside the restaurant. "And now you're mad."

"I'm not mad."

"I know you, you're mad."

"I'm not mad! Don't tell me I'm mad when I'm not mad! What the heck, Josh? Why did you even have to bring him up?" She turned the ignition off and exited the car, frustrated. Joshua unbuckled and raced to meet her before she made her way into the restaurant.

"Renae." Joshua called to her as he caught up to her and grabbed her arm to turn her towards him. "Renae! Just wait a second. Look, you're going to have to face him whether you like it or not. Alex is a part of your life and he always will be. You two share a beautiful daughter, someone you both love deeply, and you're going to have to figure out how to navigate through her highest and lowest moments together." Renae had a hard time focusing on her friend's face. However, the thought of her daughter and the relationship they all had with her softened her attitude. "I'm just suggesting maybe an apology is in order, to keep the tension at bay?" He cupped her cheeks and bent towards her to catch her eyes. "You're going to have to talk to him eventually."

Renae looked up at her friend. His dark brown eyes melted through her tough exterior. She stared at him in silence. Others would be intimidated by this cold deep stare, but Joshua knew Renae, and he knew she was earnestly thinking this through.

"Okay, fine, I'll apologize." Joshua wrapped his arms around her in a warm embrace." I hope you don't mind me drinking in front of all of your church friends," she mumbled.

"Believe me, no one will judge. A few may be jealous." He released her from the embrace and wrapped his arm around her shoulder to escort her to the door.

"Well, I really don't give a crap what people think-"

"Well I think that's obvious," Joshua replied, matter-of-factly. "We're here for the soccer party," he told the hostess inside the door.

"Right this way," the hostess gave them a friendly smile and walked them towards the back of the restaurant. Just over a dozen players were already gathered, some sitting, some standing. Renae scanned the group as she made her way to them and her eyes locked with Alex's. He looked annoyed. He immediately turned away from her and engaged in conversation with someone near him.

"Congratulations, Renae! Joshua!" Tabitha Benson, a warm and friendly player on one of the teams, jumped out of her seat and greeted Renae with an enthusiastic hug. "I just knew your team would win the championship when Josh said he recruited you! You're so good!" Tabitha was so cheerful. *Too cheerful*, Renae thought. She was going to need a couple drinks tonight.

"Aww, thanks," an uncomfortable Renae didn't know what to say. She didn't know how to receive compliments from people very well, especially when she couldn't reciprocate them. Tabitha was a terrible player.

"Do you have somewhere to sit already?"

Fidgeting with her hair, Renae looked to Joshua. "Um,

no, I don't think-"

"Here, sit with us!" Tabitha removed her purse from the seat next to hers and offered it to Renae. Tabitha's husband, Greg, made his way to Joshua and offered his hand, congratulating him.

"Okay, thanks," Renae said as she sat down. The empty seat on the other side of her was taken already, so Joshua claimed the chair directly across from her. The table for eight had another table set up next to it, with eight booths surrounding them. Blue and white balloons that matched the winning team's colors stretched to the ceiling from several chairs. An appetizer buffet was set up for the group in a small room next to them, adorned with the same balloons and other soccer-themed decorations, including a three-tiered cake as a centerpiece.

Renae hated functions, especially those with large groups of people. She avoided small talk because she was awful at it. She felt out of place and slightly anxious. Even talking to other people on her team was difficult for her when they weren't playing a game.

"What can I get you to drink?" a friendly server asked Renae as she laid a napkin down in front of her.

"I'll..." she glanced around to see what everyone else was drinking. "I'll have a water, no lemon, please."

"And are we on a separate check or with someone else?"

"She's on mine," Alex said as he sat down next to her with a half empty pint of beer in his hand. "You can put him on mine too," he added as he gestured to Joshua.

Renae stared at the table as her awkward situation just became worse. Outside of today's game she and Alex hadn't spent over five minutes with each other since they separated and finalized their divorce seven months ago. They did a good job avoiding each other and barely spoke when he picked up Maddy every other weekend. And now he was sitting with her, paying for her dinner five hours after she intentionally planted a soccer ball to his man parts. Was he trying to be nice? What were his motives? She couldn't concentrate on anything around her outside of the laughter of the couple next to her. Why were they laughing? She saw hands shake across the table, heard the words "winners tonight," "loser," and "chicken wings." She could only concentrate on the familiar scent of men's cologne that had suddenly filled the atmosphere around her when her ex-husband sat down, and it made her uncomfortable. "Do you want me to fix you a plate?" Joshua said as he stood up and Renae refocused her attention.

"Um, no. That's okay, I'll get something in a minute."

Joshua smiled at Renae, glanced at Alex, and gave Renae a wink only she noticed. As Joshua walked to the adjoining room, Renae noticed Carrie was cornered in a booth laughing with a couple of girlfriends. It didn't appear she was there with Alex after all. Renae felt like a jerk for jumping to conclusions and for how she had been treating him. Here she was sitting next to this incredibly handsome guy she shared a child and a life with, who did nothing but honor her and their marriage for 16 years. He was hardworking, honest, and sincere in everything he did. The pressures of parenthood, work, distractions outside their marriage, and individual ambitions just became too much to juggle, and their arguments turned into full-blown fights. Walking away seemed so much easier than working on their relationship at the time.

"Parents have Maddy tonight?" Alex asked.

"No, she's sleeping in the car." *Oh my God, Renae! What is wrong with you?!* She scolded herself.

Alex took a sip of his drink, stared at his cup, and contemplated moving to another table. He looked around for someone else to engage in conversation with.

"Sorry, yeah, um, she's with Mom and Dad. She was pretty exhausted after all that sun today so I'm sure it will be an early night for her tonight."

"It was pretty hot out today. I'm sure the sun drained

her."

"Yeah." After pausing a moment, she continued, "You got some sun on your cheeks."

"I got some on my arms too," Alex pointed out as he pulled up his sleeve to show off the tan line on his bicep.

"Mm-hmm." Renae grinned as she turned her head the opposite direction, trying to hide her smile. She liked his arms. She liked everything about him, which made the situation more uncomfortable. Alex was the first and only love of her life, and she vowed after the divorce she would never let anyone get close to her again. Today, his ongoing presence shook her. Keeping him at a distance and giving him the "ice queen" treatment would be a struggle this evening. Regardless of the hell they put each other through in the past, she still felt incredibly and undeniably drawn to him. She wished to herself he would walk away, even as much as she wanted him to stay.

"You look nice," Alex added.

"Thanks." Renae began to fidget. Alex could see her knee jumping as she started to bounce her foot up and down.

"You okay?"

"Yeah. You know how uncomfortable I am in crowds, and this crowd is just getting bigger." She had a nervous chuckle as she looked down in her lap and played with her bangles. She and Alex realized she was wearing the bangles he bought for her for their last Valentine's Day together. She put her arm down at her side.

"Will this relax you?" he offered her some of his beer.

"Seriously? Yes, please! I really didn't feel comfortable ordering drinks when no one else was drinking, especially since I don't know any of these people."

"You're fine," Alex assured her and Renae finished his beer in two large gulps, spilling some down the side of her lip. She wiped her face with the inside of her wrist and then proceeded to wipe her wrist on her pant leg. Handing Alex his glass, she let out a large breathy belch. Alex smiled at her as memories of their bar-hopping days as young adults returned to him. *Still the lady*, he thought.

"Thanks, I needed that." The server was back with Renae's water and Joshua's soda. Alex motioned that he'd take another beer. Joshua was on his way back to the table trying to read the faces of his friends. He couldn't tell if they had made amends or not and when he sat down with an assortment of appetizers, Renae didn't realize how hungry she was. She excused herself from the table and headed to the buffet.

"So, everyone getting along okay?" Joshua inquired, smiling as he cut a Swedish meatball in half. Alex leaned in with both arms on the table so he could get close to Joshua.

"What's the deal with you two?" Alex stared Joshua down.

"Um, what are you talking about?"

"I saw you outside. You seem to be getting a little closer than just friends." Alex's face became stern.

"Hey, no, man, no, it's not like that with us, you know that." Joshua put his fork down so he could focus on Alex and whatever he was being accused of.

"So you're not playing the hopeless romantic widow moving in on the divorcee best friend and trying to steal the family you never had? Because that's what it's starting to look like." The two friends were starting to capture an audience in the company around them.

"Alex, I would never...no!" He couldn't believe what Alex was insinuating and he could feel his anger rise. "Hopeless romantic widow? Dude, that's cold!"

"So is doing whatever it is that you're doing with your friend's wife."

"Ex-wife and don't forget who the real friends are in this circle." Joshua was preparing to throw verbal punches Alex's way.

Renae stood at the buffet table and looked at the food set before her. Nothing looked very appetizing, and she was trying to avoid foods that would bloat her. She decided fruits and veggies would be her safest bet. She turned to see if Joshua needed more wings and saw the boys face-to-face in a heated discussion. She put a few wings on a separate plate, grabbed some napkins and headed back to the table. Taking her seat next to Alex, she placed the plate of buffalo wings between the two men as their server placed a beer between Renae and Alex. Both men refused to break eye contact with one another. Biting on a strawberry, Renae's eyes shifted between the guys before resting on Joshua. She began to bounce her foot nervously and Alex placed his hand on her knee to make it stop. She grabbed his beer and began to indulge. She had no idea what caused the tension between the two men, but it could be cut with a knife. And it was making some people around them, especially Renae, uncomfortable.

"Alex," Renae interrupted the awkward silence, "can I talk to you for a minute?" She figured the best way to end the tension was to break it, and now was a good time to extend the apology she owed him.

"Yup," replied Alex who was still staring at Joshua. He reached for his glass and brought it to his lips. It was over half empty. Releasing eye contact with Joshua, he glanced at Renae who let out another wind-filled burp.

"Sorry," she whispered. "Can we go somewhere like a corner or an empty booth or something?"

Renae was horrible at apologizing. Just the thought of it and whom she had to apologize to made her stomach flip. She was glad she now had some liquid courage to help her get through it. Joshua took the napkin from his lap and tossed it on the table, sitting back in his chair. He looked around and found some of the players from his team to talk to. The company around them returned to their conversations and Alex and Renae quickly found themselves sitting alone at the table.

"Well it looks like everyone around us bailed, want to just stay here and talk?"

"Yeah, sure," Renee was so nervous. She could feel sweat begin to drip down her back. "Want some fruit or wings? They just brought them out."

"I'm good, I'm trying to watch my abs of steel," Alex joked while he poked his stomach out. Renae let out a short pigeon laugh and rolled her eyes. "So, what do you need to talk about? Do you need to switch weekends with Maddy? Give me full custody of her?" Renae knew as much as he would love that, he wasn't serious. They both had agreed Maddy needed more time with her mom and grandparents to fill her needs at this stage in her life.

"No, um, it isn't about Maddy. Oh my gosh, this is so hard. Why is this hard?!" She piqued his interest. Alex leaned in, feeling slightly nervous, dreading what was about to come out of her mouth. He was preparing for the day she would tell him she was moving on with Joshua and he feared this was that moment. He wasn't ready for this.

"I wanted to talk to you about what happened at the field today." Relieved, Alex raised his eyebrows, smiled, and found himself able to relax. He knew where this was going and he knew how hard and uncomfortable it was going to be for his ex-wife. She was getting frustrated and he was enjoying watching her squirm; not because he wanted to see her suffer, but because apologies never came easily or frequently during their years together. "Okay, I can do this. Stop smiling! Why are you smiling?!" She laughed and whined at the same time.

"Here, I won't smile, I'll look at you, straight-faced. Here, how's my angry face? Because I should be angry with you for what you did today."

"I know! You should be! And here you are, being...a perfect gentleman, and I...I'm sorry I was such an asshole. I just saw you and I saw *her* and you were all 'oh it's okay' with her when she tripped me and you put your hand on her shoulder and I got really pissed off, maybe even somewhat jealous, and it was hot and the game was intense, and... I took my anger out on you. And I shouldn't have. I'm really sorry." She stopped babbling and examined Alex's face, trying to decipher his thoughts. He was looking at her completely expressionless which nearly broke her heart. "I just, I don't want to make you mad or make things weird and uncomfortable between the two of us. Well, any more than it already is. I let my temper and insecurities get the best of me today and I was so rude. What I did was uncalled for and not only do I need to say I'm sorry, but I really want...I really *need* you to forgive me."

Alex grabbed her left hand and cupped it in both of his. He just sat and looked at her for a moment, unsure of what to say. If only apologies had been this easy when they were married, they might have avoided years of heartache. There had been so much time splitting the two of them apart, but he just felt so comfortable with her. Her apology, her compliments, her presence...if only she knew how intense his feelings for her still were, and that daily he dreamed and prayed for a reconciliation with her.

"Renae, don't worry about it. Of course I forgive you."

"Thank you," she said, relieved. "I didn't deserve you, you know," she nodded knowingly as she reached for her glass of water.

"You need to discover your worth," he casually replied. He let go of her hand, sat up in his chair and looked at her in the eyes. "You deserve so much more. You're beautiful, smart, and full of life, and I'm sorry I couldn't give you what you needed." Renae's heart rate was increasing. This moment is why she intentionally kept her distance from him. This was one of those moments she wished he would just wrap his arms around her and hold her. As much as she desired intimacy, she was terrible at expressing it. And when these moments passed, her silence always led to sadness and disappointment.

"There is no denying those two should still be together." Tabitha was talking to Carrie and the other girls at Carrie's table. Carrie began to burn with jealousy as she watched the man of her dreams converse with the woman who left him and least deserved him. She continued to observe them while devising a way she could break them apart tonight. Her hope rested in the relationship Renae held with Joshua: that one day they would break down their walls and fall in love. But that didn't seem to be happening by the look of things tonight.

Taking a risk, Renae decided to keep the conversation between them going. "So, you're back in church now? But now you're like, going all the time and joining soccer teams and stuff. Why?"

"I just found some really good and supportive people there who helped me walk through you know...our split. It wasn't the best of times for me and I decided to go back," Alex offered. He could see the withdrawal from Renae in her body language and facial expression as he mentioned their split. He needed to change course and reel her back in. "And the principles taught are pretty practical and you know, I just enjoy it. Helps me be a better man. And father."

"Oh. That's cool. I should probably go back sometime. Mom and Dad have been taking Maddy on Sundays when we have her. She seems to enjoy it, which is good because I do feel she needs those basic foundations to help her grow."

"I completely agree," Alex added. "Maybe the three of us could go together sometime if you're up for it."

They both heard him say it, but they doubted that would ever happen. Although Alex and Renae were raised in church, they decided to stop going shortly after they got married. Their endless Saturday night bar hopping didn't leave room for early Sunday morning services. They preferred to spend their Sunday mornings at local coffee shops or going out for brunch. When Maddy came along, they thought about going back, but never carved out the time to go, except on holidays or the occasional special services her parents would invite them to.

Renae decided to change the subject. "So, what was up with you and Joshua? You guys okay?"

"We're okay, just a misunderstanding. I owe him an apology."

"Where did he go, anyways?" Alex pointed Joshua out to Renae. She excused herself to go see him and make sure he was okay with staying longer for dinner. Joshua was glad to hear she apologized and to see the two speaking to each other again. Renae was the one person left on earth close to him and she meant everything to him. At this stage in their lives, his purpose was her happiness, whether he had the privilege to spend the rest of his life with her or not.

"It looks like Carrie found your empty seat next to Alex," Joshua pointed out to Renae.

"Are you serious? I've been gone for like two minutes." She turned to look but Joshua turned her around to face him. He was mostly concerned with her seeing something between Alex and Carrie that she didn't need to see nor read into.

"You face me, I'll watch and give you the play by play."

"Ok."

"She's smiling, she's playing with her hair and she looks like she's in distress."

"You're joking."

"I wish. He's looking at his watch. Oh, crap, he just looked this way." Renae started to laugh and hit Joshua's chest. "What are you doing?"

"Trying to be inconspicuous," Renae offered.

"It's not working, now he's staring at us. Okay, she's getting up. She's leaning in for a hug."

"Is he hugging her back?"

"He patted her back with one hand. And now she is walking back to her table and he is drinking from your water. And scene!"

"What do you think that was about if there's nothing going on between them?"

"Not sure, I'm not that good at reading lips or minds. But from the look on his face as he's staring at us, I don't think he's done with you tonight." Joshua was cautious of his body language around Renae as Alex looked on. Renae and Joshua returned to their table and the evening progressed with dinner, laughter, and conversations surrounding children, sports, and relationships. Tabitha picked up on how out of place Renae felt, so she focused her attention on Renae's interests as she engaged in small talk with her. Renae liked these people. They were good--although some of them a bit overly friendly--and she felt welcome. More team pictures were taken and Renae showed those gathering at her table how to share the pictures with each other on their phones and social media. Alex and Renae kept close to each other when they weren't away from their table for most of the evening. In between conversations with other people, the former couple enjoyed showing one another candid pictures of their daughter captured on their phones. Renae also enjoyed sitting shoulder to shoulder with Alex, and intentionally kept his attention so she could feel his presence beside her. Alex relished the time spent looking at pictures of his daughter, but he found the time in Renae's presence, who was continuously pushing her hair to the side as he looked over her shoulder, more enjoyable.

Having coached the winning team and organized the league, Joshua spent the evening talking to other coaches about ways to improve the following season and attract more talent and teams. Finally spotting Joshua alone, Alex excused himself to engage him. They still needed to clear up their misunderstanding from earlier.

"You have a minute?" Alex asked as he cornered Josh.

"Sure, what's up?" Joshua was still a little cautious around Alex after some of the harsh things he said earlier in the night.

"I, uh, I owe you an apology for the shit I said earlier. I was jealous and the comments and accusations were way out of line. I'm really sorry, friend."

"Don't worry about it. Alex, you know you don't have anything to be jealous about when it comes to Renae and me. We're friends, that's the way it's always been and always will be." Alex nodded his head. He'd known Josh and Renae long enough to know they would do just about anything for each other and would always be a part of one another's lives. "Jealous, huh?" Joshua continued with a grin. "So, does that mean you still have feelings for her?"

Alex didn't want to answer that question. He obviously had feelings for her and doubted those would ever go away. But his feelings were deeper than he let on. And they were growing stronger as the night progressed. He looked up from the floor and casually answered his friend. "Well, she's a tough one to get over. It's all still pretty fresh. So, yeah, I do."

Joshua stared at his friend and nodded his head. He tried to digest the thought of an Alex and Renae reunion. A reunion between the two of them would mean he would have to relinquish a part of her that he didn't want to let go of. He had no interest in giving up his treasured time and relationship with her, not even for Alex. Without a response to offer, Joshua turned their attention back to the table. Renae was carrying on a conversation with Tabitha, but her attention was focused on the two men as they began to walk towards her.

"We good?" Joshua extended his hand to Alex.

"Of course," Alex assured him as he shook his hand. Having smoothed out their misunderstanding, the two felt they were on good terms again. However, Alex still held suspicions on the future of Joshua and Renae's relationship.

Renae looked around and noticed the crowd was slowly dwindling. She glanced at the time on her phone. It was still pretty early, but it had been a long day and she was getting tired. Alex sat next to her as he closed the tab.

"Thanks for picking up dinner tonight," she said to him, smiling. She really enjoyed being in his company throughout the evening. For a moment she forgot about the space they had put between them. She examined every part of his face, stopping at his eyes. Those eyes held her heart for so long. She remembered why she kept her distance; she was afraid of becoming dangerously close to giving into her feelings for him again.

He recognized the look she gave him. It was soft and caring, without walls or boundaries. He missed this look and the affection that came with it.

"Thanks for the talks tonight," Alex replied. "We haven't spent this much time together in what seems like forever. It was really nice."

"Yeah, it was," Renae agreed with a smile.

The former couple stared and smiled at one another. The air between them disappeared and they felt as if they were the only two in the restaurant. *My God, it would be so easy to fall in love with him again,* Renae thought to herself. In spite of all the fights, all the distance, and all the pain, Alex longed to hold her again, especially in this moment.

He felt a hand squeeze his shoulder. He lifted his hand to squeeze the hand back. Renae sat up straight in her chair, her expression shifting from soft and loving to cold and suspicious. Alex snapped back into reality and looked at the young woman the hand on his shoulder was attached to. Carrie was standing next to him, smiling innocently. He quickly let go of her hand.

"Hey, Alex, I'm all set. I'm ready to go when you are," Carrie said in her sweetest voice.

Alex looked at Renae, speechless. Renae cocked her head and gave him a deathly stare. That was the look he was most used to seeing towards the end of their marriage. Usually it preceded harsh language and accusations. He hated being on the receiving end of this side of her. "Yeah...just give me a minute." He began to dig in his pockets for his car keys.

"Renae, I'm really sorry about what happened at the game today. I didn't mean to trip you. I felt so bad. I hope there are no hard feelings." Carrie batted her eyes and gave Renae a sweet smile.

Joshua sat across from the drama, intrigued, and watched as it all played out. He checked for the quickest route to the other side of the table in case he needed to pull Renae off Carrie.

Renae shifted her eyes from Alex to Carrie. She wanted to punch her smile off her perfect little face so bad. Instead, she half smiled and focused back on Alex who was still looking for his keys. Renae slid a set of keys from behind his plate to his lap. She had known him long enough to always know where he laid things down. "Better get your girlfriend home, Alex, it's getting past her bedtime." Her tone was bitter, her voice flat and deep.

"I have to get up early on Sunday mornings. I serve in children's church," Carrie said innocently.

"Of course you do...you can probably relate to them since you're so close in age." Renae stood up and grabbed her bag. She looked to Joshua, who took the cue as "time to leave."

Alex stared at his ex-wife, feeling helpless. The wall was back up and she was cutting him off. "Pray for me," Joshua said to his friend before following Renae out the door.

Renae was intercepted by Tabitha on her way out. Renae forced a smile and hugged her, fighting back emotions. Tabitha had good, strong hugs--unspoken hugs that spoke volumes and softened the hardest of hearts. Renae broke away and smiled at her, wiping away a tear. "It was so good talking to you. I hope we can do it again."

"Yeah, me too," Renae agreed as she wiped away another tear. She was eager to leave before she broke down crying.

"Bye, Josh. Again, congratulations!"

"Thanks, Tabitha." Joshua picked up his pace to catch Renae. They walked to her car in silence. Renae quickly wiped away tears that were streaming down her face to her chin. Joshua knew he was in Alex's view, so he resisted comforting his friend. She needed a moment alone to regroup anyways. She despised pity parties.

Renae took a minute to breathe and collect herself before pulling out of the parking space. "You want me to drive?" Joshua offered.

"No, I'm okay." Renae took a deep breath and proceeded to the exit. She struggled to keep from looking in the rearview mirror, but she couldn't resist. She caught a glimpse of Alex walking out with another guy and Carrie walking behind them. Renae's insides burned as the sight of them made her nauseous. *Was Carrie going back to the house with him? Were they together?* Talking to him tonight was one giant mistake. She let the tears flow down her cheeks and neck. It felt good to cry. Joshua decided the best thing to say was nothing at all. She was having a moment in her head and she needed to work this out in her own silence.

They pulled into his driveway and she put the car in park. Joshua stared at Renae as she looked forward. Her eyes and nose were red. She had stopped crying, but he could tell she was still deep in thought.

"Want to come in for a drink?"

"No," Renae whispered, still staring straight ahead.

"You going to be okay tonight?"

"Yeah." Again, a whisper, but accompanied by a short nod.

"You know I'm here if you need to talk."

"Thanks." Renae turned her head to look at Joshua and gave him a fake smile.

"Come here," Joshua beckoned and Renae reluctantly gave in. She unbuckled her seatbelt and gave him a hug. "Love you little, love you big."

She began to laugh. "No!"

"Say it!"

"I don't want to."

"I'm not letting go until you say it."

"Okay. Love you like a little pig." She brought a smile to Joshua's face. "Happy now?"

"I'm happy when you're happy. So, you hurry up and get happy so I can be happy." He kissed his friend on the forehead and exited the car. Renae watched as he headed to the front door, fiddled with his key, and opened the door to a waiting Milo.

Joshua waved and watched as the taillights of Renae's car disappeared around the corner of his street. He closed the door and shut off the porch light. Staring into the living area of his house, he realized Renae was right. His house needed a woman's touch. He picked up the picture of his family and sat down on the couch. He missed everything about Angie. Her touch, her smile, the way she looked at him. Losing her right after they experienced a major loss together almost broke him. He focused his attention on Renae through her divorce and never fully recovered from the pain of his own loss. He traced Angie's silhouette on the picture with his finger. Her hair, her infectious smile, her perfectly chiseled shoulders and arms. Her belly. His finger stopped as her stared at the picture of his hand on her belly. It was a reminder of their love. Their hope. Their future. Their loss. He wished he could go back in time and freeze it on this one moment of so much happiness and unconditional love.

"Angie, I'm a mess," he said out loud as he laid back in the cushions of the sofa and rested his head and closed his eyes. He held the picture close to his chest and wrapped his arms around it. "Goodnight, Sweetheart. Kiss our little boy for me."

Milo jumped onto the couch and curled himself next to his owner, and they both drifted off to sleep.

T WO

Renae lay wide awake in bed between her cold sheets. She had a difficult time shutting her brain down. All she could do was replay the events of the day involving Alex over and over in her head. Every time she reflected on how much she enjoyed being around him tonight, a vision of Carrie's face appeared in her mind. Renae wished she had hit that flawless face with a soccer ball instead of hurting Alex. But that's pretty much what Renae did, hurt Alex. She never thought the two of them would have the opportunity to enjoy each other's company again like they did tonight. She certainly hadn't thought about them as a couple in so long. Her nose began to itch at the idea of him rounding out his evening with Carrie. Did they go back to his house since Maddy was with her? Did he stay at Carrie's? Does he drive her to church? How long has this been going on between them?

She leaned over to her nightstand, opened the top drawer and pulled out a book, a picture taking the place of a bookmark. She withdrew the picture from its place, the moon providing her only source of light. Turning the picture towards the window, she stared at the happy couple captured in the photo. Alex was looking down at her and smiling adoringly, one arm wrapped around her shoulder. She was leaning on him, her hand on his chest, looking at the camera. This was the only picture of the two of them that she didn't store away. It was taken hours after she announced she was expecting; the radiance on his face reflected his joy, the contentment on hers showed her happiness. She would do anything to relive that day. Gradually, the thick clouds began to shield her light, so Renae placed the picture back in the book and hid it back in her nightstand. She leaned back in her bed, grabbed her pillow and hugged it tight as she closed her eyes and daydreamed about one of the happiest days of her life, hoping it would put her to sleep.

Her thoughts were interrupted by the moonlit bellowing of their backyard bullfrog. He had been extremely vocal about finding a mate over the past couple of weeks, and tonight he started to sound desperate, like the fate of his species was resting entirely on his shoulders.

She heard a series of beeps disarming the alarm on the downstairs keypad. Dad! She jumped out of bed, threw on a hoodie over her pajama top, and went downstairs to check on her father.

Phillip Rivera tiptoed through his backyard dressed in a camouflage cap, vest, and pants with a pellet gun at his side. He crouched behind a tall boulder near the bushes and positioned himself strategically so he could spot the enemy without being detected. He slowly pulled the gun to eye level, just over the boulder. He then spotted the intruder, whose brownish green neck was now protruding as he was engaged in his deep bass call.

"Oh my God, Daddy! Have you lost your mind?" Renae whispered loudly from behind him. Phil held his hand in the air for her to stop and remain quiet. Renae remained quiet but she ignored the call to stop. Crouching next to him, she began to whisper. "Are you really trying to shoot that frog in our own backyard? Daddy that's illegal and inhumane!"

"I'm not trying to shoot it, I'm trying to scare it away. Look, if I shoot there," he pointed a red laser to a place on the rock the frog was resting on, "he'll jump there. And if I shoot over there, he'll jump that way. I need him to jump *that* way so I'm trying to determine where I should aim."

Renae stared speechless at her father. He had lost his mind.

"Look, at my age, this is the only excitement I get

other than when your mom wears a pair of clam diggers and shows off her calves." Renae laughed at her dad. He was blunt, cute, and a complete blast to be around. And he still used the term 'clam diggers.'

"Okay, Daddy, just don't shoot him."

Renae and her father began to orchestrate a way to rid themselves of their backyard guest and to deliver him to their neighbor's yard unnoticed.

"Can't we just catch him and toss him over the fence?" Renae snickered. It sparked an old memory and they both started laughing. "Remember when we first moved in and we used to rescue frogs from our backyard and toss them over the fence so our dogs wouldn't eat them?"

"They would stretch their legs out as they flew through the air over the fence to safety." Phil had a hard time getting the words out, he was chuckling so hard. "What happened again, why did your mom make us stop?"

"Josh..." Renae was laughing to the point it hurt. She finally blurted out, "Josh tried it and didn't make it over the fence! Mom was so mad!"

"Oh, that's right, that was horrible. Terrible, very, very sad." They wiped the tears from the corners of their eyes. They looked behind them as the kitchen light turned on and saw Renae's mother spying out the window at the two of them with a disapproving look on her face.

"We're bad people, Dad."

"Yeah, but we're fun!"

The two kept laughing until their sides hurt.

"Wait, where did the frog go?" Phil shined his flashlight in the yard to locate the perpetrator. The pair squinted, with no frog in sight. Their concentration was so keenly focused on finding the loud amphibian that neither of them noticed the visitor who came to investigate them.

"Crooooooaaaaaakkkkkk" bellowed the bullfrog, two feet from Renae.

"Dad!!!" she screamed as she grabbed her father's arm.

He yelled back, unaware of what she was screaming at. They looked at the frog and burst into laughter again.

"Come on, let's get out of here before the neighbors call Mom again." Renae stood and helped her father off the ground. She scooped up the frog and ran through the yard with him, depositing him in the next-door neighbor's flower bed. She crouched down as she quickly headed back to the house, but not before the neighbor's porch light turned on.

"Dad!"

"Get down and crawl, soldier!" her father called to her.

Renae immediately went down to her belly and started to crawl through the tall grass, looking wide-eyed at her dad. She didn't want to think of the critters that were crawling in the grass with her; her father kept putting off cutting it and she was terrified something would slither her way. Phil watched from around the corner of the house as his neighbor's porch door slowly opened. "Rivera?" Phil ran into the house, leaving his daughter frozen on the ground. Renae flipped over and saw her family's neighbor of twenty-two years standing over her. "What's up, Mr. Reeves? What brings you out at this time of night?"

Renae walked through the door to her kitchen and armed the house. Phil sat at the table and tried his best to keep a straight face.

"You're a terrible commander, leaving me to die with the enemy."

Phil started to chuckle. "He's not the enemy; he's a pastor, a good man."

"Then why did I toss a horny toad in his backyard, Dad?!"

"It beats me! I was trying to scare it off to the neighbor behind us! If you'd just left me alone you wouldn't have embarrassed yourself."

"Yeah, well, now he expects that I will be joining you in church tomorrow."

"Well good, you could use some church after what I

heard you did to poor Alex today."

"And I may have told him you're coming to first service to start serving in the nursery."

"An evil one you are."

"And I wonder where I got that from," Renae joked with her dad.

"Hey, don't talk about your mother like that."

There were two cups of hot cocoa cooling on the counter waiting on them. Ruth had encouraged her husband earlier in the evening to talk to Renae, and she knew the two couldn't pass up a cup of hot cocoa. They had enjoyed their late-night father-daughter talks over the years and it was apparent that Ruth believed it was time for another one.

"So, do you want to talk about what happened today?" Phil asked his daughter.

Renae grabbed the cups and set them down on the kitchen table. She pulled out the chair across from her father and sat. "Which part, Dad? When I physically abused my ex-husband? When he offered to buy Josh and me dinner? When we talked, like *really* talked for the first time since before the divorce and we connected like we used to? Or when he blew me off for his new girlfriend?"

"Sounds like you had quite the emotional roller coaster of a day."

"Yeah," Renae agreed.

"I always liked that boy, Alex. Love him like a son, in fact. He's turned into quite an admirable man and father. It broke my heart when you two decided to separate and not having him around, well, I'm not too macho to admit I miss him. I guess sometimes things just don't work out the way we want them to, and sadly it's easier to cut ties than focus on making things work."

Renae was silent. She was examining her heart to determine exactly what it was she felt for Alex as well. So many feelings had risen back to the surface tonight, feelings she hadn't recognized in years.

Her father's cough snapped her from a daze. "Now, I don't know what the future holds for you and Joshua-"

"Dad, we're just friends."

"Friends don't act the way you two do. You'd think you were a couple, the way you go everywhere together and with how physical you are with each other."

"Dad! No! We're not like that. We're just comfortable with one another and yes, I do love him and he loves me, but not like that. And we're not *physical* with each other. Ugh! Can we not talk about me and Joshua? We're best friends, you know that."

"I've known from the first day he walked into our house that he was smitten with you, but once you met Alex, Josh knew his chances with you were over. I'm a man myself, honey, I can pick up on these things."

"Dad, please don't crush my relationship with Joshua right now."

"Two things: his lost love can't ever come back, yours can. And being with you doesn't hurt Angie, but your being with Joshua hurts Alex. I can see it in his face, dear. Alex hasn't stopped loving you."

Renae's bottom lip began to quiver. Tears began to well in her eyes. Phil stood and walked to his daughter, wrapping an arm around her shoulder. "Daddy, I think we really messed up." She was unable to hold back the tears any longer.

"It's alright, Punkin." He turned and coughed again. "Relationships can be tricky, especially when two people love each other so much but are surrounded by so many distractions. You two just need to come together and find common ground."

"Dad, I was so mean to him." Phil sat next to her, listening intently to every word. "Not just today, but over the last few years we were together. He worked hard and I know he loved me. He loves our daughter. We spent so much time alone together but when Maddy came, I don't think we knew how to focus on each other anymore. I began to lose whom

I thought I was, and I became an absolute bitch to him. He tried so hard to put up with my attitude, but I kept pushing him. Our arguments, our fights, he didn't start them, I did, and you know, he was always the one to apologize. He would try to come up with ways to fix our issues and I refused to listen. And when he wasn't on board with my dream, I decided it was time to leave. Who does that?! I didn't even consider giving him another chance when he asked for it. I just saw him as this authoritarian figure who told me what I could or couldn't do with my life. And that was such a lie! He wasn't like that at all. I see now that he was just trying to work out logistics for our family, but I was so bull-headed that we couldn't communicate. I shut down, and he shut down because that was better than Maddy watching us break things." Renae paused for a moment and gazed into her hot cocoa mug. She concentrated on the tiny bubbles that were slowly bursting around the edge of her drink. "I never told anyone, but there was a moment before the divorce when I think we could have ended the proceedings and pursued our marriage. It was this unspoken moment we shared and all it would have taken was for one of us to submit and speak up, but neither of us could do it. I know I was too proud or scared to say anything, so we ended it. We ended us." Renae turned to her father as she released her heart to him. "Dad, I wish I could go back to that moment and tell him how sorry I was and let him know I still loved him. But I also know I'm so scared of rejection from the one person who always accepted me. Well, the one other person besides you. Deep down I wish I could have a glimmer of hope, but I don't think there's a way to fix it. We're just so damaged now." She rested her head on her father's chest as he cradled her and brushed her hair with his fingers.

"You've always been a tough shell to crack, little one. But I guarantee if Alex knew there was the slightest chance to reconcile with you, he would be here in a heartbeat. Men and women weren't created for all this conflict with each other.

They were created for companionship and compassion. And to complete each other. And when you find 'The One,' and love is rooted deep like yours and Alex's, that love will persevere. He's a man of integrity and believe me, he won't be moving on unless you've sealed the deal with another man. He doesn't just toss away a treasure like you. Talk to him. When you two can get past all the hurt and pain and just be real and honest with each other, I believe you will work things out."

"I wouldn't even know where to start when I see him."

"'Hello' is usually a good beginning. Just don't start by abusing him." He cleared his throat and excused himself to get some water. "I told him I wouldn't tell you, but if you're going to church with us tomorrow, I want you to be prepared to see him and not be shocked. He's been visiting our church whenever we have Maddy. If you want to go with us in the morning, we'll be leaving at 8. Looks like I'm helping in the nursery, but we'll go to the later service if you want to just meet up for that. It starts at 11."

Renae grabbed the half empty cocoa mugs and took them to the sink. She wiped her face with her sleeves. "Okay. I'll just meet you at 11. Do you think he'll be okay with me being there?"

Phil cupped his daughter's chin in his hand. "Sweet girl, he'll be the happiest man alive when he sees you there."

Renae smiled and nodded her head. "Thank you for listening, Daddy." She gave him a tight hug. "I love you."

"I love you, too."

"You might want to wash these clothes, though; they stink."

"It's my lucky hunting vest. Can't wash it, it'll lose its charm."

Renae smiled. "Goodnight. I'm going to wash these mugs, so I'll shut everything down."

"Goodnight, Punkin." Phil disappeared into the dark room as Renae turned the water on to wash the mugs.

She smiled at the thought of her dad. He was her hero,

no matter what happened, and he always made himself present to help cheer her up. Tonight he was trying to help her find that little glimmer of hope she needed.

Suddenly, Renae felt a chill pass over her. She looked to the dark room and dropped the mug into the sink. A thud struck the floor from near the stairs. She rushed to the room, turned on a light and slid next to her father. His limp body was lying at the bottom of the stairs. "Daddy! Mom! *Mom!*"

* * *

Alex was awakened to the sound of his phone vibrating on the dresser next to his bed. The light from the TV was bright. An infomercial indicated it was very early Sunday morning. He rolled over to check his phone. He had eight missed calls from Renae. He sat up and threw his legs over the bed, opening the text message she had sent.

Renae:
Maddy ok. It's Daddy. Pls call when u can

Alex grabbed his jeans and shirt off the dresser as he dialed Renae's number. He looked at the time. It was almost 2 am. She had been calling since 11:30.

"Hey, I hope I'm not bothering you," Renae answered his call on the first ring, her voice small and quivering.

"Hey, of course not, what's going on?"

"Alex, it's Daddy. We're at the hospital. Can you come? Maddy's here and I'd rather she not be." Her voice was still quivering. Alex knew Renae well, and from the sound of her voice he could tell it was serious and she was scared.

"Yeah, of course," he responded tenderly. "Tell me where you are and I'll be right there."

He heard her talking to someone at the hospital. "My

husband is on his way here to get our daughter; can you tell him where we are?" She returned to talk to Alex. "Hey, Alex, the nurse is going to tell you how to get to our waiting room. We're at the hospital by the house." A friendly nurse gave him directions to get to the correct floor and lobby. He wrote everything down on a scratch piece of paper and put it in his pocket. The nurse gave the phone back to Renae. "You still there?" She sounded so small and helpless on the other end.

"Yeah, of course I'm here. You okay? What's going on with Dad? Is Mom up there?"

"Mom's here. She's with him. He, um...he had a massive heart attack." Her voice broke as she finished her sentence.

Alex's heart sank. He wasn't prepared to say goodbye to his father-in-law. It wasn't his time to go. "Hey, he's a strong beast of a man; he's going to pull through this."

"Mm-hmm." He could hear the doubt in her response.

"I'll see you soon."

She hung up.

Alex grabbed his keys and locked the door behind him. He felt cold. Not because of the environmental atmosphere, but because of the situation. Phillip Rivera was the only father he had left. Alex's own father had passed away while Alex was in college. Mr. Rivera helped him push through the pain and heal through all the heartache. And now Alex suspected he might be facing the same walk with his wife. His ex-wife. His mind shifted to what she had said on the phone. She had referred to him as her husband. Not ex. No, now wasn't the time for him to analyze what she had said. She wasn't thinking straight right now. Regardless of how they had ended their evening earlier, he was committed to walk through this crisis with her and to be there for her in any capacity she would allow. He sped through the back roads to get to the hospital quickly, wondering if he had fresh milk for Maddy in the morning as he passed the grocer. He couldn't remember if he had locked the front door. Would Renae object to him hugging her when he got there? He wanted to hold her and tell her everything was going to be okay, but that was a promise he couldn't guarantee. Did Maddy know what was happening? Was she awake? Was Joshua there with Renae? He probably was. She needed someone to stay with her tonight. Had anyone call Eric? Oh God, when was the last time Eric had seen his dad? Alex began talking to God, asking for healing, peace, comfort, direction, reconciliation, and restoration.

Alex pulled into the hospital parking lot and found a spot close to the door. He rushed to the building and quickly made his way to the elevator. He took out the instructions the nurse had given him and pushed the button multiple times for the fourth floor. The elevator doors seemed to be taking their sweet time to close. Alex nervously bounced on the balls of his feet as the elevator slowly lifted. "Please hold on, Phil," Alex whispered under his breath. He finally reached his floor and followed the nurse's directions to find his family. He approached the locked set of heavy double doors and took a deep breath. Not knowing what to expect on the other side of those doors, he asked for strength as he buzzed to be allowed through. As frightening as the situation was, he placed one foot in front of the other and proceeded towards the unknown. Alex had his ID out even before he reached the desk. He presented it to the nurse and then put on his visitor sticker.

"Your wife and daughter are right around the corner in the waiting room to the right," the nurse informed him. He made his way to the room and found Renae seated in a chair with Maddy's head in her lap. She was biting her nails and staring at the muted television. She hadn't noticed he had walked in yet.

"Hi." He quietly approached her so he wouldn't startle her and wake their sleeping baby girl.

"Hey." She looked relieved to see him. He removed his jacket and offered it as a pillow. Renae carefully slipped it under Maddy's head while Alex adjusted the blanket and kissed his daughter's smooth forehead before turning his attention back to Renae. He could see she had been crying all night. Her eyelids were heavy and swollen. In all her pain, she was still the most beautiful woman he ever laid eyes on.

"Thank you for coming to get her."

"Of course. I'm sorry I didn't answer when you first called. What happened?"

Renae stood to her feet, grabbed his hand, and pulled him away from Maddy and closer to the door. "The doctor said it was a heart attack. One minute he and I were laughing and crying together, and then a couple of minutes later I found him on the floor, unresponsive." She started to shake and felt cold. Tears were welling up again.

Alex pulled her close and wrapped his arms around her. Initially hesitant, Renae released any hard feelings and doubts she held towards him and surrendered. She buried her face in his chest and sobbed. His embrace and his presence comforted her, and as her tears began to subside, Renae lifted her arms behind Alex's back and held on tight. Alex secured his hold around Renae and fought back his own emerging tears. Renae turned her head and pressed her ear to his chest so she could feel his heartbeat. She focused on slowing her breaths to the rhythm of his heart.

"I don't know what I'll do if I lose him, Alex."

"Shhh, don't think of that right now."

"He's my rock, you know."

"I know. He's an incredible man."

They stood in silence and held each other through the fear and waiting. They were reestablishing unity in their heartache and as they stood together in a solid embrace, neither found they could let go of the other. Renae wanted to freeze this moment in time forever; the peace of his embrace was overwhelming. She was snapped back into reality at the sound of the double doors closing in the corridor down the hall. "Do you think you should take Maddy home now?" Renae asked, breaking the silence.

"Why wake her up when she's sleeping soundly where she is? Besides, I don't want to leave you alone here."

Should she tell him she had called Joshua and he was on his way? Why did she have to call Joshua? If her dad was right, and she was afraid he was right, this would hurt Alex. She needed him to leave before he saw Joshua.

"I'll be okay," she said as she pulled away. "Plus, she doesn't look very comfortable."

"If that's what you want." He rubbed her slightly trembling arms.

"Yeah, you two get some rest. I'll keep you posted if anything changes."

"I really don't want to leave you to deal with this on your own."

"You should go, Alex," Renae almost pleaded with him. Her eyes shifted to the person who had just joined them in the waiting room and then she looked away.

"Hey, guys. Any word?" Joshua affixed his visitor tag to his shirt as he approached his friends. Renae realized how uncomfortable this was becoming for all of them.

"No. I'll catch you up to speed in a minute, okay? Alex, let me help you with Maddy."

He was already scooping up his little girl in his arms. "Do you need help with your jacket?"

"No, just drape it over her. I'll get it."

"Can I help you to the car?"

"Nah, you need to stay here in case the doctor comes in. I've got her."

"Hey." She stopped him before he headed out the door. "Thank you."

"Yeah." He turned his back to her and carried his sleeping princess to the double doors. He felt like he was being forced to leave so his ex-wife could find comfort in the arms of another man. Although he had anticipated Joshua being there to stay with her, he wasn't anticipating the emotional pain he would carry facing the reality of it. Renae was no longer his, so he had no right to be mad. But anger really wasn't what he was feeling. He felt hurt and rejected. Alex paused to turn to look at her one last time. She had followed them to the doors. As those doors were closing, he watched her redirect her attention to a doctor who approached her. It must have been Phil's doctor. He wanted to go back. He needed to. But she didn't want him there. That was obvious when she told him he needed to leave when Joshua entered the room.

Alex made his way to the car and woke up a sleeping Maddy so she could sit in her booster seat. The groggy little girl looked around the car, frowning and confused.

"Where's Mommy?"

"Hey, Princess, you can go back to sleep. Daddy's taking you home to his house tonight. Mommy will call you in the morning."

"Okay." Alex covered her up again and kissed her cheek. She laid her head down and quickly drifted back to sleep.

The trip home took longer than the trip to the hospital. Alex was exhausted, physically and emotionally. So much had happened over the course of the day. The events of the soccer game were a distant memory. Feelings and emotions were revisited over the evening, and just as sparks were beginning to ignite between Renae and him once again, his hope was quickly extinguished. The heartache and uncertainty of the events overnight brought them physically and emotionally close. Not only did he want to be there for Renae, but he hurt too, and he wished he could have stayed to walk through this nightmare with the woman he still considered the love of his life and best friend. But there was Joshua. He knew Joshua would always be a part of her life; he knew that from the day he laid eyes on her. It had taken him two years to ask Renae out on a date, only because he always thought she was in a relationship with Joshua. When he found out they were just friends, he jumped at the opportunity to take her to the prom and that's where their romance began. Yet, Joshua stuck around. He was there for every celebration, every event, every big moment in their lives. He stood on the sidelines, eventually with his own bride, and always cheered them on. Alex couldn't help but feel threatened by Joshua once Angie passed and Renae stepped in to comfort him. And he couldn't help but feel suspicious about their intentions and future with each other once he and Renae divorced. He had to get the visual of the two of them together out of his mind. He shifted his thoughts from them back to Phil, and he said another prayer for him and the family as he parked the car in his driveway.

Once he got his princess tucked into her bed, he checked his phone. Joshua had called and left a voicemail. Alex had a sick feeling in his stomach as he retrieved it.

"Hey, man, it's Josh. I'm sorry to be the one to tell you, but...Phil's gone. Renae's with her mom. She said she would call you in the morning."

Alex hung up the phone and tossed it on his dresser. He sat down in the red oversized chair in the corner of the bedroom. Phil had bought this chair for Alex and Renae as their ten-year anniversary present. Memories of the two men coming up with a plan to get the chair into the room occupied his mind. "Son, you won't be able to make her happy 100 percent of the time. But it's the priceless joy in those moments in which you do make her happy that makes the hard work worth it. She wants this giant chair in your room so you two can curl up and watch a movie on it, then this chair needs to go in that room. Treasure the happy moments, kid. They get you through the tough ones." Tears were rolling down his cheeks. He couldn't hold the sorrow back any longer. Alex sobbed until he felt numb. He crawled into his cold and empty bed. And that's exactly how he'd remember that night, cold and empty.

THREE

The sun was starting to shine through the blinds of the family room window at the Rivera house. The morning light was bright and its intrusive rays woke Renae. She had fallen asleep on the recliner while sitting with her mom. Ruth Rivera was still asleep, curled on the sofa and covered with her favorite red-and-black plaid throw, using her husband's jacket as a pillow. Renae pushed herself up to a sitting position and looked around the room, her eyes resting on her mother. Tears slowly rolled down her cheeks as she realized last night's nightmare was indeed reality. She rested her head on the cushion on the chair, the tears still flowing. She was careful not to wake her mother. Ruth had taken a sedative, but Renae wasn't sure how long it would last. She felt the last thing her mother would need was to wake up and confront her new existence, and Renae certainly didn't want to go through this with her alone.

She tossed as she tried to fall back to sleep, but it was useless. She couldn't get the image of her father lying on the floor out of her mind. She quietly slipped out of the squeaky recliner and made her way to the kitchen. Her father's pellet gun was still on the table. One mug was drying on the counter, the other laying in the sink. As she picked it up, she noticed a crack from top to bottom. It must have broken when she dropped it. She tossed the mug in the trash and exhaled. Taking a paper towel off the roll, she wiped her face and neck. She couldn't stop crying. As she poured herself a glass of water, it occurred to her that her father took one with him the night before. He probably dropped it as he collapsed. She couldn't let her mother find that. Renae grabbed the roll of paper towels and headed toward the stairs. To her surprise, she found the half-empty glass on the tall table at the bottom of the stairs. He had laid it there. He must have known something was wrong. If only she had gone to bed when he went...

Renae took the glass to the kitchen and scrubbed it, her cheeks again becoming washed by her tears. She made a cup of coffee, grabbed her phone and the pellet gun, and headed to her room. Usually she drank her coffee at the kitchen table or on the back porch, but the memories were too fresh. She locked herself in her room and checked her phone for messages.

Mr. Reeves:
Hey kid. We just heard. Our hearts are breaking with and for you. Please don't hesitate to reach out to us. We'll call later. Praying for you.

Joshua:
Thinking of you. Call me when you feel like it. I'll come over if you need me. <3

Eric:
We got a 6 am flight out. We'll be there around 11.

How did Mr. Reeves know already? Joshua must have told him. She couldn't remember if she asked him to call Alex or not. Oh God, what was she going to tell Maddy? She looked at the time again. 8:17 a.m. Eric would be there at 11. She would rather not talk to Maddy alone, and she needed to talk to Alex to see how to approach her. She texted him instead of calling to see if he was awake.

Hey. You awake?

She put her phone down, not anticipating a quick response. Immediately, it lit up.

>Alex:
>*Yeah, I've been awake for a few.*
>
>*Did Joshua call you?*
>
>Alex:
>*He left me a vm. Renae, I'm so sorry.*
>
>*Can you talk right now?*

Renae's phone began to buzz.

"Hey," Renae answered on the first ring. She sat on her bed and closed her eyes so she could focus solely on Alex's soothing voice.

"Renae, I'm really sorry."

"I know. Did you tell Maddy already?"

"No, that's something I thought we should do together."

"Yeah, me too. Is she awake?"

"Not yet, but I was about to go check on her. When do you want me to bring her over? Or do you want to meet somewhere or come over here? I'll do whatever you want."

"I really don't feel like driving anywhere. Eric said he'd be here around 11. Should we talk to her before or after he gets here?"

"I don't know. What do you think?"

"I was thinking before. I don't know. Maybe she shouldn't be here when Eric gets here. It would be nice to do it while there's peace in the house."

"How about I wake her up and bring her over now then?"

"Can you give me an hour? I'd really like to shower."

"Yeah. Do you need anything?"

"I don't know. Maybe a valium, cigarettes, a joint, and a

giant bottle of whiskey?"

"I was thinking along the lines of a coffee, but if I can find any of that on the way I'll pick some up for you."

Renae smiled and rubbed her itchy eyes. "Thanks. I'll see you soon. Be careful."

"I will. Bye."

"Bye." Renae stared at her phone as she hung up. *Daddy was right about you, Alex Murphy, you are a good man*, she thought to herself. She was very lucky to have him in her life again, even if it was temporary.

Renae looked in her bedroom mirror. She didn't feel like showering. She fell onto her bed, wishing she could just stay there all day. She smelled her hair, relieved it still smelled fresh from the night before. She'd be able to put it up and let it go. That would cut some time off her routine. She forced herself out of bed and headed to the bathroom.

After her shower, she put on her most comfortable jeans and oversized sweatshirt. Her brother hadn't seen her in a couple of years, so she put on foundation and blush. Grabbing her mascara, she looked at her eyes and noticed how swollen they were. Feeling defeated, she re-capped her mascara tube and tossed it in her makeup bag. Her hair was hopeless, so she grabbed a headband and positioned her hair back and up, pulling some loose curls out to frame her face. After spritzing herself with her favorite choice of Chanel, she headed down the stairs with a half-empty cold cup of coffee.

When she got downstairs, Renae looked to the sofa, the flannel throw the only thing left resting on it. "Mom?" Renae spotted her dad's jacket back on the coat rack. She found her mom seated at the kitchen table, frozen in her thoughts. "Mom." Renae went to her mother and sat next to her, rubbing her back. Out of her two parents, her mother was the least affectionate, so Renae didn't always know how to approach her. "Eric said he would be here around 11. Alex should be here soon with Maddy. We wanted to tell her together, preferably before Eric got here."

"Is Andy coming too?"

"His text said '*we*,' so my guess is yes."

"It's probably a good idea you aren't home when he gets here. I wish Alex could stay. Could you take Maddy somewhere and leave Alex with me?" Ruth was emotionless. Renae wasn't sure if she was being serious or not about wanting her own daughter to leave so her former son-in-law could stay.

"I'll have to see, but Mom, I'd really like to be here with Eric. He's my brother."

"Sure." Ruth's demeanor immediately shifted from soft and numb to control-freak mode. "Well, I better clean up if we're going to have all this company. There's a frozen lasagna in the freezer. We'll have that for lunch when they get here. We'll need to make some fresh iced tea; your brother likes it sweet." Ruth stood from the table, pushed her chair in, then proceeded to go upstairs. Renae's eyes followed her in shock. How could her mother just turn off her feelings like that?

The lock to the front door turned and Alex walked in with a bouncy 6-year-old behind him.

"Hi, Mommy!" Maddy met her mother in the doorway separating the family room and the kitchen. Renae bent to her knees and held her daughter tight.

"Hey Stinker, I missed you!"

"Daddy got breakfast!"

"He did?"

Her little girl nodded her head. "He got...he got...biscuits and...and he got...Daddy, what did you get?"

"Biscuits and a muffin sandwich," Alex replied.

"Mmmmm, sounds yummy!" Renae tickled Maddy's tummy and Alex gave his little girl the fast food bag. "Take it to the table. I'll be there in a minute; I just need to talk to Daddy."

"Ok." Maddy skipped to the kitchen table, carefully pulled out a chair, climbed into it and sat down, her elbows barely reaching the top.

"How are you holding up?" Alex asked Renae. She shrugged her shoulders in response and placed her hands in her pockets. Alex immediately understood that the intimacy shared between them the previous night was temporary and he couldn't expect her to long for him to hold her again. "Here, want your coffee? Where's your mom?" Alex handed Renae the cup of coffee he'd picked up for her.

"Thank you. She went upstairs to clean up. I'm a little worried about her; she's acting so weird. Like, a few hours ago she was crying herself to sleep, and then I find her here frozen and numb, and then she's switching into control-freak mode. Is this normal, because I'm scared of what comes next. Oh, and get this...she doesn't want me here when Eric and Andy get here; she wants you here."

"Andy's coming? Well, I can see why she wouldn't want you around for all that."

"Seriously? I can be a nice person."

"Mommy, did the ambulance bring Grampy back?" Maddy interrupted her parents.

"You ready for this?" Alex asked his ex-wife.

"No, but I wasn't ready for any events of the past twelve hours either, so..."

The couple had a "no physical touch or affection" rule around their daughter because they never wanted to give her a false impression that her parents were reuniting. Renae was the one who suggested it and right now it was killing her.

"Hey sweetheart, your mom and I have something we need to talk to you about," Alex led as Renae followed him to the table, fighting back her already emerging tears. Alex pulled a chair next to his daughter so he could talk to her on her level. Renae pulled a chair to the other side of Maddy and rubbed her back and kissed her on the top of her head. Maddy had a special relationship with Phil, and both Renae and Alex were afraid that telling her he was gone would destroy her sweet little spirit.

Maddy stopped eating when her parents came to sit

with her. She was too young to know when it was time for a serious conversation; sadly, she was accustomed to having more than her fair share of them at her age.

"How's that biscuit, Captain?" Alex began. Maddy shrugged her shoulders. "Not very good, huh?"

"I'm not all that hungry anymore. I can save it for later."

"You know, I think it may taste better with honey butter," Renae offered. "I'm sure we can find some honey once we're done talking."

"It's on the top right shelf of the pantry," Maddy replied. "That's where Grampy gets it from."

"He does? Do you two have honey together a lot?" Alex found a good segue to start the conversation.

"Yes. He likes to have tea parties with me, and we have honey and jam with our crumpets. He always makes a mess of my tea set though. Don't tell him I said that."

"I promise your secret is safe with me. It sounds to me like those tea parties are pretty awesome. Crumpets, huh? Sounds like they're pretty fancy parties."

"They're just English muffins, Daddy. Grampy calls them crumpets because he says I'm a princess and princesses don't eat ordinary English muffins."

"He really likes to take care of you, doesn't he?" Maddy nodded her head yes. "You know, Grampy likes to take care of other people too. He takes care of your grandmother, and of Mommy, and he sometimes takes care of Daddy too. But that's not all."

"It's not?"

"Nope. When Grampy talks to strangers, it's usually because he's taking care of them in some small way. He asks people how they're doing; he gives directions when they're lost; he's even taken his jacket off and given it to people that didn't have one. You know, he even mows lawns for people who can't mow their own lawn."

Maddy's eyes grew wide as Alex told her of different

ways Phil offered a hand to help his community.

"He takes care of a lot of people, doesn't he, Daddy?"

"He does. But you know, sometimes we're so focused on taking care of other people that we don't think about making time to take care of ourselves. And that could mean we may not even realize when something may be wrong in our own body."

"Is that why Grampy fell down? Because his legs weren't working?"

Renae could see the hesitation in Alex's face. As incredible as he was at explaining this, she couldn't imagine how difficult it must be to look at Maddy's innocent face and give her this painful news. She reached around Maddy and grabbed his hand and squeezed tight. Her small act of encouragement gave him strength to proceed.

"Well, it wasn't his legs. Grampy is so strong and he felt great, so he didn't know that a part of his body wasn't working right. Nobody knew. So last night, that part of his body stopped working."

"But we can pray, and he can be healed," Maddy said, matter-of-factly.

Renae blinked away some tears and quickly wiped the ones that fell. Maddy needed her mom to be strong. Alex looked at Renae for affirmation. She smiled and nodded at him, assuring him he was handling it well. Alex took a deep breath and continued.

"Praying is exactly what we should do. And we all prayed last night. But sometimes, when we pray for something, God has a different plan and those prayers are answered in a way that looks different to us than how we thought they would look. When Grampy's body stopped working the way it should, God saw it was time to give him rest. God knew that Grampy did everything he needed to do to help Mommy, you, me, and everyone he met become the very best versions of ourselves, and now he's in this incredibly beautiful place called Heaven living and dancing with Jesus."

"Does that mean Grampy won't be coming back home, then?"

"No, baby," Renae added. "Grampy won't be coming back home."

Maddy's bottom lip stuck out and began to quiver. Renae quickly pulled her to her chest and began rocking her as they both cried together. Alex's eyes turned red as he was unable to hold back his own tears. Renae looked to him and held her arm out, inviting him in a comforting family embrace. He quickly accepted and held the girls through their deep moment of grief.

* * *

Ruth was sitting in her rocking chair in her bedroom staring out the window when Renae popped her head in the door to check on her.

"Do you need some coffee or anything, Mom? Eric should be here soon; he texted me from the airport."

Ruth didn't turn to look at Renae. She sat silently in her chair and stopped rocking. Renae leaned on the doorframe, hands in her pockets, staring into a room of memories. Ruth had already laid out Phil's best black suit on the bed.

"We need to take his suit to the cleaner's today," Ruth finally spoke, still not looking at Renae. Renae knew it was best to let her mother handle her grief on her own terms. "I heard Maddy and Alex come in. Are they still here?"

"Yeah, they're downstairs. She's going to pack some things up and he'll take her back to his house."

"He won't be here when Eric gets here? I'd rather him be here than you."

"Mom, he's my brother-"

"Yes, and I'm afraid you'll say something again to make him leave." Renae was the sibling with a sharp tongue. Eric was easily offended and thought all her jabs were aimed at him.

"I'll go talk to Alex." Renae turned and left her mom, tight-lipped, rocking again in her chair.

Downstairs, Alex was packing Maddy's unicorn covered backpack. "Maddy do you need these papers for school?"

"I don't know," Maddy replied softly and slowly.

Renae looked at her daughter sitting on the couch, combing her favorite doll's hair with her fingers. "Think she'll be okay to go to school tomorrow?"

"I figure we'll play it by ear," Alex said softly to Renae. "I can take the week off to help take care of things if you need me to. What about you? Were you planning on being in town this week?"

"I'm supposed to speak at an event in Chicago on Tuesday. I need to call and cancel. I was planning on my parents watching her over the next three days."

"We'll work it out; she can stay with me."

"Thank you. So, Mom was serious about you being here today. She's afraid of me saying something to Eric and I guess she wants your voice of reason here. I hate to ask-"

"I'll stay."

"I'm really sorry, I hope you didn't have plans today or this week."

"Renae, don't apologize. I'm here. This family is my focus right now. You are my focus. Nothing and no one are more important to me than the people in this room. I'll be here in whatever capacity you need me."

Renae nodded her head and gave him a quiet "thanks." Although having him around again was temporary, she was overwhelmed by his thoughtfulness and kindness. He still loved her family like his own and it showed. "Mom wants me to take Daddy's suit to the cleaners. I can take Maddy with me. Do you need anything?"

"No, I'm good," Alex replied.

He tossed Maddy's backpack down near the sofa and

sat down beside his daughter. Renae headed up the stairs to retrieve her father's suit when a knock sounded at the door. Renae froze at the top of the stairs and looked to Alex.

"It'll be okay, he's your brother," Alex assured her. She nodded her head and he proceeded to open the door.

"Hey, Eric, good to see you," Alex greeted Eric, inviting him in. Eric shook his hand and gave him a short hug.

"Surprised to see you here. Thought the battleax chased you off." Eric walked in, dropped his bag, and delivered a sinister smile to his sister, who was still standing at the top of the stairs. He turned to Alex and invited his tall, handsome, dark-skinned companion in. "Alex, I don't believe you've met. This is Andy, my husband."

F OUR

Ruth sat at the kitchen table, slowly drinking her morning coffee. It was Thursday morning and the family was preparing to say their final goodbyes to the beloved patriarch of their family.

"Morning," Renae greeted her mother with a kiss on the forehead and a tight squeeze as she headed to the refrigerator for creamer. "What in the world are we going to do with all these lasagnas? Why would so many people bring lasagna?" There were three lasagnas in the refrigerator and eight in the freezer. Friends and neighbors had been calling and dropping off food all week.

"Well, people must have known it was your father's favorite," her mother replied.

"Yeah, well it's not like he's gonna be here to eat it." Renae voiced sarcastically.

Andy joined the ladies and poured himself some coffee. "The limo should be here in about forty-five minutes."

"Thanks, dear," Ruth said as she hugged Andy. "And thank you for all your help this week. I don't know what I would have done if you and Eric hadn't been here."

Renae stood and looked at her mom in disbelief. What help? Was she invisible and completely helpless? What about Alex? Alex had handled all the funeral arrangements for the family and watched Maddy for them while doing it. She grabbed her coffee and headed to her room, intentionally knocking shoulders with Eric on his way into the kitchen. She knew why her mother said it. She knew her mother wanted to make them feel as comfortable and welcome as possible so they would stay longer and come back to visit more often. She knew her mother knew Renae had a tough interior and could take the indirect jabs. But what her mother didn't realize was that Renae was getting fed up with the preferential treatment of her brother and the pressure inside her was building. She picked up her phone to text Joshua.

> *Please tell me you will be there today...*
> *Idk how much longer I can watch my mom kiss E and A's asses*
> *She likes Alex more than me*
> *This week has been sucktastic*
> *I miss you*

She set her phone on her bed and went to her mirror. She pulled a two-toned cross out of her musical jewelry box, both trinkets gifts from her father, and fastened it around her neck. "I miss you, Daddy," she told the mirror, imagining he was once again behind her, fastening the necklace for her. She blinked back the tears and dabbed under her eyes, trying to keep her makeup in place. Her phone vibrated behind her.

> Joshua:
> *You know I'll be there*
> *She likes Alex more than me too*
> *Miss you more <3 C U Soon*

His texts calmed her spirit. She rested her head on her pillow and curled up in a ball on her bed. They hadn't seen each other since the hospital, and she was having best-friend withdrawals. Alex had been around, but he was helping plan the funeral and taking charge of affairs more than anything else. He was good at it and Renae admired him for it. Out of respect for him and what her father told her, she didn't bring Joshua around. And without Joshua to talk to or Alex being available, Renae felt she was walking through her father's passing alone.

"Limo is here!" Eric yelled from downstairs.

Renae opened her eyes. She must have been daydreaming; the time went by so fast. "Okay, Daddy, this is it." She put on a pair of black heels, looked in the mirror, straightened her dress, and after a deep, long breath, she proceeded downstairs to join her family.

Eric was already escorting his mother out the door. Ruth looked small and frail today, not bold and confident. Like the rest of her family, she was in all black, a drastic difference from the trendy ensembles she usually put together. Andy held the door open and waited for Renae to grab her purse before closing the door behind them. Outside the Rivera home, dew covered the green blades of grass still longing to be cut. The wetlands surrounding them were covered in a thick white vapor, and the cars were covered in beads of water. This was an unusually cool morning, which Renae was grateful for. The atmosphere matched her mood. She couldn't understand why the service was referred to as a "celebration of life," for she didn't feel like celebrating.

Andy had rented the limousine, his way of gesturing that he wanted to take care of Phil's family in any way he could. Ruth insisted he not put up a fuss over her, but he persisted and won. The two of them were getting along well. Eric sat on one side of his mother, holding her hand. She motioned for Andy to sit on her other side. Renae felt a twinge of jealousy towards them, but she and her mom were never as close as Ruth and Eric. Renae sometimes felt her mother would have loved her more if she had been born a boy. The four of them were silent during the twenty-two-minute ride. Any attempt at small talk would have been a waste of breath.

The fog began to lift as the limo turned into the Florida National Cemetery. Phillip Rivera had served in the United States Air Force for seven years, part of that time fighting in Vietnam, and Alex ensured he had a hero's send-off. The cemetery was beautiful. Luscious green grass blanketed fields carefully landscaped with symmetrical rows of headstones. Renae's gaze swept over the expanse of white and green; her heart filled with pride and honor. She was so proud that her father had dedicated time to the country he loved so much and honored that she now would be able to spend her time with him here amongst heroes.

The car pulled to a stop curbside near a pavilion prepared for the Rivera service. The family had requested donations to the Vietnam Veterans Association in lieu of flowers, so the only flowers present were the ones Ruth and the family had picked out for the service. Renae spotted Pastor Reeves standing beside the pavilion with another minister. "Well, this is it," she quietly announced to her fellow passengers. The limo driver made his way to the back of the car and held the door open for her. Pastor Reeves was quick to greet her and the family as they exited.

"Hey kid," he said as he hugged Renae. He smiled and shook Andy's hand as Renae introduced him.

"Pastor Reeves, this is Andy Crawford, Eric's, um..." she turned and looked at Andy, not quite sure how she should introduce him to their pastor.

"Partner," Andy added.

"Husband," Renae blurted out at the same time.

"It's so good to meet you. Thank you for everything you've been doing to help the family this week. I know Ruth appreciates it and has really enjoyed your company." A visibly uncomfortable Andy did his best to return the warm and friendly smile given to him. Ruth let Eric out next, and he was greeted with a tight hug from his former neighbor and pastor. "I'm so sorry, son." Eric blinked away tears as he returned the embrace from someone he'd once held so dear. "It's good to see you," Pastor Reeves assured him as he pulled away. Andy helped Ruth out of the car just as Alex pulled up behind them. "Ruth, I don't have the words. Phil meant a lot to so many of us and I know the love he had for his family and friends will be felt throughout the service today."

Renae left the family with the pastor and headed to the grey Jeep parked behind them. She opened the back-passenger door as Maddy jumped out and wrapped her arms around her mother's hips. Renae hadn't felt this happy in days. Maddy looked up at her mother with a huge grin on her face. "Hi, Mommy, I missed you."

Renae bent down to Maddy's height. "Missed me?! Well, I bet not as much as I have missed you! It's been like 18 hours!" Maddy giggled as her mother hugged her tightly and tickled her under her arms.

"Mommy, look, Daddy got me big girl shoes! They have high heels!"

"Let me see those fancy shoes."

"They're special because today is special," Maddy said as she twisted her feet to show off her shiny new heels.

"It is special. Why do you think it is special?"

"Because we are celebrating Grampy; because he was a good person. And he is with Jesus now," Maddy said, matter-of-factly.

Renae smiled and hugged Maddy one more time before rising to greet Alex. He was standing over them, admiring the two most important people in his life. Although he felt Renae had withdrawn from him since her father's passing, he couldn't help but want to hold her close today. Finalizing the funeral arrangements was hard, but not nearly as hard as saying goodbye to your father. He wished they could walk through this together, but the reality of their divorce kept him distant.

"Hey, you." He didn't know what to say in this moment. Here she stood, facing the worst day of her life, and he wanted to tell her how beautiful she looked, how sorry he was, and ask how she was doing. He really should have prepared something to say to her at this moment, he thought to himself.

"Hey," Renae said back to him. She stood face to face with him for only a moment before giving in to her emotions, wrapping her arms around him and hugging him tight. He squeezed her back, returning the affection. They both desperately wanted to mourn this loss together; they both wanted to be together and to leave together. Just neither one could say it, both afraid of inevitable rejection.

"Everything going okay?" Alex asked as they released from their hug. They remained standing close, with just inches between their faces.

"Yeah, we just got here."

"I need to go talk to Pastor Reeves; I have something for him."

"Alex, thank you. For taking care of everything. You worked miracles this week and made things happen faster than any of us could have. We all really appreciate all you've done, and we so appreciate you." She was sincere in her words and acknowledgement. The family could have been fine on their own arranging the service, but he made it so they didn't have to.

Alex cleared his throat. He wanted to tell her he would do anything for her and how honored and humbled he was to help when suddenly they were both tackled by a loving six-year-old who almost knocked them both off balance.

"Group hug!" It had been over a year since the small family had experienced a group hug outside of their sorrow and this one was long overdue. Alex scooped up his little girl and the three squeezed each other tight, Maddy laughing between her parents until she spotted a familiar face. "Uncle Josh!" She hopped out of her Daddy's arms and ran up to Joshua, giving him a hug too. The three friends greeted each other, then Alex left the girls with Joshua to talk to the pastor.

Ruth, Eric, and Andy were standing under a tree welcoming guests as they arrived. Renae and Joshua escorted Maddy to her grandmother's side.

"So, that looked intimate," Joshua noted once Maddy was no longer in ear's reach.

"Shut up, I really don't want to talk about that right now."

"You know, nothing would honor your father more at his funeral than you and Alex reuniting," he teased.

"I'm starting to regret missing you and asking you to be here today," she shot back, smiling. They wrapped their arms around each other for the remaining walk to join the family, throwing all cares about appearances aside. They had truly missed one another's company.

Joshua walked up to Ruth and gave her a long embrace. They had a special relationship, becoming closer when Angie died. He would never forget how she was there for him as a listening ear and a shoulder to cry on. He turned to Eric, shook his hand, and gave him a short hug. Eric introduced him to Andy, for a moment forgetting they had met before.

"This is my husband, Andy," Eric stated matter-of-factly.

"We've met," Joshua reminded him. "He was the doctor on call the night Angie went into-"

"labor." Andy finished the sentence for him and examined Joshua, recalling tragic details from the night he couldn't save Joshua's son.

Joshua made eye contact and quickly extended his hand. "We need to stop meeting under such crappy conditions. It's good to see you."

Once again, words were best left unspoken. Renae took her place next to Andy and greeted the army of guests who began to flood in.

As the seats began to fill up, Alex escorted Ruth, Eric, Andy, Renae, and Maddy to the front row. He then took his seat behind them next to Joshua.

"There's a sixth seat up there, why aren't you sitting with your family?" Joshua pressed.

"Nah, I'm okay. It's a family thing."

"And you were his son. His family. Your kid is up there. And you have more of a right to be in that row than Eric or

Andy, in my opinion. Go."

Renae heard Joshua's whispers from behind her. She stood to her feet, walked to the row behind her, and approached Alex. She crouched down and whispered in his ear. "He was your dad, too. Come, sit with us." She grabbed his hand and pulled him behind her as she led him to the front row. Alex sat on the end of the aisle with Maddy separating him and Renae. His chest felt heavy. Not only did he feel honored to have helped plan Phil's funeral, but he was honored to sit in the front row with his immediate family. Phil was the most respectable and honorable man he knew, and Alex would give anything to be half the great man Phil was.

* * *

Phillip Rivera was remembered for his love for God, his family, his country, and people. Mr. Reeves, Phil's pastor and neighbor for over twenty years, considered Phil a best friend. He spoke of fun times the two had shared, the hard times, the sorrowful times, and the spiritual times. He recounted stories of Phil's generosity and compassion for strangers and the lost, how he knew that generosity stemmed from his love for God and people, and that the acts of service he did were examples of God's love flowing through him. As he wrapped up his portion of the service, he opened Phil's Bible and began to share.

"I asked Alex, Phil's son-in-law and son-in-love, if he knew or could find Phil's favorite scripture, and after scouring through Phil's personal Bible, we concluded this was amongst his favorites. It comes from Romans 8-"

"38 and 39" Renae whispered. She turned to Alex and smiled.

Pastor Reeves began to read from the New King James Version:

"**38** *For I am persuaded that neither death nor life, nor angels nor principalities nor powers, nor things present nor things to come,* **39** *nor height nor depth, nor any other created thing, shall be able to separate us from the love of God which is in Christ Jesus our Lord."*

Renae looked at Ruth, who was mouthing the verse as he read it. Eric sat in reverence for the pastor, and Andy listened intently, hanging onto every word spoken. Renae felt bad for Andy. He didn't know her dad the way everyone else did. And from his body language and reactions, she could tell he wished he had. He was enjoying the stories told by people from different seasons of Phil's life. She liked Andy. She needed to make sure he knew that.

"Phil knew that no power could separate us from the love of God, and he shared that with strangers he spoke to. Phil knew beyond a shadow of a doubt that the most powerful force in the world is love and he did an outstanding job during his time here on earth expressing that. I'm going to miss you, good friend, but the good news is, we'll see each other again in Heaven."

Confirmations of "Amen" were spoken from the people behind the family as Pastor Reeves made his way back to his seat and the church's worship leader began to sing "Amazing Grace." Her voice was angelic. Alex told Renae this was Phil's favorite singer at the church, and that she was honored to sing at his service.

A piercing sensation ripped through Renae's heart at the sounds of gunshots during the close of the ceremony. Her father had taken her to the shooting range numerous times in her life. It was one of the many ways she and her dad had bonded over the years. Traditionally, the firing of the gun meant her father's weapon was no longer hostile. To her, it symbolized so much more. Many tears were shed as "Taps" began to sound throughout the cemetery. As Renae cried, she started to chuckle, reflecting on all the times her father would play it on a cassette player in the hall between her and Eric's bedroom doors and yell, "Lights out, soldiers!" She looked at Eric and she could tell he was recalling the same memory. He caught her eye and they both laughed as they wiped the tears away. Maddy walked over to Andy and crawled in his lap as the color guard lifted the flag and began to delicately fold it with precision and care. Maddy had grown quite fond of Andy over the past couple of days. Renae turned to Alex, who now sat alone. She shifted to Maddy's chair, and patted her now-empty chair for Maddy to sit in. Maddy obeyed, clinging onto Andy's arm as Ruth was presented with the folded flag.

As they concluded the service, it was Renae's turn to address the friends and family.

"On behalf of my mother, Eric, Andy, Alex, and Maddy, I want to thank you all for coming out to celebrate Daddy with us. I can see by the amount of people gathered here, and by how many lasagnas we have in the freezer, how much Daddy was loved, admired, and will be missed. He was our lighthouse, our counsel, our joy, and today he is our sorrow. He loved his wife of forty-three years unconditionally and he showered her with that love every day. Eric and I feel incredibly blessed to have been raised and loved by such an honorable and admirable man who deposited so much wisdom and love into the lives of his kids. Please, remember him for his kindness, generosity, and love. And if you ever see the opportunity to lend a hand to a stranger in need, think of Daddy and take action. It's going to take an army to fill his boots." She choked on her last words and took her seat before she began to release more tears. Andy reached over for her hand, squeezed it, and mouthed "thank you" to her. She nodded to him with a smile, took a deep breath, and smiled at Pastor Reeves as he led and released the crowd in prayer.

The family and friends stood to their feet and slowly headed to their cars. It took the Riveras a little longer than the rest to exit.

"Well, I don't know about you guys, but I could use a beer and a burger. Who's down for lunch?" Eric left the family speechless for a moment.

After contemplating his suggestion, Renae shrugged her shoulders and agreed. "I really can't think when I ate last. I'm down."

"Alex, you joining us?" Andy smiled at Alex as he stood and put his blazer on. Alex, unsure of his welcome, looked to Renae and replied with hesitation.

"Um, I'm not really sure."

"You should come," Renae offered as she helped Maddy buckle the shoe that she just couldn't seem to keep on during the service. "If you don't already have plans afterward. No pressure or anything." She was so eager to invite him, she had to back down and try to act casual about wanting him to join them.

"No, I don't have any plans," he hesitated, unsure if he was really welcome based on the way Renae responded.

"Then have lunch with us, my treat," Ruth added.

Renae stood with her hands in the pockets of her dress as she turned back to her father's urn. She was a little shocked at how quickly the conversation moved to lunch, but that was Eric. He hadn't been handling their father's death very well the past couple of days and she believed this was his way of distracting himself from coming to terms with saying his final goodbye to his father. Renae walked up to the urn and placed her hand on it. She knew her father wasn't there. She knew his soul was in Heaven. She knew his broken body was just now ash and the cold black container was just a representation of him. But she couldn't help but feel closer to him as she touched it. An arm extended across her shoulders and pulled her close. Joshua came to comfort her and say his own farewell to a man who had been a second father to him for so many years.

"Are you coming to lunch with us?" Renae offered as she laid her head on his shoulder.

"No, I really need to get some work done. Besides, you and the family have things you need to work out, and I have a feeling some of that is going to come to light today now that all this is over."

"I don't know if he'll understand. I don't see how he would."

"I think you should let Alex explain it to him. If it comes up."

"I'm sure it will. You know I just wanted to make Daddy feel loved. He was under attack on all sides, and when it came down to it, I just wanted Daddy to know someone was standing beside him, no matter where he stood. He truly loved Eric, you know that."

"I know. If you need to talk, call me. Or if you need re-inforcements. But I think if it all comes to a head tonight, it's best that you and Alex explain what happened and why. You two are a powerful force that went through this with your dad together. You should be able to explain it best. I'll be praying for you guys. And I'll be ready to bail you out of jail if you need it." Joshua kissed her on the head, released his hold around her and placed his hand on Mr. Rivera's urn. "Thank you. For investing in me and loving us all unconditionally-...I'll see you again." He patted the urn, turned to Ruth, and departed after giving her another long hug.

After saying their individual, heartfelt goodbyes, the family headed to their respective cars and departed for lunch.

FIVE

Lunch progressed into an all-day affair, with the family finally ending their evening at home after a trip to a cafe for dessert and coffee. It wasn't an outing filled with celebration, but of reflection and contemplation of next steps. Maddy rode home in the limousine with Ruth, Eric, and Andy. Ruth put Maddy to bed and sat with her in the silence, enjoying some time alone with her thoughts. Renae, in desperate need of water after consuming many stiff drinks with her brother-in-law, rode home with Alex, who offered to stop at a convenience store on the way.

Alex pulled into the driveway behind Renae's car and put his jeep in park.

"You coming in?" Renae was hoping he would say yes. Not only was she afraid of topics that still loomed un-answered with her brother and having to answer them with-out Alex, but she was enjoying his company and she wanted to spend more time with him.

"I was really hoping to get out of this suit."

"Oh, I can get you out of that suit. Oh my God, that came out completely wrong." Alex was trying his best not to laugh, but he was completely amused. "What I meant to say was that you have some clean clothes in Maddy's room from when you took her to the beach. I found them in her bag."

"And you kept them here for this exact moment when you knew I would want to go home to change, but you would want to keep me here so we could hang out and talk until the sun came up, like when we were dating."

"Well, you figured out my diabolical plan. Whatever

shall I do?" she laughed.

"You could invite me in for a drink. Or to let me use the bathroom. I could really use a bathroom break."

"Okay, Alex, would you like to come in and use my restroom facilities, followed by a stiff drink and a rendez-vous on the back porch to watch the sunrise?" She was gig-gling, an effect of the drinks she'd had during the course of the day.

"Why, Ms. Rivera, I would love to do that," he said. He loved that he could still make her blush and bring a smile to her face. They stopped talking and stared at each other.

"Alex...okay, I've been drinking, so I feel kind of vul-nerable, extremely honest, and I may have lost my filter for now. Just, don't talk, let me get this out really quick before I lose my nerve."

"Okay."

"Shhhhh. I said don't talk. Okay. I'm just, I'm curious. And I'm okay with whatever your answer is; I won't hate you or like you any less than I do right now.... at this very mo-ment... in time. Am I rambling again?"

"A little."

"Shhh. Okay. Sorry. Okay. Alex, when we were at the restaurant the other day and Carrie came up...and you took her home...was there, *is there* anything going on between you two? Like are y'all together or dating or flirting or do y'all like each other? It's cool if you do and everything, I mean, we don't have anything going on between us, so it really doesn't matter, but I was just wondering." She gave him a sheepish smile as she finished speaking.

Alex was quiet for a moment before answering. "Is it okay to speak now?"

"Yes! Please! Sorry, proceed."

"Saturday evening Carrie approached me at the res-taurant and asked for a ride home. Her friends backed out on her and I was the first person she asked. I agreed, as long as I could get another person to ride with us for integrity purposes. She and I have nothing outside a friendly acquaintanceship that stemmed from sitting near her at church and her joining the soccer team. I kind of think she wants more but I'm not going to entertain that. Ever."

Renae knew he meant it. She felt uncomfortable for asking. She certainly didn't know how to respond or what to do next. "Um...did you still need to use the bathroom?"

"Yeah, if you don't mind."

"Okay."

Alex followed Renae into the house. Renae made her way upstairs to change and to grab the change of clothes for Alex as he headed to the downstairs bathroom. Andy and Eric were standing in the kitchen discussing travel plans when Alex joined them.

"Are you guys planning on staying a couple more days?"

"Yeah, I think we're going to leave Sunday morning sometime. I want to stick around as long as I can for Mom and make sure she's well taken care of."

"Sure. I mean, not that I want you two to leave--it's been great having you here--but I'm pretty sure Renae will do a good job taking care of her too."

"Oh, come on, my sister take care of my mom? I'm seriously thinking about staying around next week so Renae doesn't screw anything up."

"What am I going to screw up?" Renae asked as she entered the kitchen and gave Alex the clothes she'd gathered for him. "Mom's sitting in Maddy's room, by the way. She's going to get dressed and she'll be down after that. I imagine she'll be sleeping on the couch again."

"See, that right there," Eric pointed out. "Our mom doesn't need to be sleeping on the couch, but you've let her ever since Dad passed. She should be in her room, in her bed, and starting to move on with her life without Dad."

"Dude, what the hell?! She lost her husband like what, five days ago?! And she buried him today and you're like,

'Time to pick up the pieces and move on, Mom!' Can you give her a little time to mourn? I would think *you* would be the child who coddled her."

Alex walked over to Andy, spacing himself between Renae and Eric. "I just want to warn you, this could get ugly, but it's been a long time coming," Alex whispered. Andy looked at Alex, confused and somewhat scared. He had heard horror stories of his sister-in-law's temper and physical strength; he had just never experienced it.

"You're the one who's coddling her, Renae! Unlike you, I want her to move on with her life. Her world doesn't have to stop because her husband died. I just want to see her get back on her feet and start functioning like a normal human being again."

"So do I, but in her own time, Eric." Renae started taking steps towards her brother. "You weren't here to listen to the screams and cries of your mother when she learned the love of her life passed away. You weren't here to see her cry herself to sleep her first night without him. She's a little upset, Eric, and if she wants to sleep on the couch, then by all means, let her sleep on the couch!"

"I knew you would throw that in my face. That I wasn't here. I got a flight the second we hung up the phone. Don't think for a minute that I didn't want to be here. That I didn't regret not being closer."

"At what point do we break this up?" Andy whispered to Alex.

"When she looks like she's going to tackle him or throw a punch."

"For real?" Andy was shocked.

Alex nodded his head and shrugged his shoulders. "It's what they do. They bottle everything up until they can't take the pressure any more. It's gotten mildly violent before, but they never break anything or shed blood or anything like that."

"And just like that this conversation became about

you, Eric. If you knew what was so good for Mom, why did you stay away for two years? Why didn't you check up on her and Dad? Who knows, Eric, maybe if you were here to help them function like normal human beings Dad would still be alive, because obviously I didn't know how to take care of him." Renae was pushing Eric. She knew she was being mean. She knew he had his reasons for staying away. Reasons that probably broke his heart more than she knew. But she kept pushing. She was mad and she was ready to start throwing blows.

Eric could feel his temperature rise. He stepped closer to his sister, narrowing the space between them. "You know damn well why I stayed away. And don't you *dare* insinuate that Dad would still be here if I had been here."

"You're right. If you'd stuck around, we would have buried him a long time ago."

"Why are you so mean? You know what's comical about all of this? Dad skipped my wedding for whatever stupid reasons he could give and bent over backwards for his precious little girl-"

"Watch yourself-" Renae warned.

"-who failed miserably at her marriage and chased away the perfect guy."

"Okay, you two, that's eno-," before Alex could finish his sentence, Renae pushed Eric to the floor, her fists clenched at her side, and stood over him. Andy let out a short scream and jumped on the kitchen counter with his hand over his mouth.

"Say it again, I dare you."

"What are you, eight?! You're a freaking bully!"

"You're a jerk," Renae walked away from her brother and Alex helped Eric to his feet. Andy sat on the counter, still in shock over what he had just witnessed. Renae walked past him and headed to the liquor cabinet. She pulled out four crystal tumblers and her father's favorite whiskey. She chose the tumblers carefully. They were the ones Eric had bought for their father for Christmas with his first paycheck. They held sentimental value to both men and she knew it. If she couldn't hurt him on the outside, she was going to make sure it cut deep on the inside.

"This was Dad's favorite whiskey. Anyone care to join me? Otherwise I will get very drunk on my own while finishing this thing off tonight."

"Oh, yes, please, I'm in need of a drink right now," Andy was quick to respond. "I have no idea what I just witnessed, but I need a drink to scrub that from my mind."

"Alex? Eric?"

Alex shook his head to decline.

Eric stared at the tumblers and after some careful consideration, he broke his silence. "You know, I don't know what Dad's favorite whiskey is." Renae began to pour a third glass. "I thought he drank bourbon. When you offered me his pellet gun yesterday, I thought it was a real gun. Like a .38 or something. I never went shooting with him; that was your thing. Almost everything that he did, he shared with you. And every milestone of yours, he was there for, celebrating right beside you. What I said about your marriage sucked, and I'm sorry, especially to you Alex, because you've been nothing but awesome and I still consider you a brother. But, Renae, I can't help but be jealous of the relationship you had with Dad, and the fact that he died not knowing I loved him and wished for so much more between us tears me up inside. But he just couldn't accept me." Eric began to sob. There had been so many things that needed to be said between him and his father over the years, and now it was too late. Revealing her sensitive side, Renae walked over to her brother and held him. Alex felt butterflies in his stomach. This was the moment the family had anticipated, and he knew it was up to him to talk to Eric. Andy hopped down from the counter and walked to Eric and Renae. He rubbed Renae's back and began to wipe away his own tears. He had been hurt in all of this, too. There was more history with this family than just his and Eric's marriage, and he ran from his circumstances, taking Eric with him. It was time for him to come face-to-face with some issues that had been troubling him, too.

As Eric began to calm down, he pulled away from his sister and wiped his tears. "I hope he knew I loved him and wanted nothing more than to rebuild our relationship. It's ironic, but I called him the night he passed away. I called his cell and left him a message saying those exact things, about loving him and wanting restoration between us. And when I found out he had spent his last hour with you, it burned me. The thought that he missed my call or never listened to the message because he was bonding with you broke me. I was jealous of you. I *am* jealous of you. I mean, you may be a divorcee living with your parents and a complete witch, but I am jealous of your relationship with our dad, with our pastor, with your friends. I mean, look, you completely ruined your marriage but here stands Mr. Wonderful, right by your side during the worst moment of your life. I just wish I knew whether Dad got my message or not."

"Well why don't you check his phone?" Renae suggested. "You can look at his phone and see if he checked his voicemail. Then you'll know and you won't have to live with the what-if's in case he did listen to it."

"Do you know where his phone is?"

"I do." Alex offered to get it so he could get away and change into his jeans.

"While he gets that, how about we raise a glass to your dad, in his honor?"

"Good call, Andy." Renae grabbed the tumblers, Eric again wiped away his tears, and the three raised their glasses high. None of them could think of anything to say, so they clinked their glasses together and partook. Andy devoured the drink in one shot, while Renae and Eric took a sip, both shivering as they laid their glasses down.

"Holy crap, what is that?! Jet fuel?!" Eric looked to Renae, who gave a short cough.

"I think so, maybe that's why he always told me to steer clear of his whiskey."

"It burns!! Oh God, it's burning!" Andy leaned over the counter and started to hit it. "Ahhh! Why does it burn so bad?!"

"Well it wasn't intended to be a shot!" Renae started to laugh at Andy, with Eric quickly joining in once he saw Andy's empty glass. "Do I need to call 911?"

"Nooo!" Andy squealed.

Alex walked into the kitchen to see Renae rubbing Andy's back, her face in Andy's face, with Eric on the other side of him laughing. "What did I miss?"

"Andy decided to shoot about three ounces of Daddy's rocket fuel and right now he's trying to recover from the burn." Renae grabbed her glass and poured the remaining contents into the kitchen sink.

Eric turned his attention away from Andy and noticed Alex was standing in the room with the phone in his hand. Alex held it up so everyone could see. The siblings quickly redirected their attention to it.

"So?" Eric tried to act like it was no big deal whether the message had been heard or not, but internally, his stomach was flipping.

"Well, there are 96 missed calls on here; all of them from your mom."

"She wanted to hear his voice," Renae spoke quietly.

"And there is one new voicemail...it's from an 888 area code. The message from you was saved."

Eric sighed and fought back tears. "So, he heard it. He knew. Good."

Alex figured this was going to be the best way to lead into the conversation he needed to have with Eric tonight. He and Renae had agreed that he should do it alone. "Eric, can you and I talk? There are some things you really need to know."

Eric nodded his head.

Renae grabbed a six pack from the refrigerator, locked elbows with Andy, and led him outside to the back porch. "That's our cue to leave." She turned to look at Alex before shutting the door behind her. He was staring at the bottled water in front of him. She could see his lips moving, but he wasn't talking; he was praying. She was grateful Alex had stepped into this role. She recognized that she wasn't as strong, patient, and level-headed as he was, and he would be more successful at getting the message across than she ever could.

❋ ❋ ❋

"You know, the last time I sat on this porch was with your father. It was the night Eric and I told him we were engaged," Andy reflected.

"Oh, if you're looking for a camp counselor to talk to tonight, I am *so* not the person you need to talk to."

"I'll never forget the sting in his eyes. They squinted in pain to reveal his hurt."

"And yet, you're still talking."

"Your mom began to cry. I'm still not sure if they were tears of joy or disappointment. She hugged us so tightly after Phil got up to leave."

Defeated and knowing Andy was going to keep talking no matter how much she told him she didn't want to hear it, she downed her first beer and offered him one.

"I wish I'd gotten to know him, other than the two times we had dinner here or when he came up to the hospital. He had this fun energy to him. You could see how much he just enjoyed being around people. And the stories told about him today were inspirational. What I wouldn't give to be a part of a family unit like what you all have here."

Renae didn't know what to say to Andy. It wasn't that

she didn't care. Offering him words of affirmation would be pointless. Agreeing with him would be like pouring salt into an open wound. She leaned back in her chair at the long patio table and stared at him sympathetically. She knew her father would have loved Andy, just as she was beginning to. She also knew she didn't want to reflect on any circumstances that might bring more sadness. Not tonight. She wasn't emotionally stable enough to balance more feelings.

"Sorry to vent," Andy added. "I know you have the emotional sensitivity of a rock. I just needed to release that to someone who wouldn't get offended or defensive."

"It's okay," was all Renae could offer. She rested her foot on a bar supporting the table and rocked as she brought the bottle to her lips and looked outdoors. The frogs were beginning to conduct their evening melody. Some of the noises she had never been able to identify, unsure if she was hearing a weird breed of amphibian or bird. She was so lost in her thoughts, she didn't hear the pending question Andy had asked of her.

"I'm sorry, that was too intrusive," she heard him say.

"I'm sorry, what? I was lost in thought listening to the animals out there. What was intrusive?"

"I asked if you and Alex were working things out and if you were possibly thinking of getting back together."

"Oh! No, nooooo...no, we're not...he's just been here...we haven't...we're not together. No." Renae was shaking her head and grabbed her drink. She held it close as she repeated "No, we're not together." She took a sip of her drink, sat up straight, and cleared her throat. She could tell from Andy's facial expression that he had more to ask than she may be willing to answer.

* * *

Alex and Eric had been sitting at the kitchen table, a

place of many family discussions, catching up on the past couple of lost years. "Yeah, and now Andy is a neonatologist at the hospital. I wasn't sure if he was going to get past the loss of Josh's baby, especially since that loss hit pretty close to home. But since we moved and he's become established at this hospital, I think he's made peace with what happened, and he's learned to press on and celebrate the victories, no matter how big or small they are."

"Man, I can't even imagine how difficult it was for him when baby Ian died. We never even thought of how it affected him. We were so focused on Joshua and Angie and trying to help them cope through the pain. I know Renae probably wasn't the warmest when he came around after that."

"She was cold. A flat-out bitch to him."

"Yeah, but I don't think she realized it."

"I can't believe you're still defending her. You weren't here when I introduced him to the family. Renae walked into the room, waltzed right up to Andy, gave him one good look-over, told me she freaking hated me, then grabbed her keys and left. Can you imagine being a gay black man walking into this house for the first time to meet the family and getting that reaction? From the woman who was best friends with the father of the baby he'd promised--yet failed--to save? Believe me, she knew she was being a bitch."

"Well, Andy seemed to get past it. Have you?"

"Get past how nasty that girl out there can be? I'm not past it; I'm just used to it. I think the hug she gave me today was the first one I've received from her since your wedding. I don't know what happened to her growing up. She used to be cool. I certainly don't know how she ended up with an upstanding guy like you, but I can certainly see how she couldn't keep you around."

Alex was quiet for a minute. He wanted to offer a rebuttal, but he refrained. Things between him and Renae had been moving well this week; he didn't care to reflect on the past or what brought them to separation.

"Well, I'm really glad things are working well for him. And you. How are you holding up through all of this?"

Eric paused for a moment. "I knew this would come up eventually."

"What's that?"

"The distance between Dad and me. How I'm coping. You're kind of macho; are you sure you want to talk about feelings and stuff? You might get a little misty-eyed. I'm not sure I've ever seen a jock cry before."

"Yeah, we're not in high school anymore; I hope you can get past looking at me as a jock now," Alex joked.

"So...wow. Yeah, I'm just gonna say it. I'm still hurt that Dad didn't come to the wedding. I'm hurt he didn't call, send a bottle of wine, a card. None of that. I watched him throw an extravagant wedding for you and Renae. It was joyous; he invited friends from all over the country, put them up in a hotel, served the most delicious food, and celebrated past midnight. You would have thought you two were royalty, the way he doted on you. Man, he loved you and was so excited about giving Renae away to you. I was so proud he was my dad. I thought, man, I can't wait until I meet my forever person. I knew customarily Dad wouldn't throw a wedding for me, but I couldn't wait to have my dad show me and my spouse off to his friends and celebrate us the way he did you. And you know what, Andy is an amazing person who should be celebrated. He freaking saves babies! And Dad missed it, and Renae missed it, and you missed it. And I couldn't forgive any of you for turning your back on us but screw you; I have friends and family who chose to be with us and accept us. You know, all I could imagine for the past two years or so was Dad on his knees trying to pray the gay away. I couldn't call him, Alex, and he never called me. He never tried to explain why he didn't come. He didn't try to come visit. He and Renae have always been so close, closer than he and I ever were. And when I found out you two were getting divorced, I thought for sure she would be shunned by Dad. She would finally get the treatment she deserved, being the horrible person that she is. But he let her move back home with him!" Eric laughed and shook his head. He noticed Alex was a good listener but was curious as to what he was preparing to share. "You know, Alex, I think Dad would have liked Andy. And I wish Andy knew you while you and Renae were having problems. He would have moved heaven and earth to keep you two together. Y'all are missing out on a pretty incredible person."

Alex took a moment to digest everything Eric had just laid out before him. He felt for Eric. He didn't appreciate the way he talked about Renae, but they were always pretty harsh with each other. He wasn't sure if Eric would ever understand Phil's reasons, but for Eric's sake, he needed to explain.

"So, Eric," Alex began, "what, besides Andy and your deep-rooted loathing for your sister, do you feel deeply passionate about? A cause you would give up everything--your friends, your house, your family, your lifestyle--for."

Eric looked at him and thought about it. He proceeded with caution. "I doubt there is any cause that I would sacrifice my family for."

"This isn't about sacrificing your family; it's about sacrificing yourself. Something you would lay it all down for so they wouldn't have to suffer?"

"Okay, then, the Pride movement. I'd be willing to sacrifice spending my life with my family so others could love whom they want to love."

"You'd be willing to give up friends, jobs, family, your life for that?"

"I already have," Eric responded coolly.

"Ok. Your dad felt that same way about his relationship with God."

"I've heard this."

"I know you have, I know you were raised in church and I know you know what the Bible says. That's not what I'm getting at."

"Okay," Eric didn't want to hear Alex preach to him, especially since he knew the lifestyle Alex and Renae used to live.

"This relationship Phil had with God molded him into the incredible man all those people remembered today. Honoring God was at the forefront of every thought and every action Phil made. I'm sure you can remember how much he helped people. If someone was asking for money on the street, he would give them money *and* the jacket off his back. He mowed lawns for widows, constructed houses for the homeless; he couldn't watch a tree get cut down without planting a new one."

"Yeah, he was always pretty considerate of the environment and people around him. I'll never forget the hissy fit Renae had after she collected a ton of live shells when we were at the beach and he made her put all her new friends back. He was protective over all life, even if it meant breaking his precious daughter's heart."

Alex laughed with Eric. "I've never heard that story; you'll have to tell me about that one."

"She cried for hours. She also killed a starfish; she found it in the ocean and hid it in her swimsuit so Mom and Dad wouldn't find out. They found out a week later from the funky smell emanating from her room."

"Really?! She won't let Maddy disturb anything at the beach or in the water. I thought she was just afraid of Maddy contracting diseases."

"Yeah, no, she probably feels remorse after killing that starfish. Dad made up some crazy story about the mommy starfish looking for her baby and Renae lost it. She cried and wore black for two days. Anyhow, that was way off topic. Sorry."

"No, that's pretty funny, and probably explains a few things. Anyways, back to your dad. He put so many people's needs above his own, and I think it's because he knew God would supply all he ever really needed. He reiterated to me once what Jesus said was the greatest commandment of all. That is to love God, and then love your neighbor as yourself, in that order. So, for Phil, to love God meant to honor God, His Word, and His commandments. And as someone who walked with God, he felt that to do or knowingly be a part of something that God was explicitly against in His Word meant he would have separation from the One he committed to follow. It split Phil's heart in two when he searched his own soul and concluded he couldn't be a part of your day. It wasn't that he didn't love you nor that he couldn't accept Andy. It was that he believed with every fiber of his being that what you were doing was falling outside the will of God, and Phil couldn't celebrate that. He couldn't sit in the presence of your choice and the Holy Spirit at the same time."

Eric sat in silence and stared at his drink for a moment.

"And what about you and Renae? What do you think? You didn't come either and I know neither of you were attending church, so what's your excuse?"

"Eric, your mom and dad were at odds over this. Renae was worried these differences would split them apart. As you may recall, his position was the unpopular one and he didn't have many people outside his inner circle applauding his decision to skip the wedding. So, one day your sister came home and told me she was going to stand beside her father and support him. She felt he needed assurance from someone close to home, that regardless of his beliefs he was still loved and respected as the head of the family. And with everything we were going through, I felt I needed to stand by my wife's decision. It wasn't that she and I were protesting or hating you. It was about loving your father when he was under attack by more people than you know."

"I guess he and I could relate there."

"He loved you. He prayed for you every day. And he wasn't 'praying the gay away.' He was praying that you would one day love God like he did. More than he did. He prayed for your protection and prosperity, and for the words to say to you when he saw you again. Eric, do you know how many times he would sit down and show people pictures of you on his iPad? And he'd share pictures of Andy that he could find on social media. Your dad didn't disown you or dislike you. He loved you. He just had no idea how to show you. I'm just really sorry it's tonight that you're finding all of this out."

"Yeah, me too," Eric said softly. He wasn't sure if he fully understood his father's position. He knew he didn't agree with it, but he also knew how much he needed to hear that his father loved him. "Thanks for that, Alex. Dad was lucky to have you for a son-in-law. I hope you two got some time together before he passed away."

"Well, nobody is ever prepared for that, but yeah. We saw each other occasionally."

"That makes me happy," Eric began as he wiped some tears away. "Not just the fact that you guys were seeing each other but because I'm pretty sure you were doing it behind my sister's back."

"Do you think you two will ever get along?" Alex inquired.

"I love my sister, and I know she loves me. I think our tough exteriors toward one another keep us hard. I'm not sure if it's a good or a bad thing."

"Yeah, I wouldn't exactly call that a good thing."

"I wonder what they're talking about out there. You think Andy's still alive?"

"Alive, yes. Passed out, more than likely."

✲ ✲ ✲

Had it been any other night, Renae may not have felt so comfortable sharing her innermost feelings with Andy. But tonight she was throwing caution to the wind and willing to answer pretty much anything he threw her way.

"When Angie passed away, Joshua pretty much lost his mind. He sheltered himself and became a recluse. I probably spent more time with him than I should have, now that I look back at it. There were definitely times when I could tell Alex was suspicious of us. Nothing ever happened, but I'm still not sure whether Alex believes that."

"How did she pass? Eric never told me."

"She overdosed. I don't think anyone recognized that she was so depressed after baby Ian passed away-" Renae stopped mid-sentence when she realized guilt was pouring over Andy. She immediately understood why Eric never told him; he was protecting him. She reached across the table for his hand. "Andy, I'm really sorry for how I treated you during all of that. Hey, you need to know *none* of this was your fault. Any doctor that worked on that baby would have had the same result, you *know* that. I look back and that tiny little person was so lucky to have you for a doctor that night. You did everything you could. Angie and Joshua tried for years to have a baby, and they knew trying to have him was a risk. But for his short time here on Earth, he knew true love. Ian was *so* loved. And I thank you for the time you were able to give his family with their little boy. They *did* have a son, and their story and his life may look different and be something most of us don't understand, but you know what? He came into and left this earth knowing the most important force in the world, thanks to you."

Andy released his hand from Renae's grip and covered his face as he cried. His tears weren't tears of sorrow, but of release. He had been carrying a burden for so long, and as Renae spoke, he felt the burden being lifted off his shoulders. Renae walked over and embraced him.

"I'm so sorry," she whispered in his ear.

"Thank you. I really needed to hear that." Andy rubbed his eyes, took a deep breath, and turned to Renae, giving her a warm smile. "Here, a hug is best when it isn't one-sided." He reached to wrap his arm around his sister-in-law when the chair suddenly gave way, the pair screaming as they fell to the concrete floor.

"She's killing him!" Eric jumped from the table and ran outside, Alex right behind him.

Eric and Alex ran through the door to find Andy and Renae laughing uncontrollably on the floor, two pieces of a chair underneath them.

"Oww, it hurts, it hurts!" Renae cried out as she laughed. "I think I broke my spleen!"

"Your spleen is on the other side!" Andy blurted out with a laugh.

"You are so wasted," Eric said as he attempted to help Andy up.

"I'm not, I promise," Andy replied, still laughing, as he got to his feet and helped Renae up.

"I'm going to have a bruise. I hit the arm of the chair," Renae whined.

"Were you two fighting?"

"No, just the opposite," Andy answered Alex. "We were trying to hug, and the chair busted from underneath. I took her down with me."

"You can't even hug people without hurting them," Eric lashed out at his sister.

"Piss off," Renae gave her brother a piercing glare as she rubbed her side and walked back to her chair to sit down.

"Eric, we were having a moment, one of many tonight." Andy looked at his sister-in-law and their expressions turned soft as they exchanged smiles. "I am feeling far from hurt."

"Yeah, we connected tonight and I, um, I really regret not getting to know Andy before this week," Renae admitted, her focus still locked on Andy. "He really challenged me this evening and I'm pretty thankful for that." She was still rubbing the pain on her side from hitting the chair in the fall.

Alex, exhausted not only from the activities of the day but also from being released from the pressure of the conversation with Eric, pulled a chair from the corner of the patio and sat next to Renae. "Where does it hurt?" He felt Renae's side where she'd been rubbing. She jumped at his touch and sat up straight in her chair.

"It's okay, I'll be fine." She shifted in her chair to close off her body position to him. He had hoped for any reaction but that to his touch.

"You know, I think we need to get going," Andy locked eyes with Renae. They'd had a serious conversation about her and Alex's relationship tonight and she could tell from his facial expression that he was urging her to talk to her ex-husband. "We'll be back pretty early tomorrow morning."

Feeling emotionally drained, Eric agreed. The duo quickly said their goodbyes and then retreated inside to gather their belongings and say goodnight to Ruth, if she was still awake.

Alex and Renae sat in silence on the back porch. Neither of them knew what tomorrow would hold since the funeral was over and Alex was free of any further obligations or duties with the family. Neither was eager to say goodbye to one another after the events of the past week. They were enjoying each other's presence, even though they couldn't bring themselves to admit it. After hearing Eric's car doors shut and the car pull away, Alex broke the silence.

"You know, as much as I enjoy the company, I don't think I'm going to make it to sunrise."

"Me neither." Renae started to shiver, not just from the chill in the air, but also from the release of much emotional stress.

"Are you cold? We can go inside."

"No," Renae shook her head. "I'm a little chilly, but I feel like I'm coming down from an intense adrenaline rush or something. How did it go with Eric?"

"It went pretty well, I think." Alex stood up, and Renae, wanting him to stay, felt her heart sink a little. "I'm going to run to the bathroom, I'll grab a blanket for you when I come out and we can talk about it. Unless you're ready to call it a night."

"I can stay up a little more. A blanket would be great." She was relieved and grateful for more time with him. As he closed the door behind him, dread sank in as she thought of being alone with haunting thoughts and memories of her father. The silence was taunting her, and she felt as if her chest was being crushed by an unknown force. She looked over at the Echo sitting on a small table on the patio. "Alexa, play Dad's playlist," she instructed. Still shivering, she laid her head on the cold tile table as one of her father's favorite worship songs reverberated through the speaker.

> *When darkness comes*
> *And my eyes grow dim*
> *You know the way*
> *It's by Your grace*
> *That my spirit sings*
> *You show the way*

Renae closed her eyes and absorbed the words of comfort surrounding her.

> *Should mountains fall*
> *Crash into the waves*
> *You know the way*
> *Refuge and strength*
> *Though the earth should change*
> *You know the way*
>
> *Be still and know*
> *That He is here*
> *Be still and know*
> *Jesus forever in control*
> *Be still and know*
> *He's Lord of all*

The pressing feeling on her chest was being lifted as her fear turned to a sorrowful peace, and tears streamed down the corners of her eyes.

When my mind shakes
Full of anxious thoughts
You show the way
Light up my path
Heaven send Your fire
You show the way

Overcome by the sadness of the events earlier in the day combined with the conversation she'd had with Andy, she was no longer able to stabilize her emotions. She buried her head in her arms as she began to cry. Alex walked outside with an oversized blanket and, seeing her emotional breakdown, raced to Renae's side.

"Come here," he whispered as he reached for her arm and pulled her close to him. She stood to her feet and buried her head in his chest. He placed the blanket over her shoulders and wrapped his arms around her. The comfort of his embrace eased her sobs, but the tears didn't stop flowing. "Is this okay?" he asked her quietly.

"Yeah," Renae whispered back. "Can we sit down?"

"Sure." Alex led her to the small loveseat on the porch. He sat down and Renae curled next to him, again resting her head on his chest. He wrapped his arm around her and rubbed her shoulder as she covered them both with her blanket. Worn down, they sat and listened to the music as peace began to envelope them.

Day by day
With joy and strength
We will sing
Who is like our God?

Lifted high
To bring You praise
There is none
That is like our God

Recognizing the sound of slight sniffling above her, Renae lifted her head to look at Alex. They stared into one another's eyes as tears streamed down both their faces. Gently, she wiped the drops from his cheeks. He was just as affected by this loss as everyone else in the family, and tonight they were reunited in the midst of their pain. Renae rested her head back on Alex's chest and laid her arm on his stomach. He bent his head forward and kissed the top of her hair. Renae closed her eyes and sank into familiar comfort. Within minutes, she drifted off to sleep, Alex not far behind her.

Both slept so soundly, neither were disturbed by the serenading of the backyard bullfrog.

* * *

Renae opened one eye and moaned at the daylight. She was dreaming of her father making french toast and bacon for her and Maddy. She closed her eyes and tried to return to her dream to no avail. She wiped her cheek, which was covered in a thick slime. Looking down, she realized she had drooled on Alex most of the night. As she sat up, her head reminded her of how much she had drunk the day before and how much she needed water and some pain killers.

Alex, awakened by Renae's movement, reached for his neck and started to rub it. He could barely move it without wincing in pain.

Renae noticed he was awake. "Holy cow, I feel like crap."

"I can't move my neck."

"What in the world did we drink?"

"I had water, you had tequila, whiskey, and beer. Why is my shirt wet? I can't see it."

"I may have drooled all over it."

"That's pretty disgusting."

Renae slowly stood up and tossed the blanket behind her onto the loveseat. "Oh God, I hope Maddy isn't up right now."

Alex received that as Renae hoping Maddy wouldn't see the two of them together. What Renae meant was that she just didn't want to have to take care of her daughter in her current state of physical agony. "Yeah, I should get my things and get going."

"You're not staying for breakfast? Nope, can't talk about food." Renae held her fist over her mouth and stopped moving. When the urge to throw up subsided, she looked at Alex and smiled as she shuffled to the door that led to the kitchen. "Do I look smexy?"

Alex looked at his ex-wife and grinned. Her hair was every direction, dried drool was crusted on her cheek, and yesterday's makeup was smeared around her eyes. "My dear, you are the definition of smexy."

Renae smiled and nodded in agreement, which sent a serious throb through her forehead and temples. "Ow." She grabbed her forehead and made her way through the door to the house.

"Mommy!" Maddy greeted her mom as she opened the door. Alex heard Renae moan her most colorful expletive as she closed the door behind her. He looked around the patio. The broken chair still lay in pieces on the floor. Empty beer bottles cluttered the table. Ruth was going to be beside herself if she walked outside to this. He began to clean up the mess as the door swung open and his little girl ran out to see him.

"Daddy!!" She wrapped her arms around his legs, almost tackling him to the ground.

"Hey, Princess!" He peeled his little girl off his legs and

picked her up to squeeze her tight.

"Did you and Mommy camp out here last night?"

"Kind of. We were up talking, and we got so tired we fell asleep out here."

"What were you talking about?" Maddy started to trace the features of her Daddy's face as he talked.

"Well, we talked about Grampy mostly."

"I miss Grampy. I miss his hugs."

"Me too, baby, me too."

She looked at the broken chair behind her daddy. "Did you and Mommy have another fight last night?" Her big brown eyes held so much innocence, but she had witnessed more fights between her parents in her young years than any child ever should ever have to endure.

"No, baby. Not at all. The chair broke last night when Uncle Andy was in it."

"Did he get hurt?"

"Nah, he's a pretty tough guy. Want to help me throw it in the garbage up front?"

Maddy nodded her head and helped him pick up the heavy pieces of the chair. They took them through the yard to deposit them in the trash can by the garage. As they closed the lid, Eric and Andy pulled into the driveway. Maddy jumped with excitement. Seeing Alex still at the house and in his clothes from the night before, Andy jumped out of the car when it came to a stop.

"Well, good morning! I can only assume you and Miss Renae had a really good talk last night."

"We just fell asleep on the couch outside," Alex explained as he shook Andy's hand. "Nothing too eventful."

"You two need to go out and have dinner," Andy said as Eric walked up.

"Why, so she can poison him?"

"Eric, please, don't." Alex glanced at Maddy to remind Eric his daughter was hearing everything they said.

Eric looked at his niece and held his hand out. "Hey

cutie, is your grandmother up yet?"

Maddy took his hand and smiled. "She woke up early. She slept with me last night."

"I saw that when I tucked you in last night. But you were sleeping."

"You saw me when I was sleeping?"

"I did." The four made their way to the front door. "And you probably didn't hear me, but I promised you bagels this morning." He held up a brown paper bag filled with bagels and tubs of cream cheese. Maddy looked at her uncle and showed him her toothy grin. She reminded him of his childhood best friend, his sister. He pinched her cheek and led her inside.

* * *

Renae lay on her bed, regretting the choices she had made the night before. The water and painkillers hadn't kicked in yet. She just wanted to go back to sleep so she couldn't feel the effects of her behavior. Alex entered her room, slightly knocking as he snuck in.

"Hey, mind if I come in?"

"Come in." Renae was barely audible, her face buried under her blanket to her nose.

Alex walked into the room he hadn't seen in years. He looked around and recognized some of the items they had accumulated together, and some he hadn't seen since they were dating. Her mirror was adorned with pictures of Renae and Maddy, Mr. and Mrs. Rivera, and Renae and Joshua. Not seeing his face with her in pictures but seeing Joshua's brought a slight heat to his cheeks.

"How are you feeling?" he asked.

"I regret decisions I made last night. Mostly everything I consumed. How are you feeling?"

"I'm fine. Hey, I wanted to find out what you have planned today." He sat down on the side of her bed and pulled the covers away from her face. "Want me to take Maddy?"

"Are you off again today?"

"Yeah, I took the week off in case you needed me for anything."

"Oh my gosh, I would love it if you took Maddy. Do you want to bring her back Sunday? I think our weeks and weekends have gotten mixed up somehow. I don't know whose weekend it is to have her."

He reached for her hand and held it in his, staring at it and rubbing her scarred ring finger. "I was actually wondering if we could get your mom to watch her tomorrow night." He was trying to work up the nerve to ask her out on a date. The idea had consumed his thoughts for the past two days and Alex knew he couldn't leave the house without suggesting it. He couldn't get over how nervous he was and how ridiculous he felt. He had known Renae for over half his life and he felt like he was once again a teenager asking her to the prom for the first time. "Maybe if she could watch Maddy we could go out for dinner. Just you and me."

Renae couldn't get over how cool he was. She wished she had an ounce of his confidence. She also couldn't believe how much had changed between them in the course of a week. He had changed so much, but she was still the same woman who she now wondered was worthy enough to be with him. She was course, argumentative, and quick to anger. All those things affected their relationship during their marriage. She rubbed his hand with her finger. "Can I ask her and let you know?"

"Of course."

The thought of going on an actual date with Alex took her mind off how horrible she was feeling. Not letting go of his hand, she rolled onto her back and stared at the ceiling. "A date, huh?" She began to recall the conversation she'd had with Andy the previous night. She shared a lot of her feelings with him, shared her and Alex's shaky past, and her fight to stay separated from him. Andy had scolded her about how ridiculous they were being. He could see in five days that they still loved each other, especially on Alex's part. But this notion of consciously staying apart to avoid stirring up feelings was the dumbest thing he had ever heard of. Regardless, she feared the thought of letting her guard down and the risk of being hurt again. "I don't know, Alex. There are some things we need to talk about and I'm not sure if we should before, during, or after this date. What's the point of going on the date in the first place? Is it to argue about our differences? To bring up past hurts? To navigate our separation in the future?"

Alex felt defeat trying to penetrate his hope, but he wasn't going to allow it to, not after all the progress he and Renae had made this week. Every sacrifice, every choice, every action had been made by putting her first. He pushed away his insecurities and took a chance at being honest and raw with her. "I just want to take you somewhere nice, treat you to dinner, watch you smile, hear you laugh, listen to your dreams, and just spend some one on one time with you. You deserve a nice night out and I'm afraid I neglected to treat you to enough of those when I had you."

Renae turned her head to look at him. She was speechless. She'd always known he was pretty incredible, but now he was placing his focus solely on her. She strained to remain emotionless. Alex continued, "I don't know, maybe we could have dinner first and then go to the pier to talk. We can see how the evening plays out. What do you think?" Alex held her hand to his mouth and Renae studied his face. She knew every scar, every wrinkle, every line on that face. When it was soft, it brought her comfort. When it was harsh, it brought her resentment. He'd been doing an amazing job at bringing her comfort over the past few days.

"Yeah."

"Yeah?"

"Yeah," Renae repeated with a smile. "I'll talk to Mom and if she can't, maybe Joshua would be able to."

"Or we could find a sitter."

"Ok... What should I wear?"

"Something like what you had on at the team party is fine. Dressy, but casual."

"Ok. You remember what I had on at the team party?"

Alex gave her a flirtatious wink and tried to contain his excitement. He stood up and gave her a quick kiss on the forehead. "I'll have Maddy get dressed. You get some rest. I'll see you around 5 tomorrow?"

"5 works," Renae agreed with a smile.

"Ok, if I don't see you before we head out, I'll see you tomorrow. Just let me know if I need to bring Maddy here." He stopped to look at her one last time and gave her another kiss on the forehead, bringing a fresh smile to her face. They locked eyes, smiling at one another as he walked backwards out of the room.

The despair and sorrow that had filled the house was quickly being choked out by hope and joy.

S IX

Hours had passed since Alex left for his house with Maddy. Renae had showered and was feeling much better, so she made plans to go out with Joshua. They had spent so little time with each other over the past week; she wanted to catch him up to speed on the week's events and get his advice. She needed another person's opinion, someone outside her family who knew the history of her and Alex. Joshua was there when she fell in love with Alex and when she called it off. He was there to hear of every fight, every heartbreak, and every triumph. Renae felt he could tell her if she was making the right move spending more time with Alex, or if she was making a dire mistake. She was desperate to see him.

Andy and Eric were with Ruth in her room, cleaning out Phil's personal belongings as Renae entered to talk to her mother. She was shocked at the sight of her father's clothes piled in boxes, memories of him being stored away.

"What's going on here? What are you doing with all of Dad's stuff?"

"Well, look who's back from the dead," Eric greeted her.

"Honey," Ruth began, "your brothers and I talked about it and we decided it was best to sort these things out before they left. They knew it was a huge task for me to do on my own, and all of us knew you would try to hold onto everything."

Renae was ready to lose her mind. How dare they try to erase Daddy a week after he passed away! They had just laid him to rest yesterday. How on earth could her mother be so cold and callous towards the memory of her husband? This was such a horrible idea; it had to be Eric's. She fixed her gaze on her brother as those around her could feel the tension quickly escalate.

"What do you plan on doing with all of this, then?"

"Donate it to veterans," Eric replied. "There are some great organizations out there that I'm sure Dad would love to see his things go to. I can't wear any of it and it's all good stuff so I'm sure it will all get some good use."

Renae couldn't argue with that. Her anger began to subside as she realized Dad's belongings could be passed to people in need, people her father deeply cared about. Scanning the room, she saw they weren't trying to rid the house of all his belongings, just the things that would be of good use to others. Renae looked to her mom, who she noticed was taking in the scent of articles of clothing before folding them and placing them in a box. She kneeled down next to her mother and leaned against her. "You're a very strong and brave woman, Mom." Renae put her arm around her mother and squeezed tight as Ruth accepted and returned the hug.

"I don't know about that. I'm just trying to keep busy and surround myself with people right now. Your Daddy always carried enough strength for the both of us; I'm not sure where I'm finding the strength to just keep moving each day." Ruth fought back her tears. She had stopped folding the clothes and started to stare at the floor. "I'm afraid I don't even know how to react without your brother telling me how I should feel right now." She quickly snapped out of her daze and started to sort and fold clothes again.

Renae began to realize how lost her mother felt. She didn't have the words or encouragement to offer her. She knew that despite her distaste for her brother, his presence and guidance were exactly what her mother needed right now. The two of them had a special bond that no person, action, or word could ever break. Renae decided now wasn't the time to ask her mother to watch Maddy. She didn't want to seem selfish or insensitive. She was also unaware that Andy had already done it for her. As she stood to her feet, Andy spoke up.

"Oh, Renae, we talked to Ruth. She's happy to have Maddy tomorrow night."

"How did you know I needed someone to watch Maddy?"

"Oh, yes! I figure we can make ice cream sandwiches and watch a princess movie or two. It'll be fun!" Ruth added with enthusiasm. She was happy to have something to look forward to.

Renae was perplexed. How would Andy know she needed her mom to watch Maddy? Unless he and Alex had talked. Oh my gosh, they talked! Did Andy tell Alex anything she told him last night? What *did* she tell Andy, by the way? Renae knew she was loose-lipped when she drank too much, and she knew she'd definitely drunk too much the day before.

"Um, thanks, Mom. I appreciate it. We shouldn't be out very late," she said cautiously.

"Stay out all night. I don't mind," Ruth replied with a wink.

Eric and Andy exchanged smiles before turning those smiles to Renae. She was feeling suspicious of a conversation they all may have had with Alex, but to save herself from embarrassment, she didn't inquire about any details. Renae began to back out of the room. She couldn't handle being away from her closest confidant any longer. She needed to get to Joshua's.

"Okay. I'm going to leave you all before I shove all Dad's stuff in the attic, and I'm going to head to Joshua's house."

"Don't you go screwing things up with Alex by messing around with Joshua now," Andy warned.

"What? There's nothing going on with Alex and me to screw up, and I'm not messing around with Joshua."

"Mm-hmm," replied Eric as he tossed a sweatshirt at

his sister. It was their dad's favorite grey Air Force sweatshirt and her brother knew she would appreciate it more than anyone else ever could.

"Thank you," she said after she opened it. She gave Eric a tender smile and headed toward the stairs. She really wished they'd had more moments like this in their lives. She just couldn't stand being around him for very long. Still, she had hopes that one day they could really reconnect and be friends again. Perhaps her relationship with Andy would help that.

* * *

Joshua stood in his master bathroom and rubbed his freshly-shaved face dry with a towel. He was happy to have some alone time with Renae today. With the passing of her father, Alex in her life again, and Eric and Andy in town, he knew she had to be close to a mental meltdown. He was preparing himself to walk her through it; it was what he always did, and he was more than happy to be the one to fill that role in her life. He walked to his nightstand and placed two devotional books he had been studying in the top drawer. One was on grief, the other relationships. He knew navigating through everything Renae was facing would be tricky, so he was equipped to guide her through it.

As he headed down the stairs, Milo's head lifted off the couch and focused on the front door. His wagging tail alerted Joshua that Renae was approaching. Milo could always tell when it was her at the door, and his excitement always gave her away. Just as she was about to knock, Joshua opened the door. Seeing one another took their breaths away and they quickly engaged in a long, heartfelt hug. "Where have you been all my life?" Joshua teased.

Renae laughed as she broke their embrace and kneeled down to give Milo the attention he was demanding to receive. "Hey, boy! I know! It's been too long!"

"He's been pretty bummed the past couple of days. He's not used to going more than 48 hours without seeing you. I'm pretty sure my dog loves you more than he loves me."

"Did you miss me, boy? I'm so sorry. I missed you, too!" She picked him up and let him give her doggie kisses as Joshua led her inside. Renae took Milo to the kitchen for a treat and saw a colorful spread of vegetables on the counter along with cutting boards, knives, and pans. Since Joshua wasn't fond of clutter, she knew what his plans were for them this evening. "What's on the menu tonight?"

"Chicken Marsala with sides of brussels sprouts and jasmine rice. But first, a beautiful mixed green salad with...these nutty-and-seedy things," Joshua said, as he picked up a premade package of dressing and salad toppings, investigating the contents.

"You got a bag of salad, didn't you" Renae laughed at her friend. Together they had tried cooking many dishes they'd found appetizing on The Food Channel, but either their taste buds were off or something usually went terribly wrong. They couldn't even get a fresh salad right. They both knew it wasn't because they were terrible cooks individually; it was because together they were too distracted to pay attention to what they were supposed to be doing.

Joshua tossed down the package and opened the refrigerator to a bowl of salad ready to go. "I figured we wouldn't want to spend all night slicing tiny pieces of cabbage and kale, and I can never remember what goes into the stuff."

"And the sauce for the chicken? Did that come from a package?" Renae teased.

"Nope, we're going to make that from scratch tonight."

"Oh no, this could end badly."

"And if it does, frozen pizza is our back-up." Joshua smiled and winked at his friend. He knew just as much as she did this would probably be another disaster. But the time spent together and the memories they made were precious, so neither of them really cared.

Renae walked to the sink and washed her hands. "Ok, what can I do?"

"You can start by opening the wine."

"Yes! That I can do. Is there a special one you want me to open?"

"Yeah, the one in the corner of the counter behind you."

"Perfect," Renae said as she located the wine. She looked at the label and didn't recognize it as one they had shared before. New dish, new wine, she was game.

"What movie do you want to watch tonight?" Joshua started to cut and peel onions.

"I can't do anything sad or a rom-com right now. Brainless comedy?" Renae suggested as she pulled the cork out of the wine.

"How about something that doesn't make me feel like I lost two hours of my life? *Braveheart? Gladiator?*"

"That Sparta fight was pretty epic."

"That's *300.*"

"No, I don't want to watch that. One of the other two is fine." Renae swirled her wine in the glass she'd poured for herself.

"Ok. I think I can stream one of those. I'll check when I'm done with these onions. There's a measuring cup near the wine, can you see how much we're supposed to use?"

"Of what? The onions?" Renae lifted the wine to her lips and took a sip.

"No, the wine," Joshua answered as he saw the pained expression on Renae's face.

"Oh my God, this stuff is awful!" she exclaimed, her mouth still full of wine. Joshua couldn't speak, he was laughing too hard. Renae walked to the sink and spit out the wine. "What in the world?! What was that? Like three-dollar drugstore wine?!"

"No, it's the wine for cooking the sauce, you lush."
Joshua grabbed the glass from her, placed it on the counter,
and embraced her. He adored her quirkiness and the random
things she did that made him laugh.

"I'm glad you're amused."

"I'm sorry, I didn't pay attention to what I bought
since we're cooking with it. Here, drink some water. I'm sure
your liver would appreciate it tonight after what you said
went down yesterday." Joshua poured her a glass of water
from the tap and Renae gladly accepted it.

"I can't believe that was yesterday. You know, it seems
like days since I last saw you. So much happened this past
week."

"Well, I understand if your days have been messed up
lately. You've been through a lot. And hey, I'm here to talk
when you're ready. In the meantime, the good wine is in the
usual cabinet. You get that; I need to get these mushrooms
and onions into the wine."

"Do you have any idea what you are doing?" Renae was
skeptical and tired. She really didn't feel like spending the
evening over a hot stove in the kitchen.

"Not really." Joshua wiped his hands on a cloth after
washing the mushrooms and looked at Renae, who had
grabbed a better bottle of wine. "But that's kind of our thing,
isn't it?" Renae couldn't help but think he was absolutely
adorable. And the fact that he went through all this trouble
for them to have a fun night together warmed her heart. She
decided to push through and cook with him, no matter how
much she didn't want to. It was important to him, so it was
important to her.

An hour and a half later, the friends were seated on
the sofa, eating their dinner and sipping wine. "I don't know,
maybe if we'd added some sugar it might have cut the bitterness," Renae suggested as she took a bite of pizza.

"Maybe. I thought we followed all the directions."

"Did we, though? Were we supposed to reduce the wine

with the mushrooms and onions in it as they caramelized?"

"Is that what we did?" Josh winked at her as he took a sip from his glass.

"I have no idea." The pair chuckled as they raised their pizza slices to toast.

"To us. And frozen pizzas," Joshua proclaimed.

"Thank God for frozen pizzas! Hey, are we going to watch the movie?"

"Yeah, let me see what we've got. What did we decide? *Braveheart?*"

"Sure."

"Sure that's not too much rom-com for you?"

"I think I'm good." Joshua had remembered that Renae said no rom-com and she loved that about him. He was a good listener. Communication was something she and Joshua were so good at and oddly, it was one of the defining failures in her marriage with Alex.

Renae watched Joshua as he flipped through the menu to see if the movie they'd chosen was available. She remembered what her father had said about him and wondered if there was any truth to it. Did he love her? And if she got back with Alex, what would it do to her relationship with Joshua? She was at home here and she didn't want to think of spending her days without him or Milo; she loved them both so much. Living without him was unimaginable, but how would that affect her relationship with Alex, if there was a relationship in their future. She needed to talk to him. She needed to find out his opinion about her and Alex, and to find out if he felt they were at a place in their relationship other than where she thought they were.

"Here it is. We can rent it. Or should we buy it?"

"It's up to you. It's one of your favorites; I think you should buy it."

"All right, then, purchase." It was a good pick for the two of them for three reasons. One, it was a classic movie. Two, it was long, and that meant they were committed to spending some time together. Three, if they wanted to talk or miss any of it, it wouldn't matter because they already knew what happened. Renae took her usual place on the corner of the sofa, with Milo cuddled next to her. Joshua seated himself next to them. Ten minutes into the movie, Joshua could see Renae's focus was on something other than what they were watching.

"Hey, do you want to watch something else?"

"No, this is fine. It's good. Sorry, I was just zoning out there for a bit."

"Well, you've had a lot to deal with the past few days. It's okay. Do you want to do something else other than this? Want to go somewhere?"

"No, this is good. I really don't want to be around people right now. Well, any other people besides you."

"We could turn the tv off and talk if you want," Joshua suggested.

"I kind of like it on in the background. It serves as a filler in silent awkward moments."

"Are you telling me things going to get awkward tonight?" Joshua smiled at her.

"I really hope not; I don't know how I could juggle one more emotion these days." Renae pulled a sleeping Milo onto her lap. She pulled out her hair claw and placed it on the small table next to her, along with her wine and plate. Joshua put his plate on the table and turned to face Renae so he could give her all his attention.

"What's going on? Is it Eric and Andy? Your mom? You doing okay?"

Renae hesitated telling Joshua about her relationship with Alex and how it had been progressing. It's all she could think about, which made her feel somewhat selfish. She looked at Joshua and saw the genuine concern in his face. She had to tell him.

"Josh, Alex and I are going on a date tomorrow night." Renae studied his facial expression, not sure if he would be happy for her or disappointed. It looked like both.

Joshua tried to gather his thoughts for a moment. He had planned a response for most all other situations that could arise tonight, but not this one.

"How do you feel about that?" he slowly began.

"I don't know. Nervous. Excited. Apprehensive. Scared.... At peace. Like, the universe is trying to set things back to how they're supposed to be." There was a long silence before Renae began to speak again. "Things just seem a little different now. I don't know what happened. You know, this week his entire focus has been on me and our family. He's always been pretty freaking awesome, but now he's just amazing and he is sweeping me off my feet again. Staying away from him is a fight right now, and I'm tired of trying to resist being with him. But I'm so scared of letting my guard down and getting hurt again. Should I be skeptical about his intentions? And then, what about our jobs? We're going to face the same challenges with our jobs that we faced when we decided to divorce. I don't know. I'm just so freaking torn. But I'm *really* looking forward to being with him. Does any of that make sense?"

Joshua thought about everything she said and searched his own heart for his feelings on the matter. He had to admit, he feared that once she got into a relationship with anyone else, he would lose her. They had become as comfortable as a familiar married couple and he didn't want to let her go. But he knew beyond a shadow of a doubt she belonged with Alex. He always knew, even in high school, when he had to release his deep feelings for her so he could pretend to share her joy when Alex asked her out. If he didn't tell her all of this, she would never know. But did she need to know, since she had a chance to be back with Alex?

"It all makes perfect sense. Renae, I can't make this decision for you, you need to. This is about your family, and I have no reason to believe why you shouldn't give him another shot. You and Alex are better together. You two were made for each other. I don't think he has ill intentions at all. He still loves you, and I really think for a guy of Alex's integrity to come to you and ask for another chance, well, I don't think you have to worry about letting your guard down with him."

"Josh, I don't think it's him I'm afraid of; I'm pretty sure it's me. I'm afraid I won't be happy enough, that I'll be sitting there waiting for the ball to drop again, and I'll completely miss out on moving forward because I'm too focused on the hurts of the past. I'm afraid I'll keep comparing myself to him and trying to outdo him, outrank him, belittle him. And one day he'll get sick of me and walk out and shut the door. I really don't want to make the wrong choice here."

Josh looked at his friend. She was desperately looking for answers he couldn't give. He wasn't prepared for this. And he certainly wasn't prepared for the question that followed.

"And then there's you." Josh studied her eyes as she cautiously delivered the next question. "You've been there for me almost my entire life, and what we have is a dream. What will happen to us?" Her eyes winced at the word 'us.' He could see their relationship was equally as important to her as it was to him. But perhaps it was time they examined it to see if it was appropriate or not, especially with the prospect of her ex-husband re-entering the scene. He decided to throw caution to the wind and tell her how he felt. If they truly valued each other's friendship, they needed to be completely honest with each other. He paused the movie so neither friend was distracted and they could give one another their full attention. His stomach began to flutter as his nerves told him he had to share everything. He took a moment to look at her face, from which he drew his courage.

"Do you remember the day we met?" he began.

"I do. It was at the soccer field. We've been pretty much inseparable ever since."

"Yeah, well, I've never told you this before," he paused to clear his throat and gather his words, "I never told you this, but when you walked on the field that day, I thought you were the most beautiful human being in the world. Which was a huge deal because up until that moment I believed Mrs. MacKenzie was the most beautiful person I'd ever laid eyes on."

"Our English teacher?"

"Yes ma'am. She didn't know it, but I had plans to marry her after high school."

"You're right, I didn't know that," Renae laughed.

"Well, Mrs. Mackenzie lost out when you showed up. I loved everything about you: your hair, your smile, your laugh, your confidence. And then when you kicked a soccer ball...no one had seen a girl play like you. So, that day I decided to dump Mrs. MacKenzie and I dreamed of the day Renae Rivera would become Mrs. Renae Levingston."

"Josh-"

"Shhh," he lifted his finger to her lips. "I need to get this out now or I never will, and I'll regret it. Anyhow, I never told you how I felt. Being your best friend and doing *everything* together was enough for me. I think it was because of our up-bringing in church and how we were encouraged to not date so young."

"Mm-hmm."

"Well, I remember the day in high school when you first laid eyes on Alex. You asked me who he was, and I told you it was that Alex kid that we'd been going to school with since we'd moved there; he had just been working out and be-come a star athlete. And your reaction brought jealousy into my life for the first time I can remember. You said, 'I'm saving myself for marriage...or that guy Alex.'"

Renae buried her head in her hands. "Ohhh my gosh, I can't believe I said that."

"I can totally believe you said it. Anyways, I followed you everywhere you went as you chased after this jock who didn't even know you existed. And through it all, I loved you. I wanted you to chase me the way you chased him. I wanted you to look at me the way you did him. I wanted you to desire to go to prom with me like you did him. And when he finally noticed you and asked you to prom, I was devastated. But I loved you regardless. And I swore that if that jock ever hurt you, I would be by your side to pick up the pieces. As you two stepped into a committed relationship, I gave up hope of ever being with you. You and Alex were just this perfect couple and everyone around you could see it. So, without you even knowing, I released you. I decided I would have to release you fully to Alex and pray for you both in order for me to live a full life with whomever I could find to love me. And that's when I met Angie. And I loved her, man, did I love her. But when she passed away, I doubted her love for me, and it killed me. And then you and Alex split and here you are in my life again. I won't lie, sometimes I feel like it's fate. We're both single again, doing life together, loving and supporting each other. I often feel like we're getting our second chance, that the universe is setting things back to the way they need to be with us. But then when I see you and Alex together, or hear of you two together, I know beyond a shadow of a doubt there are big plans for the two of you somewhere down the road. My heart is breaking at the thought of letting you go again, but I know it's the right thing to do. Renae Dawn, you belong with Alex."

Renae just stared at Joshua, her heart racing. Was she so oblivious to what love looked like that she couldn't see it right in front of her all this time? Or did she know all along that he loved her, but she just chose to ignore it?

"Renae, go on this date with Alex. Be open with him. Let him be open with you." Joshua pushed Renae's hair behind her ears and held her face. "You want my opinion? Here it is. Alex has changed. You may change, you may not, but he doesn't care. He wants you, just as you are. So, go! Get your man! But don't y'all dare forget about Uncle Josh. I expect best friend time at least twice a month. And you still have to play on my soccer team next season. Okay?"

Renae smiled as she pulled him close into a hug. "Thank you. God must love me to have sent you to walk with me all these years."

"He loves you big time. And I always will too."

"And hey, don't ever doubt for a second that Angie loved you. You were the absolute best husband any girl could have dreamed of. She was just so grief-stricken that she couldn't look beyond her pain to see her future. You, you're a prince. She knew it and she said it, and she loved you for everything you are. You need to believe that. You're going to make some beautiful girl out there a very happy woman one day. And I'm going to have to fight hard to not be jealous of her."

Joshua looked at her, holding her cheeks in his hands. "What would happen if I kissed you right now?"

Renae looked into Joshua's eyes, her breaths becoming heavy at the thought of what could happen next between the two of them if her lips met with his in this moment. No one had lifted her up, spoken kinder words, treated her better, nor supported her more than this perfect soul in front of her. As tempted as she was, her thoughts shifted to Alex. She would never be able to look at him if anything happened between Joshua and her. And no matter how charming Joshua was, she never had feelings for him the way she did for Alex.

"We'd go upstairs and enter into a night of intense passion...and then wake up to a world of regret."

"Then you need to go home." He pulled her head close and tenderly kissed her on the forehead. Renae closed her eyes and squeezed his arms. She wouldn't reciprocate the kiss, but she would let him know how much it meant to her.

"I should." She stood to her feet and located her shoes. "What about this mess we made in the kitchen?"

"I've got it. I can clean it up while I watch this movie I just bought for $14.99."

"Okay. Thank you for tonight. Damn it, Josh, I told you I couldn't handle anymore emotions," she laughed as she blinked and wiped away tears. Her sensitivity to his revelation left him somewhat satisfied. It let him know she cared. "Anyways, thank you for dinner, the talk, and loving a mess like me. And for encouraging me...and Alex. You're a pretty noble and stand-up guy."

"I try, but it's been the encouragement from a strong woman like you who keeps me honest." He got off the sofa and walked her to the front door. "Text me when you get home, so I know you made it safely."

"Always." Renae opened the door, took a step outside and turned to her friend. The way he looked at her had already changed, and she realized she had to be okay with that.

"Hey, I love you little, love you big," he started.

"Love you like a little pig," Renae finished. They smiled and gave each other one final hug goodbye before she turned to walk to her car. As always, Joshua watched until her car was no longer in his sight. He walked into the house and slowly shut the door, certain he was ending a significant season in his life. He leaned his back on the door, tears streaming down his face. Once again, he had released the love of his life, but this time he felt much more at peace about it.

SEVEN

The sun was rising Saturday morning and the cool morning breeze made the weather perfect for a run, so Alex decided to take Maddy and her bike to a local park for some exercise. He had a dozen things on his mind--work, exercise, where to eat tonight--but all of his thoughts returned to Renae. His only regret about asking her out for dinner was that he had to wait all day to see her. He couldn't wait for the evening to arrive, so he'd planned a full day with his daughter to help the time pass quickly.

"Alright sweetheart, we're going to keep a steady pace. I'll run and you ride. Just don't drive too fast and get far away from me. Got it?" Alex tightened the chin strap to Maddy's helmet that matched her bright pink bicycle.

"Got it, Daddy. And I'll try not to fall too many times this time."

"And what do we do when we fall?"

"We get right back up and hop on the bike again."

"Good girl. You ready? If you're ready, give me a thumbs up." Maddie put her tiny thumb in the air. "What are you doing? Didn't I say to keep both hands on the handle bars?"

Maddie started to laugh. "Daddy! You said to give you a thumbs up!" She had her mother's vocal chords, and if their inside voices were loud, their outside voices were louder.

"I know, I'm just messing with you. Alright, we're going to make three loops and then you can go on the playground. Let's go, Captain."

The pair began to circle their way around the large

park. For a Saturday morning, it wasn't very busy yet. Vendors were beginning to set up their white tents for the local market in a nearby parking lot. Locals brought their dogs out to enjoy the fresh morning air. A few couples were testing out the terrain with their toddlers and jogging strollers. Alex really enjoyed living in this community and city. He felt it was a safe place for his family, and he enjoyed the eclectic people they were fortunate enough to do life around.

Maddy did an excellent job staying on her bike and keeping pace with her father. She had been riding without training wheels for two months but was unable to get much practice in due to her parents' soccer schedules. Alex took her riding when he could, but it was Phil who convinced her to take the training wheels off, and he took her out every other weekend. They traveled under mature oak trees and over the raised concrete that the tree roots were breaking through. They passed duck families and watched as the native sandhill cranes flew over their heads and came in for a landing. Maddy had spent a lot of time at the zoo with her mother when she was a toddler, so she was able to identify all the animals and tell her father at least one fact about each of them. Today, he learned sandhill cranes mate for life. As they approached the point where they began, Maddy slowed down, positioning herself behind her daddy.

"Daddy, I think we need to stop for a water break."

"Already? We've only made one lap."

"I'm so exhausted, Daddy. I really need to rest."

"Ok," Alex laughed to himself. She was dramatic, like her mother. They pulled over to the side of the path and parked Maddy's bicycle. As she walked to the front of her bike to get her water out of her small backpack, Alex scanned the people around them. A few other walkers had entered the trail and a couple of young kids on longboards joined the mix, but what caught his eye was the disheveled gentleman picking up trash around the park. Alex watched the man investigating the contents of the things he picked up, separating some into a trash bag, some into a blue recycle bag, and some into his canvas backpack. As the man walked toward the playground, Alex's curiosity was spiked and he felt led to see what the man was up to.

"Hey Maddy, you ready to take a break and head to the playground?"

Maddy was more than excited to head to her favorite place in the world. After packing her water bottle back into her backpack, Alex led her along a path to get to the kid's area. Maddy ran to the slide and Alex parked her bike next to the bench closest to where he could watch her. He sat on the bench, opened Maddy's backpack, flipped through his wallet that he had placed in there, and put bills in each of his pockets. He waited as he watched the older gentleman make his way around the playground to where Alex was sitting.

"Daddy! Watch me go down the slide!"

"Okay sweetheart, I'm watching," Alex said, for the sixth time. He loved that she found so much joy engaging in a simple activity and that she could entertain herself endlessly by doing it. As she reached the bottom, Alex congratulated her while she jumped up and down in excitement.

"Hey, you want to race down the slide?" Maddy asked another child her age she found entering the stairs. If only adults could easily interact with one another as kids do. At what point did we stop having fun with people we just met and close ourselves off, Alex wondered.

Alex wanted to be sure he didn't ignore the gentleman cleaning the park. He wasn't wearing a county uniform or anything to identify that he worked for the parks department. He looked like he could use a shower and a washing machine. And more than likely he could use a good meal. As the man got closer, Alex sparked a small conversation while reaching down to grab a piece of trash littering the playground.

"It's no wonder there is trash everywhere around here;

it doesn't look like they've emptied the trash can in a week."
He dropped the garbage he'd found into one of the man's bags.

The man thanked Alex, smiled and nodded, and kept about his business. "It takes a lot of dedication to get up early on a Saturday morning and come clean up the park. We really appreciate all the work you do here in the community."

The older man had thinning grey hair that reached the middle of his neck. His smile was inviting and his eyes were kind. "Oh, I don't work here," the gentleman replied. Keeping one eye on Maddy, Alex decided to get the man's story.

"Oh, so you come up here and volunteer?"

"My friends and I just like to keep the place clean an' get the trash before the wildlife does. Park gets busier, ponds get dirtier. Just lookin' out for the little ones who cain't look out for themselves." He picked up a plastic ring that once held a six pack of soda, pulled out a small knife from his backpack, and cut the rings before disposing of it.

"Tell me something," Alex stood up to talk face-to-face with him, "do you live close by?" He could tell the man was hard of hearing by the way he turned his head but watched Alex's mouth as he spoke.

"We stay in the woods." The man pointed to the woods closest to the park. Alex had heard of stories of wild pigs in those woods. He couldn't imagine this guy lived there.

"Your house is in those woods?"

The man shook his head and kept cleaning up. "No, no house. Just a tent. We camp."

"Oh, you're camping?"

"Mm-hmm."

Alex immediately caught on. "You and some people you know have a camp or shelter back there? You live in some tents?" The stranger nodded his head and smiled. Alex extended his hand. "My name is Alex, what's yours?"

"Larry."

"Larry? Well, it's nice to meet you Larry. That's my little girl right there, Maddy." Larry nodded to acknowledge her. He had caught her interest and she slowly started to make her way to her daddy and his new friend. "Larry, is there anything you need? Food and water? Clothes? You've been helping the community out so much by cleaning this up, I really would like to help you out in return."

Larry shook his head and smiled at Maddy as she approached. He waved at her and began to make his way to pick up more trash. Maddy grabbed her father's hand.

"Daddy," she pulled him down to her level so she could keep the conversation private. "I saw that man taking an orange from the garbage and putting it in his bag. I want to give him money for lunch so he doesn't have to eat out of the trash can."

"I think that would be a really nice thing to do, Madeline. Give me a minute." Alex turned to Larry and walked to him. Alex reached into his pockets and carefully pulled out the bills from each. He grasped his hands together and began to address Larry. "Hey, it was so nice to meet you today, and like I said, I want to thank you for what you're doing here; it really means a lot. My little girl here really wants to make sure you get a good lunch when you're done; I've heard the place up the street has great chicken and dumplings." Maddy broke out into giggles. "She thinks the words dumplings is the funniest word invented."

Larry gave Maddy a sweet smile. He probably had children or grandchildren of his own, Alex thought. He was happy she could spread a little sunshine in this stranger's life this morning.

"Anyways, it was a pleasure meeting you, Larry, and I just want you to know God sees you; He cares about you, and He loves you. He couldn't love you any more or any less than He does right now. And He will always make sure your needs are met. Stay focused on Him. I hope we continue to see you around, and we'll be praying for you." Alex reached his hand out to shake Larry's one last time, but this time he slipped some folded bills into the palm of his hand. Phil Rivera used to call it the 'Pentecostal handshake' in church. Alex learned this form of generosity from the man himself.

Larry accepted the money which brought him to tears as he received far more than what he needed. "Thank you," he said as he wrapped his arms around Alex. Alex returned the long hug. He wondered to himself how long it had been since Larry was embraced. When Larry released his hold, he looked to Alex and stated, "God is good."

"All the time," Alex replied as he escorted Maddy to grab her bike so they could finish their laps on the trail. As they began their last two miles, Alex turned and saw Larry continuing to pick up the trash, but now he had a small dance in his steps. He reflected on a message he'd heard once, that if God gives you something, it's God's to release. And whatever the recipient does with it is up to him and God. He knew from the look of relief in Larry's eyes that God would abundantly meet whatever Larry needed at that moment.

Gratitude filled Alex's heart as he felt humbled to be used in some small way to help fill the need of a stranger. He was honored to be the father of a little girl who saw the needs of people and wanted to help them in return. He concluded that if he and Renae had done anything right, it was the way they were raising their precious daughter.

* * *

Renae spent over an hour trying to find the right outfit for her night out with Alex. She finally decided on a pair of wide-legged striped capris with a cute wrap around top, finishing with a pair of pointed black flats. As she headed down the stairs, she was abruptly stopped by the evident disapproval of her brother-in-law.

"Oh, no. No, no, no. That's not going to work."

"What? Is it my hair? My shoes? What do I need to change?"

"Everything!" He stood up and marched to the stairs, grabbing her by the arms and leading her back to her room. "We're trying to woo him, not scare him. We want more Sophia, less Audrey. Show those curves. These bottoms look like something my dad would wear to bed. You might as well throw on a white t-shirt, grab a tub of ice cream, and watch some old 80's movie if you're going to wear those pants."

"That isn't a bad idea, actually."

Andy walked into Renae's closet, shock bringing him to a halt. "How do you find anything in here?"

"This is my go-to pile, that's the stuff I don't like, and that's the stuff I can't fit into but one day I might."

Andy began to sort through a massive mound of clothes piled in the middle of the closet. He laid aside mostly jeans and soft tops and then hung items he didn't want to get wrinkled to one side of her closet.

"I'm going to organize this for you when we come back, and you're going to get rid of everything you don't wear. Here. We're going to try on things from this pile." Renae headed into her bathroom while Andy continued to sort her clothes and dig for some shoes. After six wardrobe changes, the duo fought and then agreed on fitted white capris, an oversized grey and white V-neck blouse over a peach lace bralette, and strappy kitten heels. Andy convinced her to wear her hair down and he constructed loose waves while she touched up her makeup.

"You know, you're acting like the typical gay best friend right now. I always wanted a sister."

"Well I have two older ones, so I'm an expert at helping girls get dressed."

"Because you're obviously not an expert at getting them undressed. Hahaha, laugh with me, that was a joke; it's funny."

Andy smiled at Renea's reflection. "You know, you're not as bad as your brother tries to make you seem."

Renae was silent as she looked at her reflection in the

mirror. Andy's words stung a little, and they opened a portal to her negative thoughts. How could she actually think she was capable of making Alex happy? She didn't see worth in the person she was looking at. What she saw was a conflicted mental mess, incapable of loving other people unconditionally. She saw someone on the brink of self-destruction. She saw sadness and brokenness: someone who was undeserving of this person Alex was becoming and undeserving of having a sweet girl like Maddy as her daughter. She thought of times she'd wanted to escape into her work trips and never come home, leaving Maddy and Alex on their own. She saw herself as someone who was rigid and cold, and her reflection was ugly. Her thought process was interrupted as Andy showered her with hairspray.

"You, my dear, are date-ready." He joined her in looking at her reflection and saw the sadness in her face. "What's the matter? You don't like it?"

"No, it's really pretty, thanks. I just need some time to gather my thoughts tonight. Alex should be here any minute." She faked a smile and gave him a weak hug.

"Hey, you are a strong and beautiful woman, always remember that."

"Thanks, Andy. I really appreciate that." Shutting the door behind Andy, Renae curled up on her bed. She reached for her phone and once again played the familiar song from her father's playlist. She closed her eyes as she plugged in her earbuds and just listened. No tears were shed, no heavy weights pressing on her chest. She just lay in her own silence, cleared her thoughts, and existed.

Day by day
With joy and strength
We will sing
Who is like our God?

Lifted high

To bring You praise
There is none
That is like our God

She could understand why this song was on her dad's playlist. The words and melody carried so much peace. She began to focus on the person she was and whom she wanted to be. Maybe all this time her thoughts should have been focused less on changing the hearts of others and focused more on changing her own heart. Wrapped in her revelation, she didn't hear the knock at her bedroom door.

Eric poked his head into her bedroom and saw her laying on her bed. "Hey, beast, your beauty is downstairs." He realized she didn't hear him, so he sat on her bed and gently touched her leg. Renae opened her eyes and turned her head to see her brother. "Hey, Alex is downstairs. You okay?"

She wasn't sure if it was the question 'you okay?' or his soft tone that touched her spirit, but she couldn't resist sitting up and wrapping her arms around her brother's neck. Although he was initially shocked by the rare display of affection, he slowly returned the embrace.

"I love you, sis."

"I love you, too."

He stood up and helped his sister off the bed. "We can have our moment another time. Right now, your prince charming is downstairs waiting for you. And he's going to be speechless when he sees the beauty standing before him." He straightened her top for her and smoothed down the hair that had been moved out of place by her pillow.

"Eric, I've been such an asshole. Not only to you, but to Alex. I'm so scared I'm going to rehash things that happened in the past and completely ruin everything again."

"Renae, you can't move on with your future if you're going to live in your past. You're getting a fresh start and it begins the moment you walk out that door. So, you can either let fear and anxiety win, or you can walk in confidence and hope. That guy down there loves you just as you are. All he wants is for you to love him back."

She stared at her brother for a moment and looked deep into his eyes. Those eyes were a reflection of her father, something she'd never noticed before. In this moment, he sounded like their father, too.

"Will I see you and Andy again before you leave?"

"I don't think so; our flight leaves tomorrow so we need to get back to the hotel to pack our things. We'll be back soon, though, to check on Mom."

"I like Andy. He's a really nice guy. And I can't express how wrong I was to-"

"Don't apologize. That was a while ago and I should have given you a heads-up before bringing him over. We just need to move on and push forward. And you need to get downstairs!" He smacked her bum to get her moving.

She extended her arm to him. "Will you escort me?"

"It would be my pleasure, baby sister."

Alex stood in the family room with Andy, Ruth, and Maddy as Renae and Eric began to walk downstairs, arm in arm. They stood in disbelief as they watched the dueling duo approach.

"Okay, I didn't know we'd have an audience," Renae muttered to Eric as she let go of his arm.

"Me neither. Now I feel awkward and gay." Renae broke into laughter at his comment.

"Mommy! You look so pretty! I like your hair!" Maddy broke the moment of silence. She was dressed in a cute sundress with matching sandals, her hair combed and sprayed back in flawless ponytail held with a matching scrunchie.

"Look at *you*! Can I borrow your outfit tonight? You look so pretty!" Renae picked Maddy up and gave her a kiss. As she received a hug from her little girl, she looked to Alex and gave him a smile. He never dressed their daughter up, and he and Renae had occasionally fought when they were married about how he would never match her outfits. Trivial, but to her this symbolized one step he was purposefully taking to improve things between the two of them.

"It won't fit you, Mommy! You're too big! Daddy took me shopping, look!" Maddy wiggled out of her mother's arms to run for her shopping bag full of clothes.

Ruth could see in Alex's face that this wasn't quite how he imagined the evening would start. He still held the flowers he brought for Renae in his hand. And they hadn't even greeted each other yet. Focusing on one another was hard with a six-year-old wanting one hundred percent of both her parents' attention.

"Here, Maddy, how about we take these clothes to your room and hang them up. And maybe tomorrow you can have a fashion show and we can let Mommy see everything you got then." Ruth winked at Alex, grabbed Maddy's hand, and escorted her with her bag upstairs after she gave her parents a quick hug goodnight.

"Well, I'm hungry. You hungry, Eric?" It was evident in Andy's fidgety behavior that he was making up an excuse to leave the room and let Renae and Alex have the time and space they needed.

"Yes! I'm starving. We should warm a lasagna. Um, you two have a good night. Alex, hurt my sister and I hurt you. Ah, who am I kidding, you're huge, I'd never win. Take care of her. And you, sis, remember what I said. I love you." Andy and Eric said their goodbyes and headed to the kitchen. Renae and Alex stood in the family room, finally alone.

"Hi." Alex's eyes were locked on Renae.

"Hi." She couldn't stop smiling at him. She would be completely content if they stood in this moment for the rest of their evening.

"You look absolutely stunning." Renae couldn't speak. The most handsome, courageous, and honorable man she'd ever known stood before her. His presence and charm left her without words. "These are for you." Alex handed her a creative bouquet of flowers wrapped in brown butcher paper.

"Maddy and I picked them from a mobile florist this morning. Each flower has a special meaning, but I won't tell you what those are. You're going to have to figure that out on your own. But we chose them based on their meaning, and they represent how we feel about you." They were the most beautiful assortment of flowers she'd ever laid eyes on; but the thought behind their selection was the true beauty behind them.

"That's so beautiful. Thank you." She still couldn't take her eyes off him. She was swept away in this moment. He had this tender strength, his demeanor powerful, but soft.

"I'm just going to put these in some water; I'll be right back."

On cue, an arm with its hand outstretched appeared from the kitchen door. Renae and Alex grinned as she placed the flowers in the hand that then immediately disappeared.

"These walls have ears. Let's get out of here," Alex suggested as he placed his hand on Renae's back to lead her to the front door.

Alex relaxed as he realized that tonight, in this moment, she didn't pull away or jump at his touch; instead, she leaned in towards it. As he closed the door behind him, he silently prayed that this marked the moment they could walk out of their past and step into their future.

EIGHT

"So, what are you in the mood for?" Alex fastened his seatbelt and started the jeep. Renae's thoughts immediately shifted to the numerous times they fought during their marriage about how Alex always left the decision of where to eat up to her. She realized now how ridiculous those fights had been, and she also realized she was going to struggle with the past tonight, fighting hard to keep those past offenses from affecting the present.

"I honestly could eat a hot dog or chicken wings and be completely content right now," she replied, smiling at him.

"Hot dogs or chicken wings." He stopped and stared at her as she looked at him with a mischievous smile on her face. "That's really not what I had in mind tonight."

"What are you in the mood for?"

"Well, see, tonight is about treating you, so I'm in the mood for whatever you're in the mood for."

"Okay," she started, while twirling her hair around her finger, "well, I had pizza at Joshua's last night, so no Italian. I threw up everything from Thursday's meal yesterday morning, so nothing fried and no burgers...so...seafood?"

"Creole?"

"Oh my gosh, yes." They both enjoyed it, but rarely ate it even though it was one of their favorites. "Do you know a place around here to get some?"

"I do. I haven't tried it yet, but it's down south. We're driven by a couple times and it has good reviews. We have 6:30 reservations, so we should be good on time." Alex mapped the route on his GPS and headed out the driveway.

"Wait, how did you know I would pick seafood?"

"I didn't. I just have 6:30 reservations at seven different restaurants throughout the city tonight and that was one of them."

Renae leaned back on the headrest and studied Alex while he focused on the road and its surroundings. She asked herself what they were doing. After this week, there was no doubt that the two of them still loved one another. However, love was never an issue. She turned to look out the window and watched the massive ancient oak trees pass by. He had reservations at seven different places...was that because she was indecisive and picky, or was it because he wanted to make her happy? She concluded it was probably both.

Alex found it difficult to engage in small talk with someone he knew everything about. They knew what they had been up to recently, so they had nothing to really catch up on. He was a little bothered about the pizza with Joshua comment, only because it meant she was with Josh last night, but he didn't want to bring that up. He could ask her about work, but that was always a pretty stale subject for the both of them. Before he could land on the right approach, Renae broke the silence for them.

"I can't get over how adorable Maddy looked tonight! Did you pick that outfit out or did she?"

"I'm not going to lie; she and the salesperson did. Maddy picked out the outfits and as I approved them, the salesperson brought out matching shoes and hair thingies. I was impressed with how Maddy's so conscious of what she gets and how much she's getting. She picked out two outfits and stopped. When I told her she needed at least five, one for each day of the school week, she went nuts. We narrowed it down to six from thirteen, and then she got a couple t-shirts to wear with her jeans."

"Well, I'm going to let you take her shopping from now on. She and I have a hard time agreeing on anything."

"Yeah, not sure if the bank account can handle that," he

joked. "I had no idea how much clothes for little girls cost."

"Well, I typically don't take her to those cute little specialty stores unless there's a sale. I usually take Miss Maddy to Target."

"So, she pulled one over on me today?"

"That's what little girls do to their daddies." The words escaped Renae's mouth before she realized the impact they would have on her heart. She took a quick and deep breath as the pain of losing her dad quickly returned. She turned her gaze back to the window, her eyes beginning to flood with tears. "God, I miss him." Her voice was barely audible and mostly just air being forced out of her chest, escaping her choked vocal chords. Nevertheless, Alex heard, since he was tuned into every gesture and word of hers tonight. He reached to her lap and grabbed her hand. She squeezed back tightly as tears streamed down her face. She turned to look at Alex and forced a smile and a laugh.

"I'm sorry, I didn't mean to be a fun-sucker, getting all sad and weepy on you. I'm an emotional mess."

"There's no need to apologize and you are not a fun-sucker. I wouldn't want to be with anyone else in the world right now other than you, weepy or not." He kissed the back of her hand and settled their grasped hands in his lap. "I miss him, too."

"You were one of the last people on his mind before he passed. Our conversation that night...before he passed away....it was about you."

Alex wasn't prepared to hear that. He loved and admired Mr. Rivera to the point that he prayed he could continue his legacy in any way God saw fit. He took a deep breath as he let a tear fall down his cheek. "You were so lucky to have him for a father."

They drove in silence for a few minutes before Renae spoke up.

"Hey, Alex, can we just go to a park and grab something from a food truck? No stuffy atmosphere, just somewhere we can...enjoy each other's company...and talk."

"I know a place." Alex turned off his GPS and headed towards the park he and Maddy had been to earlier that day. Renae's idea was much better. No table between them, no one to interrupt their conversation, no one to hand them the check signaling the night was over.

"Do you want your hand back?" Renae asked, as he was maneuvering the winding back roads with one hand.

"Nope."

Renae didn't want to give it back anyways.

The recreational park was transformed at night. Lights strung through the trees were now lit as the sun was making its way to the horizon. Musicians were playing on a makeshift stage in the middle of a small field covered with blankets and lawn chairs. Children were chasing bubbles provided by a clown who also delighted them with balloon animals. Food trucks lined the outside of one section of the parking lot. The park wasn't overly crowded, but there were enough people there to make a lucrative profit for the vendors. Alex turned the car off and asked Renae to stay inside as he ran around to help her out. He had to park in the grass and wanted to make sure she didn't hurt herself in her heels as she got out. Plus, it gave him a chance to demonstrate that chivalry wasn't dead. Renae kept close to Alex as he helped her out of the car. He put her purse on the back floorboard and covered it with a sweatshirt from the backseat. After locking up the jeep, they clasped hands again and began to walk toward the trucks.

"Oh look, there's the guy who has the Maine lobster rolls. He was at a festival at Mom's church once," Renae pointed out.

"Is that where you want to eat?"

Renae smiled at him, which he knew meant a definite yes.

Once they'd grabbed their dinner, they found an empty table to stand at close to the band. "This wasn't even close to my idea of where we would end up tonight, but you never cease to surprise me."

"This location was actually your idea, Mr. Murphy."

"Did you have somewhere else in mind?"

"Nope, this is absolutely perfect," Renae took a bite of her buttered lobster roll, delighted in the fact that they'd also found a Neil Diamond cover band. She watched the crowd as they sang along to Sweet Caroline, occasionally joining in herself, but quietly so no one could hear her. She was raised on this music, and it caused her to reflect on a time when life was innocent and she felt secure and safe in her father's house.

"How's your lobster roll?" Alex asked.

"It's incredible. And you know I don't even really like lobster, but these are so good. How about yours?"

"Yeah, it's really good. I could eat another one. How about you?"

"Mmmm, no; I'm good," she said with a mouth full of deliciousness. "You go ahead."

Alex was starving. He had anticipated an appetizer, salad, entree, and dessert tonight, so he hadn't eaten much during the day.

"Can I get you another lemonade?"

"Please. It's so good."

"You got it. Need anything else? You okay here by yourself?"

"I'm good, thanks."

"Ok, I'll be right back with that lemonade," Alex said, winking at her before walking away. Renae watched as Alex returned to the food truck. She hoped she hadn't made a mistake suggesting they skip a restaurant and head to a park. So far, it seemed like a good idea. She was very apprehensive, however, about the rest of the evening. She didn't want to waste this precious time she had alone with him...well, somewhat alone. After all, they were surrounded by people tonight, somewhere Renae would typically want to stay far away from. She didn't know if they had a lot to talk about. She didn't know what course the evening would take; she just knew she wanted it to last.

"Can I take your trash for you?"

Startled, Renae turned to her right to meet a gentleman standing near her with a trash bag offering to clear her table for her.

"Oh, that would be great, thank you." Renee examined him as she collected the trash from her table and helped him put it in his garbage bag. She figured he was homeless by the looks of him, but she wasn't quite sure of his intentions. Was he doing this for tips? She didn't have her wallet on her; she had left it in the car. The two made eye contact as he smiled at her, nodded, and began to walk away. "Thank you, sir. Have a good night."

"You too, ma'am," he replied as he left. Renae looked around and found two other men, similarly dressed to the one who had served her, walking around the park picking up random trash. These two were wearing caps, and although Renae couldn't quite make out what they said, she could tell they promoted a service in the military. She felt compelled to go nearer to read their caps. Alex approached the table with her drink as she started to walk away.

"Everything okay?"

"Yeah, I just…see those two guys over there picking up trash? I just wanted to read what was on their hats. There was a guy here earlier who came and took our garbage. I wasn't sure if he was doing it for tips, but it looks like right now they just want to keep the park clean."

"Where's the guy who took your trash?"

Renae looked around and pointed him out when she located him. "Right there; that's him."

Alex was hoping it was Larry so he could introduce him to Renae, but it wasn't.

"Those caps say 'Vietnam Veteran.'"

"Oh, Alex-"

"I know. I was here this morning with Maddy and met one of them. His name is Larry. Really nice guy; he had the kindest smile. Really, I think they just want to mingle with people, keep their park clean, and maybe earn a meal or something. I gave Larry what was in my pocket. Hopefully it helps him until someone else steps up."

Renae looked to the men and she was moved with compassion. She could never understand why men who sacrificed so much were rewarded with so little. Veterans held a special place in her heart, probably due to the fact that her father was one. It took a minute, but it dawned on her what Alex had just said.

"You gave him money?"

"I gave him what I had on me. Talked to him for a minute. He and his buddies live in a camp in the woods over there."

Renae's heart sank. She recognized this was the veterans' normal, and she hoped that they felt valued and appreciated by the community they lived and still served in. She faced Alex and observed, "You're a lot like him, you know."

"Who's that?"

"Daddy." Renae gave a matter-of-fact look to Alex, who in turn was humbled to think he was even half the man Phil Rivera had been. "The lobster guy is waving us down; I think your roll is ready."

Alex returned with it a minute later, suddenly not feeling hungry anymore. There was too much on his mind for him to eat. He and Renae exchanged knowing looks and walked over to the man who'd taken her trash.

"Hey, man, we just appreciate all you and your buddies do to keep this place clean. Dinner is on us tonight. Hope you like Maine lobster." Alex handed the gentleman his food as Renae offered her untouched lemonade and straw to him.

The gentleman graciously accepted the food and thanked them. He again locked eyes with Renae, smiled at her, and then walked away. "Should we buy dinner for those other two guys?" Renae suggested with a smile. Alex wrapped his arm around her waist as they headed back to the food truck.

After delivering meals to the other two men who were cleaning, Alex and Renae slowly started on the trail that led around the park. Renae's emotions began to stir when the band started playing a classic song from her father's favorite movie when she was growing up, *The Jazz Singer*.

"How are your feet holding up in those shoes?" Alex asked.

"I'm good, thanks." Although the atmosphere of the evening to this point had been relaxing, they both began to feel nervous around one another. There were things they both desperately wanted to talk about as well as topics they feared would arise. Renae decided to start with the subject that landed them at the park in the first place. "You ever feel like the ones who've left us on this earth are in Heaven watching us and just smiling down? Because I feel like that's exactly what Daddy would be doing right now if he could see the two of us."

Alex made a noise to acknowledge what she was saying but without offering his opinion.

Renae put her hands behind her back and took a deep breath as she proceeded. "I was unable to sleep that night. I couldn't shut my brain or emotions off after seeing you all day at the field and then spending the evening together at the restaurant. When you left with Carrie, it crushed me, and I wasn't ready for that."

"Renae, I told you she just needed a ride."

"Well, I know that now, but that night...that night I was convinced you had moved on and when I thought of her going home with you, it made me sick. But anyways, I followed Daddy outside; he was trying to scare off one of the bullfrogs in the back and we somehow stumbled into another crazy shenanigan like we always managed to do. When we got back inside, Mom had made us some hot chocolate and he decided it would be a good time to talk. Mom had told him how I treated you at the game that day..." Renae had to take a moment to gather her strength, for she felt she was about the expose her vulnerabilities to the one person who could hurt her the most. "He really liked you, Alex, so much that he loved you as a son. He missed having you around; you really meant a lot to him. And over the past week, I realize I've spent time with an honorable, compassionate, God-fearing man whom my father would be so proud of. You've become so much like him, and I don't think there is anyone he would rather have fill his shoes than you. His Bible is on my nightstand, the one you had Pastor Reeves read from, and I want to give it to you when we get back to the house. There is so much contained in that book: his notes, his favorite verses--you've seen it. And I doubt it will ever mean as much to me as it will to you. So, I really think you should have it. Our whole family does." She still hadn't told him everything about their conversation, but this was about as far as she thought she could go for now.

"Thank you; that means so much to me. That's really a huge honor."

They continued to walk in silence until they came upon an empty bench under an oak tree just off the trail. Alex grabbed Renae's arm, sliding his hand down to reach her hand, clasped it, and guided her to the bench to sit. They sat close, hand in hand as they watched the water ripple in the pond in front of them. The sunset over the water provided a picturesque view.

Once again, Renae's throat tightened as she was about to speak. "I told him that night I had made a mistake. I've made a lot, Alex-"

He cut her off. "Renae, I don't want to talk about our past mistakes tonight. I never would have dreamed we would ever be together like this again. Believe me, I have so many regrets, but right now I really don't want either of us to focus on them. We're not going to be able to move forward if we dig up unpleasant memories."

"Eric the Wise told me earlier that we can't move into our future if we keep living in the past. Alex, I need to be honest with you. I'm scared to death right now of moving forward with you...if that's something you're even considering. You're the one person on this earth I want to love unconditionally, and you're also the one person who could destroy me in an instant once I place my trust in you."

Alex turned to Renae and tucked her hair behind her ear. He pulled her chin towards him, causing her to look at him.

"Renae Rivera, I still love you. I never stopped. Letting you go was the dumbest thing I've ever done and if you sit here right now and tell me there is even a slight chance of the two of us reconciling and sharing a future together again, I will stop at nothing to make sure that happens. Renae, there's nothing that I want more than your unconditional love and trust, and I pray to God you could believe I would never betray that trust. You know me; I would never do that to you."

Renae shifted her body position on the bench towards Alex so she could look at him without straining her neck. "Alex, what if everything we've been feeling this week is because our emotions have been in overdrive due to circumstances we've been placed in? You've been so incredible--beyond a shadow of a doubt you've been so incredible! But what about Monday? Monday we get back to the daily grind and hustle of our lives. What if we can't withstand the pressure and everything goes back to the way it was when we were married? I don't want to fight you; I don't want to hurt you. I don't want to be hurt again, but opening myself to you would only put me at risk of another devastating blow I don't think I can take. And I don't want to be unfair to you."

"The only way you could be unfair to me is to tell me you made a mistake but then refuse to let me have another chance with you. Renae, your father was alive last week when we had dinner. I felt the connection; I think you felt it, too."

"I did. And like I said, I felt crushed when I thought you

were with Carrie. Dad held me as I cried over you Saturday night. I made a mistake divorcing you; I told him that. And he said if you thought there was a slight chance of reconciliation between us, you would be there in a heartbeat."

"Your dad was a smart man. Renae, I feared the day you and Joshua would tell me you two were in a relationship. Seeing you together when you were standing close in the parking lot on Saturday...I was pretty pissed at him. And you. But I just couldn't stay mad at you once I was near you."

Renae nodded her head. "Yeah, Daddy brought up the Joshua thing too. Alex, Josh and I talked last night. I doubt things will ever be the same between me and him, but he's cheering for us, Alex. He's always been team Ralex. That night in the parking lot, he was preparing me to see you. And he was encouraging me to talk to you and to apologize. He just wanted to see me happy and he knew that wouldn't happen if you and I had tension between us. Oh, and I just made that Ralex thing up."

"I like it; it's like a knock off Rolex."

"No, a Rolex is a knock off Ralex." They chuckled. It was a good time to slow down and lighten the conversation. "Andy and I talked the other night. He's pretty special. I have no idea what he is doing with Eric, but he is definitely a strong supporter of us. He, um...he said he really wished he'd been around when we were separating. He would have done everything in his power to keep us together."

"Eric said the same thing about him."

"I doubt I would have listened to anyone when I made my mind up. Even Joshua begged me to change my mind and stay with you when I told him we were splitting up."

"Really? I thought he was going to swoop in and take his shot at being with you the moment he saw the opportunity open up."

"There was never an opportunity with Joshua."

"I always knew he had strong feelings for you, even before we started dating. The way you two were always together after Angie passed, and how you two are always together now; you act like a couple. Chad came up to me at work one day and asked how it felt knowing my ex-wife moved on with my best friend after he saw the two of you at dinner one night. You still want to tell me nothing happened between you two? Ever?"

"No. I mean, last night we did talk, and we could have ended up in a situation that would have jeopardized everyone's relationship-"

"But nothing happened between you." Alex didn't want or need to hear details, so he interrupted her before he heard any more.

"Correct. Like I said, Team Ralex." An annoying buzzing sound approached Renae's ear and she swatted at it until she slapped her face.

"Ouch, you okay?"

"Yeah, mosquitoes are coming out."

"Want to go back towards the band? They're burning some citronella over there; maybe there are less mosquitoes that way."

"I don't think that's the only thing they are burning," Renae said jokingly.

"You're probably right."

As they headed back to the band, Renae walked closer to Alex. Their hands were still joined. "Alex! Do you hear that? They're playing the song Daddy dedicated to us at our wedding reception!" Renae pulled Alex closer to the music, but before they got mixed in with the crowd, Alex brought her to a sudden stop and twirled her around to face him.

"Hey, dance with me." He wrapped his arms around her waist, and she placed her arms on his back. They drew each other close as they began to slow dance to "Forever in Blue Jeans." She rested her head on his shoulder and he laid his head on hers, both of their hearts pounding.

"Thanks Daddy," Renae whispered softly towards the skies.

"I believe he's definitely smiling down on us from Heaven."

"You think he knew this would happen? You and me?"

"I don't think he would be okay leaving if he didn't think it was possible."

"Alex? What are we doing?"

"Dancing to a pretty darn impressive Neil Diamond cover band."

"No, what are we really doing? Should we be testing this, or should we have left it alone?"

"I think we'd prove to be the dumbest and most hard-headed people alive if we ignored what we have and kept fighting this power that keeps drawing us together."

As they continued their slow dance, Renae closed her eyes and took in that familiar cologne she remembered from a week ago. This time it didn't make her uncomfortable, but it relaxed her. "Is this how you imagined the night going?" she asked.

"Not at all. It's so much better."

As the song came to an end, they had transitioned from a slow dance to a solid embrace. Renae pulled her head away from Alex's shoulder to look at him. He returned her gaze, carefully studying her face. The time spent in the sun from playing soccer had brought out her freckles that he loved so much. The band switched gears and led into another favorite from *The Jazz Singer*, "Hello Again."

Renae choked up. "Oh my gosh, can this night get any more feely?"

Alex smiled, grabbed her hand and started to lead her around the crowd to the car.

"When I told Dad I thought you'd moved on, he didn't buy it. He said you were a man of integrity and he was right. When he told me to talk to you, I told him I wouldn't even know where to start. He said I should simply start with "hello." So, please forgive me for going through all the emotions tonight. I'm feeling extra-feely right about now. This stupid song."

"I like extra-feely. You're being real; I love that about you."

As they approached the car, they faced one another and linked hands.

"Where to now? The pier? Beach? Home? The night's pretty young; I'm not ready for it to end. I find myself really enjoying the company."

"I don't know, maybe we could find a cheap hotel like the good old days. It's been a while." Renae couldn't keep a straight face.

"Yeah, I'd say it's been about the same to the exact day and time for me, too. But I actually have a house now, so we don't have to sneak to a hotel around town."

"Oh my gosh, do you remember the time we were leaving that one dive and we ran into Daddy's golf buddy there?"

"We were so busted."

"He was so busted! The only reason we didn't get ratted out was because that woman was definitely not his wife!"

"Your dad would have killed me."

"I think he knew what was happening. He was probably just glad it was you. He thought you had good genes and he knew he wouldn't get a strapping young grandson from Josh." Renae noticed Alex didn't look as amused by the comment as she was. "Hey, I'm sorry that I may have given the impression to you or anyone else that Joshua and I were involved."

"Don't worry about it," Alex tried to sound like he could blow it off, but Renae knew his ego had been damaged at one point or another.

"I'm not worried about it, I just want you to know I recognize our behavior was at times inappropriate or disrespectful towards you, especially while we were still married. For anyone to have the impression that I had moved on with him...well, that meant that we weren't acting as friends and I'm so sorry to have acted in a way with any guy to leave that impression. It was my job to lift you up, not bring you down, and I was lousy at it."

Alex stepped closer to Renae and made intentional eye contact with her. He was standing in front of the love of his life. She was a woman of unparalleled strength exposing her vulnerabilities this evening. He chose his words very carefully. "Renae Rivera, I forgave you 16 years ago when I said 'I do'. For all of it. And even though we're not married anymore, I still made you a promise. And I won't break that promise."

She stared at him in disbelief. Tears began to fill Renae's eyes as Alex kissed her hand. Her throat tightened. The only thing that felt natural to do was to wrap her arms around him and hold on tight. "You know how you said you wanted to hear about my dreams? I stopped dreaming when you walked out of my life. I just couldn't dream without you being in it."

"My dreams always had you in them. Even after the divorce. And those dreams turned to prayers of hope. And here we are today. You, in my arms again. I promised God that if this happened again, I would never let go again. So, as God is my witness, you're stuck with me, Renae."

"That's so good to hear."

The pair decided to drive to their favorite beach so they could just enjoy walking in the cool sand, hand in hand, and enjoy being in each other's presence. They found a bench to sit on and watched the lights on the cruise ships from miles away.

"Why didn't we ever go on a cruise, Alex?"

"I think we let life and work get in the way of pleasure. I can't remember our last vacation together."

"If you went on a cruise, where would you go?"

"Probably Alaska. Because I know you've always wanted to go there."

"What about the Mediterranean?"

"Is that where you want to go?"

"I think so."

"Then that's where I want to go too. Next year?"

Renae sat up and looked at him. "Really? Like, you want to plan one?" She was too excited for him to change his mind.

"Let's do it. Let's plan a cruise for next year. You and me."

Renae grinned and resumed her relaxed position; she was leaning on Alex's arm as she sat beside him.

"Every time we come down here at night, I have a hard time leaving. The sound of the ocean waves is so relaxing. I think I could stay here all night."

"I'm not in a rush to get home; are you?" Alex replied.

"No, but I think I just hopped on the sleepy train."

"We can head back. We have a lifetime to come back and do this. Next time we'll get a room so we can just go to sleep with the door open and hear the waves."

"That sounds amazing."

Alex helped her off the bench and carried their shoes in one hand, her hand in the other as they took the long stroll back to the car.

The trip home was silent. Alex decided to turn on his favorite playlist of worship songs to break the silence and ride in a peaceful atmosphere. Renae recognized a couple of the songs from her father's playlist. She paid attention to the lyrics. It's no wonder she had seen a change in Alex's attitude since they'd split. He'd been filling his soul with so many encouraging and uplifting messages, he didn't have room for the negativity. She looked out the window, trying to figure out what to do next. She still needed to give him the Bible she'd promised him. Should she invite him in for that, or should she have him wait in the car? Would Maddy still be awake? She might want to see Alex, which would make it harder for him to leave. She wanted him to stay. Both were disappointed to see the entrance of her neighborhood. Alex pulled into the driveway and put the jeep in park. He considered shutting it off, but he wasn't sure if Renae would just get up and leave, or invite him in.

"Are you going to Mom and Dad's church tomorrow?" she asked.

"I was thinking about it. Why? Are you going?"

"Yeah, I'm thinking it's the day to make good on a promise I made to someone."

"I'll go with you then."

"Okay. Want to come and tuck Maddy in? I can give you Dad's Bible."

"I'd really love that."

Alex shut the engine off and followed Renae inside to Maddy's room. Ruth had fallen asleep on the sofa, so they tried to stay quiet and not wake her. Maddy was listening to her grandfather's playlist, and her room felt full of peace. As Alex leaned down to kiss his sleeping angel, she rolled over and hugged him, her face red and stained with tears. "Hi, Daddy."

"Punkin, what's the matter? Why are you crying? Can you not sleep?"

"Daddy, I miss Grampy tucking me in. I miss him, Daddy." She began to cry again. Renae walked from her bedroom with the Bible and stopped in the doorway as Alex tried to comfort his daughter.

"Where's Mr. Snuggles? Is he hiding under the covers?"

"He fell under the bed."

Alex bent down and reached under the bed until he retrieved a special ratted brown bunny that he'd given her when she moved out of their home. "Here he is. I think he was scared under there."

"I was too scared to get him. Daddy, can you sleep with me tonight so I don't have any more bad dreams? I can scoot over so you can fit."

"Oh, sweetie, I don't think Daddy can stay tonight. I can stay right here until you fall asleep, though."

Renae felt a sick feeling come over her as she saw her daughter's need to have her father close to her. They had really screwed up. What would the status of their relationship do to her? Especially if they gave her hope they would all be a family again and then failed? In this moment, she realized she had to dismiss the what-ifs and focus on the immediate needs of Maddy. And right now, in her grief and fear, she needed her protector. Maddy squeezed her eyes and turned her mouth into a perfect upside down "U," her tiny sniffles becoming stronger and louder.

"Hey now," Alex sat on her bed and pulled her close to cradle her. Renae saw herself decades younger being comforted by her father after many bad dreams. She walked up to the pair and sat down next to them. Alex looked at her and shrugged to tell her he didn't know what to do. Renae smiled and mouthed "stay" to him. He nodded his head and mouthed "thank you" to her. Renae rubbed her daughter's back as Alex told her he would stay with her.

"I need you to hang in there a couple of minutes, though. I need to have a grown-up talk with Mommy in the hall, but I'll be right back, okay?"

"Pinky promise." She extended her tiny little pinky to her father and he wrapped his around hers.

"Pinky promise." Alex followed Renae to the hall and toward her room. "I can leave once she falls asleep."

"It's up to you, but I would hate to be you after she discovers you ditched her in the middle of the night. She can hold a grudge like her grandmother."

"Which one?"

"Oh, God, Alex, your mom hates me. Does she have any idea?"

"Don't worry about it, I'll take care of her. I was lucky to be raised by her for 18 years, but you're my forever person that I choose to be with and she can learn to deal with it. Again." Now wasn't the time to discuss Deb Murphy's disdain for Renae. Maddy needed her father. Renae grabbed an extra blanket and pillow from her bed and handed them to Alex.

"Well, once she gets to sleep, if you find yourself wide awake you can always return these. I have a bigger bed."

She winked at him as he drew her close and sighed. "Can we just annul our divorce? Pretend it didn't happen?"

"We should be able to, shouldn't we? But why? So you don't have to sneak into my room and worry about my mom flipping out on us in the morning?"

"Well, I for one don't want to waste another night without you at our house. In our room. In our bed."

Renae looked at him and grabbed his pinky finger. She knew she had some work to do on her heart before she could love him the way he deserved to be loved. But she didn't want to ruin the moment for him. "Goodnight, Alex." Renae smiled and led him back into Maddy's room.

Before leaving, she leaned down to give Maddy, who was already in a deep sleep, a kiss on the cheek. She moved towards Alex, brushed his hair back, and kissed him on the side of his forehead. "Thank you," she whispered in his ear.

He turned to her and pulled her close for a hug. "Goodnight." He kissed her on her cheek, and she rose to switch the nightlight off and head to bed.

As she lay her head on her pillow, she quietly thanked God for second chances. She thanked Him for her family. And she thanked Him for His faithfulness. She didn't know she was about to be tested and tried. That her world was about to crumble before her. And that it would take a complete surrender, standing in a position of absolute faith, to withstand the events to come.

NINE

Renae stared at her ceiling fan as the moonlight cracked through the blinds. The moon was full and bright tonight. Her superstitions led her to believe that was the reason she was having trouble sleeping. She was thankful for the moonlight, though. She felt that was the only thing pushing away the darkness that was pressing on her. She looked at her phone. 1:52 a.m. She closed her eyes again and tried to push away the memories invading her thoughts. She squeezed her eyes tight to try to remove those memories from her brain. She heard herself yelling at Alex to go back to work so she wouldn't have to see him. She saw herself push him into a wall and watched his anger build toward her and then back down, fighting the urge to strike her. She heard Alex raise his voice before walking out and slamming the door behind him. She saw a broken mirror, shattered by a mug she threw toward Alex during an argument. She saw her bags on the floor at her parents' house as her mom prepared ice cream for Maddy, still in her pajamas with her red rain boots on, while Renae and Phil argued outside about her decision to leave her husband. The sights and sounds of the past were terrorizing her. She had instigated all of it. All the pain, the fights, the grief they went through--she was the calculating menace behind it all. She didn't deserve someone like Alex, and one day he would eventually figure that out. There was no way this could work out any differently than before. Her fears were beginning to suffocate her will to make this work. She couldn't drag Alex and Maddy through this again.

She opened her eyes as she became aware of her breathing. She was having a hard time catching her breath. She looked at her phone again. 1:58 am. This had been happening since midnight. Renae dreaded closing her eyes. She looked around her room and located a bottle of water on the dresser. Tossing her covers to the side, she stood to retrieve it, knocking down a picture frame in the process. She didn't care; she needed some relief. The bottle cap was resistant to release from her trembling grip, so she tossed the closed bottle to the floor. She sat down on the bed, her heart still pounding as she buried her face in her hands.

Alex hadn't been sleeping well, either. He was too excited to fall asleep. He kept thinking about the night they'd had, their talks, their future together. He was considering places to take Renae on Sunday for what he hoped would be another date when he heard noise coming from her room. He slipped out of bed to check on her. As he entered the room, he could clearly see the expression on her face had shifted from an intoxicated glow to bothered and scared. The light in her eyes that was sparkling for him just hours ago had been extinguished.

"Hey, what's going on? You okay?" He pulled her chin up to look into her eyes, but she pulled away.

She couldn't tell him that she was starting to feel the oxygen-robbing sensation of anxiety and fear sink in, triggered by her own memories and insecurities. Alex stood confused in front of her.

"Baby, what is it?"

Renae knelt down on the floor and tried to catch her breath. Heart racing, she put a finger on her wrist to feel her pulse and check if she was still alive. Alex had never seen her like this. Renae had never felt like this and she was quickly becoming frightened of her own body. Alex could see her hands tremble as she tried to stand up. He was quick to join her side, putting one hand over one ear and boldly whispering in the other as he held her up, "You weren't given a spirit of fear, but of power, and love, and a sound mind." He repeated it to make sure she heard it. "I believe in you, Renae. I believe in us." She couldn't make out anything else he was saying; she could just feel his breath on her cheek as he spoke.

She let out a deep sigh and felt a release in her soul. She grabbed Alex's arm covering her ear and squeezed it tight. Alex still had a good grip on her, and his face was pressed hard against the side of hers.

After a few minutes of standing like this he asked her, "Better?"

"I need my water. It's somewhere on the floor." Alex found it near the wall where she'd thrown it. He opened it up and handed it to her, still holding her arm to help her balance. "You can let go now, Alex."

"You need to eat something?"

"No."

"Orange juice? Something? What can I do?"

"Nothing; just stop trying to fix this, Alex."

Alex was taken aback and a little hurt by her sudden, sharp tone.

"What? Fix what?"

"Fix us. Alex, we can't just sweep everything that happened under the rug and pretend we've always been fine. It didn't work before; how can you think it will work now?"

"Renae don't-" he stopped his sentence short. He realized he was about to place some blame on her and that was wrong. "Can you help me understand what happened during the past two hours for us to end up here? Renae, help me understand, because I'm really at a loss right now. And I really don't want to leave here knowing I had you at my fingertips and then something weird that I will never know happened and I lost you for good."

Renae knew she owed him an explanation. She'd quickly concluded that she wasn't good enough for him or what he needed. She was a mental basket case, and he deserved someone loving who could walk hand in hand with him through life doing whatever it is that Jesus people do.

And the thought of those horrible images and memories becoming a reality once again shook her to her core. No matter how much she loved him, she was better off alone, and he was better off without her. Alex didn't understand any of this as she explained it, and he refused to accept it.

"Renae, it doesn't make sense. One moment we're telling each other we love each other-"

"I never told you I loved you tonight, Alex."

Alex turned away from her, hurt. She was right. Had he been hearing what he wanted to hear tonight? Was he imagining they were getting back together? Had he been so elated about being with her that he completely made up all the good moments in his mind?

Renae could see that this comment visibly shook him. She hated herself for doing this to him. She hated herself for doing this to herself. She was ready to walk away from him forever out of her fear of their past. What she wasn't ready for was his next proposition.

"Renae, I will let you walk out of my life if you can look at me in the face right now and tell me you don't love me and there is no chance for us again. I'll leave and you can have your life to yourself again. But know if you can't, I am going to fight for you. I'll bust hell wide open and fight fear itself if I have to."

Renae took a deep breath, determined to end this for good. As she turned to look at him, her eyes locked with his. Neither of them could break their gaze. She loved those eyes. In this moment, they were soft but surrounded by lines of worry. Her heart broke and she couldn't withstand the emptiness of the cold feelings inside of her. As her eyes filled with tears, her heart filled with warmth.

"I can't. My God, Alex, I've been fighting myself to stay away from you for so long. I'm tired of fighting. I'm tired of us fighting. I'm tired of rehashing the past in my mind. I can't tell you I don't love you, but I can't tell you I love you, either. The truth is, I can't love you wholly until I love myself, and

I really don't even like myself right now. And when it's our time, I want to love with everything I am. I want to love you wholeheartedly, because you deserve someone to love you that much. I'm just sorry I didn't recognize that years ago."

Alex was fighting back tears but didn't fight the urge to pull her close and hold her tight. The love of his life was longing to become everything he had hoped for her and more; but allowing her to find herself required patience from him. And he didn't want to wait for her another minute. But he would.

"Renae, I love you more today than I did five years ago. When you're ready, I'll be here waiting for you. Whether that's tomorrow, or next week, a month from now, or next year. I'm really hoping for tomorrow, but you take the time you need. I'm devoted to you and to us and our family one hundred and ten percent."

Renae knew he was telling the truth. She knew he loved her without conditions and would take her back regardless if she was a basket case or not. She was staring at the most incredible, loving, handsome man she'd known besides her father, and she questioned why she never saw his worth before. He had changed incredibly over their time apart, and she was in awe of the man he had become.

"What the hell happened to you to make you so awesome?" The two smiled at each other.

"Your dad. Absinthe. Mostly Jesus"

She laughed. He was relieved. "Alex, I really don't want to close my eyes again tonight."

"Want me to stay here with you?"

"Then Maddy would be upset you weren't in there with her when she wakes up."

"We can make a pallet in her room and sleep on the floor. We'll just let her know you got lonely and we couldn't all fit on the bed."

It didn't matter how many blankets they placed on the floor underneath them, the floor was hard and cold. But that didn't bother Alex and Renae one bit as they cuddled up with one another and drifted off to sleep. She was completely at ease being back in his arms.

* * *

Renae began to stir as the distinct smell of bacon crept its way upstairs. She opened one eye and saw Alex lying next to her, watching her in total contentment. She quickly closed it and smiled at him. She opened the other eye to take another peek, shutting it once she saw him again. She opened both eyes and he was face to face with her. This was a routine they had went through as newlyweds, and they both found amusement in it again this morning.

"Your mom is making bacon this morning," Alex whispered.

"Don't you remember, she makes bacon every morning. Well, she hasn't the past week. Maybe she knows you're here. Is Maddy up?"

"She's up. She tiptoed out of here about twenty minutes ago."

"How long have you been awake?"

"Maybe half an hour."

"You hungry?"

"Starving."

"Want to meet me downstairs? I need to put these blankets and pillows away."

"I'll help and we can go down together. Can we just lay here for like another five or ten minutes? Or all day?"

"All day is good." Renae replied as she pulled the covers over their shoulders and cuddled close to Alex. The events that had occurred hours before were a distant memory for her. She felt secure and full of hope.

Ruth Rivera was in lighter spirits this morning. She has seen her former son-in-law's jeep in the driveway as she opened the blinds to let the morning sun in. That meant things went well for Alex and Renae last night. She didn't care to know how well they went; she was just happy for her daughter that she had another chance with the love of her life. Disappointment almost ruined her mood when Maddy revealed that her daddy spent the night to stay with her because she was sad, but when Maddy continued to tell her that he slept on the floor with her mommy, Ruth was confident things were moving in a positive direction. Feeling in a mood to celebrate a little, she decided to treat the two of them to a full breakfast of bacon, vegetable quiche, and fresh fruit. Maddy settled for cereal. Her grandmother was treating her to the sugary kind Renae normally didn't allow, as long as Maddy let her parents sleep in and come downstairs on their own.

Ruth inhaled and exhaled deeply at the sight of the two of them walking into the kitchen together, hand in hand. She wished Phil were here. He'd be so happy. She fought the tears that were beginning to build up, then greeted the couple who were being attacked by an overly excited six-year-old.

As Renae loosened her grasp on Alex's hand and squeezed Maddy tight, Alex turned to Ruth, who looked like she needed a hug. "Breakfast smells amazing, Mom." He gave her a tight embrace and continued to whisper in her ear, "and I promise I was an absolute gentleman and kept my hands to myself last night."

"Well, that's a shame," Ruth joked with him as she pulled away. His hug felt good. She needed that. And it felt good to joke around a little. She wasn't nearly done mourning the loss of her lifelong lover, partner, and best friend. But this morning the sun was shining a little brighter on her home and she began to realize she and her family were going to be just fine.

Alex made a cup of coffee and brought it over to Renae. She turned to him and handed him a bowl of fruit. Standing inches apart, they gazed and smiled at one another as they enjoyed their refreshments.

Ruth squeezed into their space to interrupt their flirting. "I'm gonna have to grab one of your daddy's knives to cut through all the sexual tension between you two."

"Oh my God! Mom! Why?!" Renae was shocked and embarrassed by her mother's comment while Alex turned away, smirking. He and Ruth used to love to gang up on Renae and clearly Ruth was starting to feel somewhat like herself again.

"I'm actually going to take this to go, if you don't mind." Alex explained to Ruth that he needed to go home to shower and get ready for church. "Are you going today?"

"I'm not sure if I'm ready for all the sympathy hugs and 'Are you doing okay?' inquisitions," Ruth admitted.

"That's okay; I got you." Renae stopped glaring at her mother over the sexual tension comment and walked to the stove to get Alex some quiche to go.

Shocked, Ruth replied, "Are you going to church today? Do you feel okay? It's not a holiday."

"Yeah, I'm going to church with you, so what?" Renae tried to play it cool. She didn't want anyone to make a big deal out of it.

"Alex, you really do have her under a spell, don't you?"

"Wasn't him, Mom. I'm just holding up to my promise to Mr. Reeves, that's all."

"Well, okay, I guess we're all going to church this morning. Have to make sure I'm there to see everyone's eyes when they discover the prodigal has come home."

Renae rolled her eyes at her mom, who was fully amused at herself.

"Maddy, finish your breakfast so you can get ready for church. Did she shower last night, Mom?"

"No, I took a bubble bath and used your bath bombs."

"Well, I could just swear there was some unicorn glitter in those bath bombs with the way you're sparkling this morning, sweet girl." Renae gave her little girl a kiss on the head as she delivered Alex some quiche. Maddy giggled and put a giant spoonful of milk-soaked cereal into her mouth.

She grinned as she watched her mommy and daddy treat each other kindly. She loved seeing her parents so happy, and she would love nothing more in her heart than to be able to live with both of them again. Her short memory could not recall a time where they were happy together like they were in this moment.

Alex laid his breakfast on the table and bent to his daughter's height. "You feeling better this morning?" Maddy nodded her head. "Good, I'm glad to hear it." He swept some of her hair out of her face and she jumped from her chair to give him a long bear hug.

"Do you have to go, Daddy?"

"Well, I need to go home to shower and get dressed for church. You don't want me all stinky and smelly like a barn-yard animal, do you?"

"They're not so smelly. Wet dogs smell worse. But I bet if you were a goat you wouldn't smell that bad."

"You don't think so? Well, I'll have to take your word for it. I'll meet you and Mommy and Grammy at church later though, okay?"

"Pinky promise?" Maddy loved the pinky promise.

"Pinky promise."

Renae stood back and looked on with admiration. Alex loved his daughter like Renae's father loved her. And she knew Maddy would come out stronger for it. Little by little, Renae's fortress was coming down.

"Why don't you finish your breakfast so you can get dressed? How about you wear one of your new outfits from yesterday?"

"Okay, Daddy." Maddy climbed back into her seat and turned her attention back to her cereal as Ruth laid a plate of bacon next to the bowl.

"Bacon is ready; grab some before you head out, Alex."

"Is this that Million-Dollar Bacon?!" It was his favorite. The sweet and savory flavors infused with peppered heat satisfied every taste bud known to man.

"Why yes, it is, and I made extra."

"You're so good to me. I love you, Mom." Alex gave Ruth another hug and a kiss on the cheek. Ruth was truly in a good mood now. She was just sorry she had to see him go so soon.

Renae started packing his breakfast into a bag so he could easily travel with it. She found a jar and placed several strips of bacon standing upright inside, adding her portion as well, since he liked it so much.

"Do you have a travel mug I could take this coffee to go in?"

"Here, you can take mine. I'll get it back from you later." Renae poured a fresh cup for him into her favorite travel mug and stood ready to walk him out.

"Thanks for the breakfast, Mom. Sorry I can't stay and eat."

"Oh, you're welcome." Ruth gave him one last hug. "I enjoyed seeing you this morning. Don't be a stranger."

"I'll see you in a couple of hours," he assured her. "Bye, Punkin. I'll see you soon too." Alex kissed his little girl on the top of her head and then walked over to Renae.

"I'll walk you out."

Alex grabbed the bag and mug from Renae, and the pair headed to the front door. As they approached the door, neither were sure how to say their goodbyes. Renae opened the door and decided to follow him out to his car. The sun rose in the front of the house and the warmth it brought was soothing and awakening. Alex opened his car door, placed his breakfast inside, and turned to Renae.

"I'll see you soon." She crossed her hands in front of her and smiled.

"If I had my way, I'd be packing up all your things and we'd be going home together right now...but, soon."

Renae nodded in agreement. "Soon."

Alex touched her face as she smiled at him with adoration. He wrapped one arm around her waist and pulled her close, pressing her body against his. She tilted her head up as he leaned down, his lips meeting hers for the first time in over two years. She closed her eyes as she felt her breath escape her, lifting her hand behind his neck and head and squeezing it tight. Alex tightened his squeeze around her waist as he tried to pull her closer. Renae grabbed his arm with her free hand. As the kiss ended, they rubbed noses and Alex rested his forehead on hers.

"I'm definitely looking forward to more of those," he whispered.

"Me, too."

The sound of an ignition starting a nearby car interrupted the moment. They turned to see Mrs. Reeves. She was wearing a jubilant smile as she turned to them and waved before backing out of her driveway.

Renae covered her mouth and smiled as her face turned red. She returned the greeting to her neighbor, whom she absolutely adored.

"Think she'll call Mom?"

"Well, we're not seventeen and making out in my car so my guess is no."

"Be careful going home."

"I will. Meet you in the cafe before service?"

"Yeah, like a quarter 'til?"

"Sounds good." He bent forward to give her one more kiss before getting in his car.

"Dad's Bible--it's still on Maddy's dresser. Want me to just bring it to church?"

"That'll work. And I don't expect you to say it back, but I love you. And I am going to give you my last name again someday soon, Ms. Rivera."

Renae beamed as she watched Alex back out of her driveway and leave her line of sight. She turned to her house, determined to work on the content of her character, to find her worth, and to love herself again. She was committed to the idea of once again loving Alex and letting him love her in return. She was confident that the two of them could move forward and be stronger than ever before. She sighed deeply as she shut the door behind her. This was going to take some major work on her inner core to accomplish. But the end result would be so worth it.

T EN

The ride to church was about twenty minutes from the Rivera home. It gave Ruth plenty of time to ask her daughter questions about the events of the prior night and where she saw her relationship going with Alex. Renae turned the volume up on the car stereo so Maddy wouldn't overhear anything her little ears and mind couldn't process. "I don't know, Mom, it's just happened so fast. A week ago, I could barely look at him without wanting to hurt him. And now it's not a question to see *if* we can make it work; it's more like we're moving forward together and determined *to* make it work. I just...I know there are things I need to get through in order to fully give him my all."

"Like your past?"

"It really isn't even that. I can leave all that exactly where it belongs, behind us, because we're not going to let our past define our future. You know how Dad drilled into us to love God and love people like we love ourselves? Well, I don't love who I am, Mom, and I'm not sure how I can love him when I don't feel I'm worthy of him."

Ruth felt sympathy for her daughter and her face couldn't hide it. She knew her daughter had thick skin; she just didn't realize that all this time that tough exterior could have been a defense mechanism to mask how she felt about herself.

"Well, do you love Alex?"

Renae paused for a moment before speaking too quickly. She knew once she admitted it out loud to herself and someone else, there was no going back. "I really do, Mom.

So much."

"Do you love God?"

Renae looked at her mom and shrugged her shoulders. "Not sure. I know He's real; I believe in Him. And in Jesus and the Holy Spirit. I know I can count on Him when I need Him. But I don't know if I really *love* Him. Does that make sense?"

Ruth felt like she was stabbed through the chest with a dagger. She thought she'd done everything right when she raised her children: she took them to church, she read Bible stories to them, she watched them get baptized when they were young. What could have happened for them to stray so far from their upbringing and religious beliefs? Then it occurred to her. For so long, she taught them to chase after religious practices and ideals and never encouraged them to chase after a relationship with God. She looked at her beautiful daughter and her sadness turned to determination. Today, Renae was taking multiple steps in the best direction. And Ruth would do whatever it took to help her daughter discover unconditional love in a relationship with God...and with Alex.

"That makes sense, sweet girl. I'm proud of you. And I'm proud to call you daughter."

"I'm glad you're my mom." Renae gave her mom a quick smile before she pulled into the church parking lot. She preferred parking away from the masses, so she found an empty row and parked her car.

Ruth reached for Renae's hand before she turned off the ignition. "I'm just going to say this. I'm proud of you for approaching this the way you are. Your faith is going to help you get through those moments of doubt. Once you love God, your love for Alex will flourish and expand immeasurably. Together you two will form a force so strong the powers of hell will try to move mountains to separate you. But hell's power doesn't move mountains, God's does. And when you two have God at the center of your relationship, He will move mountains. When you face a giant, remember that you serve a God who conquers giants. And when you look in that mirror and see some distorted version of yourself pointing out your flaws, remember those flaws are invisible to Alex and you need to start seeing yourself through the lens he looks at you with. You're the daughter of a King, and He's calling you home. You are beautiful; you are clothed in dignity and strength; you are a masterpiece. That's how your father and I saw you; that's how Alex sees you, and that's how God made you. I love you, Renae Dawn."

"Mom, you're gonna make me cry." Renae hugged her mother in the car. "Thank you, Mom. I'll do my best to remember that. We could just go to lunch now, since you already took me to church."

"No, I think you have someone in there waiting for you."

"Jesus?"

"I was going to say Alex, but Jesus too."

All three girls exited the car and headed toward the building in good spirits. As they walked through the parking lot, Renae spotted a familiar grey jeep. She picked up her pace. "Mom, Alex said he would meet us in the cafe. Which entrance is that?"

"The one to the left. Why are we walking so fast? We have plenty of time to get seats; you got us here early enough."

Renae turned to her mom, who was holding Maddy's hand. "You know why," she said with a mischievous grin. Renae faced the greeters who were welcoming church-goers at the door. She saw faces transition from welcoming and cheerful to concerned and sympathetic as they shifted their focus from Renae to Ruth. By the looks on their faces Renae concluded this could be hard for Ruth to push through, so Renae pulled Maddy to her right and held her hand. She held Ruth close to her left and tried to pull her through the crowd of women who were beginning to gather and check on her. "Mom, you okay? I'm sorry, we should have gone through a different entrance." This foyer was where people always gathered, and it was the most crowded.

"I'm okay," Ruth replied.

"Ruth, it's so good to see you!"

"Ruth, hey honey, how are you holding up?"

"Ruth, we've been praying for you and the kids. If you need anything, you know we're a phone call away."

Renae was grateful her mother was surrounded by a strong support system. She understood that they didn't know how they could help, but they just wanted her to know they were there for her. They wanted her to know she was loved and would be taken care of. Renae was also grateful for those who were cautious and waiting to greet her mother so as to not overwhelm her.

Ruth stopped to talk to a good friend of hers and Renae, feeling protective, tried to stay close by. "You go ahead and find Alex; I'll meet up with you. He knows the area we like to sit in," Ruth assured Renae.

"You sure?"

Ruth nodded her head, so Renae grabbed Maddy's hand and began to look around for Alex as they walked toward the line of people waiting to order coffee. She was well-received by familiar smiles and greetings of 'Good morning!' Although she'd stayed away for so long and it had changed so much over the past two decades, this place and the people in it felt like home.

"Excuse me, pretty lady, are you lost?" A smile swept across Renae's face as she recognized the voice in her ear coming from behind her. She turned to face Alex.

"Not anymore." They managed to exchange a quick kiss before Maddy jumped toward her daddy, almost knocking him down.

"Hey, kiddo! You ready to go to kids' church?"

"Nope! I want to stay with you and Mommy."

"What? You have so much fun every time you go."

Renae stood back and observed as Alex reasoned with

Maddy. He was wearing a dark blue suit and tie with a blue and purple gingham-checked shirt under his jacket. She liked how he looked in a suit. She realized her cream maxi dress, half-covered in light blue and lavender flowers, matched him perfectly. They complimented each other without even planning it.

"Alright, she's going to go to kids' church. Want to go get our seats first?"

"Sure," was all Renae could say. She felt extremely undeserving of this blessing in front of her, but she was so thankful for it.

Alex grabbed Renae's hand and led his family to the main auditorium, making his way to the section Phil and Ruth normally sat in when he visited. He found three available seats, and Renae laid down her purse and her father's Bible to save them. They decided that Alex would drop off Maddy and Renae would stay to wait for her mother.

Renae looked around at the sea of people greeting one another and felt a little lonely. Funny, she had been attending this church for over half her life, but she hardly knew anyone here. Suddenly, she saw a familiar and friendly face. It was Tabitha. Tabitha saw her, too and rushed over to hug her.

"Renae!! I'm so happy to see you! I saw Alex and Maddy and asked about your mom. He told me you were here, and I had to run over before kids' church started."

"It's so good to see you too, Tabitha!" Renae returned the hug. She really liked this girl, even though they barely knew each other.

"Look, I really want to bring something over for you guys, but I heard everyone was bringing lasagnas and I didn't want to overwhelm you with more food. Can I bring you a Spanish dish sometime this week?"

"Oh, Tabitha, you don't have to do that."

"I know, I just want to. That's what friends do."

"That would be fantastic, thank you." Renae gave in. She was overwhelmed by Tabitha's generosity and kindness.

And some Spanish food sounded delightful.

"I need to run next door, but I'll get your number after the service so we can figure out which day would work best for you guys."

"Sounds great. Thanks, Tabitha."

Shortly after Tabitha left Renae, Ruth came to sit with her.

"How are you doing, Mom?"

"I'm okay. Mind if we stay a little late after the service? I have someone I need to talk to."

"That's fine."

Renae saw the musicians and choir begin to take their places on the platform. Over the years, the team on the platform had modified their look from choir robes to modern clothing. Their sound changed too, looking more like a band onstage at a concert rather than stiff men in suits showing off their skills on the brass horns and with guitars. Renae didn't understand the criticism some people had over the change, and she didn't go often enough to really care. She just knew she was able to tolerate it now. The countdown on the screen indicated there was a minute left before the service started. She looked to the doors to see if she could spot Alex coming in. She spotted him just outside the auditorium talking to someone. He looked so happy. She made a mental note to never again destroy his happiness through her selfishness.

As the music began to play, Alex made his way back to her. "You look absolutely stunning, by the way," he said as he returned. They both stood with the rest of the congregation, as was customary during the musical portion of the service.

"I had to try; I mean, look at you. You look so handsome; people are probably wondering how I landed a hottie like you."

"I'm positive that's not what they're wondering." Alex winked at her before they focused their attention to the stage and screens.

Church had changed so much from when Renae had

been regularly attending. She usually didn't know or recognize any of the songs they sang when she visited. She stood and read the lyrics as her mom sang to the left of her. Curious about attendance, she looked around to see how full the auditorium was. Typically the place didn't fill up until the last song, but that looked like it had changed. Finding a seat in the first section was becoming difficult already.

The tempo and atmosphere began to shift and slow down as the singers and musicians transitioned into the second song. It was a song she recognized from her father's playlist. If it pulled on her heartstrings when she'd heard it at home, she couldn't imagine how she would react to it at church in the absence of her father. Her emotions began to escalate, so she excused herself to escape to the bathroom before the floodgates opened. On her way, she ran into Pastor Reeves, who was on his way into the auditorium.

"Hey, kid!" He greeted her with a smile. "So good to see you." He leaned in close to her. "I saw a certain car in your driveway this morning as I was leaving, and Elaine told me something when she got here." He had a huge grin on his face.

Twenty years ago, Renae would have felt like she was about to get into so much trouble in this conversation, but today she knew that wasn't the case. "He's here today, sitting with Mom and me."

"Your Dad would be so happy and so proud. Cheering and praying for you guys," he said as he made his way to the auditorium door.

Renae had a difficult time pushing open the bathroom door. Her body was weakening as she was overcome with numerous emotions. She thought she could escape the song in the safety of the four walls of the bathroom, but the church was now broadcasting everything on the platform through the ceiling speakers. She wanted to stand in front of the sink so she could regroup to the sound of running water, but the bathroom was too busy for that. Trying her best to avoid people, she walked into a stall and paced back and forth in the tiny space. Being alone wasn't helping her push through her sorrow, either. She took a deep breath and decided to face it head on. Wiping her tears, she left the stall and washed her hands. She couldn't help but return the smiles of the friendly faces. As she looked in the mirror, she noticed the ugliness that she saw in her reflection yesterday had disappeared. Today, she saw radiance staring back at her. She faced her image for a moment as she heard the words, "my daughter, you are so worthy." With that, she turned to the door and made her way back to Alex and her mother.

"You okay?" Alex was growing concerned about her.

"Yeah, I'm great." She smiled at him and pressed her head onto his shoulder as to give him a quick hug without embracing.

The song set concluded after two more refrains, followed by a prayer from Mrs. Reeves. She was claiming victory over finances, health, marriages, and job situations. After prayer, it was a practice to turn and shake hands to greet people and welcome them to church before taking a seat. This was Renae's least favorite part. She turned around to greet the person behind her, but his back was to her. She then turned to greet the people in front of her, but their backs were faced to her as well. Alex and Ruth were shaking the hands of the people next to them, so, feeling awkward, Renae plopped down in her seat and pulled out her phone to make sure she silenced it.

One thing that hadn't changed much was the order of the elements in the service, and Renae anticipated what would come next. She recognized that this moment was time for announcements and offering. The vocalists were still standing behind Mrs. Reeves, so that pretty much guaranteed another song. Then Pastor Reeves would get up to deliver his message, and he would wrap up with a call to action or a salvation altar call. The call to action was usually a challenge over the week, such as reading a certain book in the Bible or applying something taught during the message in everyday life. The salvation altar call was more committal. It required walking to the front of the auditorium as an act of surrender to God and accepting Jesus as your personal Savior. Renae wondered which way he would close today. She was betting on the altar call. As the congregation was asked to stand for another song while the offering containers passed through the rows, Renae felt comfort in the familiar.

The next song was an original written by the music pastors. Renae never heard it before, but she was drawn to its melody and message. The girl who sang at her father's ceremony stood before them, and her powerful yet angelic voice sang words declaring the love of Jesus. The regular attendees were familiar with the song already. She saw her mother lift her hands in worship to one side of her. Renae stood silent while she studied the words.

Jesus, loving kindness in Your hands
In my place You chose to stand
On what should have been My cross
You hung as You breathed Your last, for love

Alex placed his hand on her shoulder and pulled her close.

Jesus, what a Friend I have in You
You are making all things new
You have freed me through and through
As You got up from that grave, for me

Yes I know, You loved me so I could love You
You bled and You died so I could live
There is no greater Love than this.
You shouldered my sin and my pain
You tore through the grave, so I will stand
My whole life in surrender to You
There is no greater Love than this

Renae put her arm around Alex's waist as she focused on the message behind the lyrics. When Ruth had asked her if she loved God, Renae didn't know what that would feel like. It was evident in the lyrics and melody that the writer knew exactly how it felt.

Jesus, You have been there from the start
Divinely You have chased my heart
Created things show Who You are
No rock's gonna take my place

As the song continued, Renae began to feel a tug on her heart. She missed this. She didn't recall at what point she and Alex had decided to stop attending church; she just remembered that they thought they didn't need to go. Today she was beginning to regret staying away for so long.

You're my Blessed Assurance, dressed in salvation
You have come for the world You love
You're my Kinsman Redeemer, clothed by Your mercy
Drawing close so that all could know

You're Jehovah forever, moved by compassion
Lord of all still You call me Yours
You are seated in Heaven, fullness of glory
Dearest, Jesus, You are mine

She remembered images of who she believed Jesus was and how extravagantly He loved. She had no doubt in her mind He loved her. She felt remorse for not returning that love for so long. But here she stood, once again in the four walls of her church, and she was standing with the love of her life who was beyond a shadow of a doubt completely transformed through his relationship with Jesus. God did it again, she thought. Like the story of the Good Shepherd who left the flock to find one lost sheep, He left the ninety-nine to find her.

* * *

Renae felt fortunate to have Pastor Reeves as her pastor and neighbor. She enjoyed the practicality and humor in his messages. They were relevant, timely, theological, and always inspired by Scripture. She knew that if she ever decided to come back to church, it would be here where they not only preached unconditional love, acceptance, and forgiveness, but they practiced it as well. After living with the Riveras as neighbors for the past twenty-two years, her pastor had a lot of experience demonstrating it to her family.

Today, his message related to having a healthy home. Renae stared at him and internally questioned if this message was pointed directly at her and whether he knew she would be there today. Was he reading her mind? She had been in church many times when the message was directly related to something she was going through...were his sermons just general enough to cover a wide aspect of circumstances that so many people could relate to? Were they direct? Did he have her house wire-tapped for topics that struggling Christians (or those who haven't decided to live for Christ) dealt with? She realized she was staring at the lights and zoning out. She needed to focus. Renae leaned forward, with her pen and notebook in hand. She always took notes. It helped her pay attention. She checked her phone to see if she'd downloaded the Bible app on it already. Having the Bible on the phone was easier than remembering a book. She placed her phone in her lap for easy reference.

Healthy homes are cultivated by healthy choices. She'd better jot that down since they put it on the screen. Was he referring to eating? Probably not.

We should listen more, talk less, minimize anger. Crap, this was going to sting; she could already feel it coming. She wrote it down.

Our homes, our hearts, and our emotions can be likened to a refrigerator. They can smell rancid and even become toxic. Renae considered that statement for a moment. Her home life with her parents was nothing like that, largely due to the fact her mother stayed out of her way and her father pretty much let her have her way. But her life with Alex...toxic and rancid were spot-on for the emotions that had run high in their household. Their relationship had become stale and hard. They had constantly referenced past hurts, which pretty much stunk. Playing the blame game like they'd done so often was toxic. She had to turn from those thoughts. Who they were becoming would not reflect who they used to be.

In order for us to have healthy homes collectively, we must have healthy homes individually. There it was. He nailed it. She had to clean out the refrigerator of her own heart before she could feel confident that she could share a healthy home with Alex. She had recognized this only hours ago, when she was in the midst of a panic attack because she was reflecting on all the junk in the past. But what did she need to deal with? What was it about her that was causing her to react in such a nega-tive and defensive manner toward those she loved?

Pastor Reeves offered Scripture for support to lead up to his points.

Psalm 4:23-24 "Search me, O God, and know my heart; try me and know my anxieties; and see if there is any wicked in me, and lead me in the way everlasting."

Renae shifted in her seat as she wrote down the book, chapter, and verse for reference. She'd grown up in church. She was aware of the ways God worked, but she was pretty apprehensive about inviting the Omniscient to examine her heart and strip away the parts of her she tried so hard to cling to. She was becoming increasingly uncomfortable and it showed in her fidgeting.

Alex leaned over to her and whispered in her ear. "You okay?"

"Nope."

Sensing her uneasiness, he moved a little closer to her and put his arm around her. Far too many times he had pointed out her flaws in their past. Now, he would love and accept her however she came. After all, she had his heart and he had hers; any matters that needed to be examined were between her and God at this point.

Renae relaxed at Alex's touch. She stopped fidgeting and was able to focus again. All of that led up to the first point Pastor Reeves made in his message.

1. Release the Offense. Release/let go/remove the junk from the refrigerator.
Hebrews 12:14 "Pursue peace with all people, and holiness, without which no one will see the Lord."

Renae stared at that verse, especially the beginning. Pursue peace with all people. Pursue was the same thing as chase. Chase peace. Chase peace with whom? All people. All means all. Dang it, that meant Eric, too. Renae scribbled his name down on her notes next to the verse and circled it. "Release, let go, remove." To move on, you need to ask God to reveal the stagnant funk in your heart so you can release it. Crap, she had to let God examine her heart so He could show her what she needed to let go of. Was she asking God to reveal her flaws to her? She really had to trust that this would end well.

Pastor Reeves caught her attention as he was singing the chorus to one of Maddy's favorite songs. "Folks, sometimes you just gotta let it go!" he said. She chuckled along with the congregation.

Renae grabbed her phone and looked up the given verse on her Bible app. She liked to compare different translations of the Bible, mostly because she couldn't understand most of them. She'd often found herself zoning out of messages and digging into the rest of the chapters of the Scriptures that Pastor Reeves referenced. She lifted her eyes to the pulpit as the pastor moved on to his second point.

2. Renew the Commitment.

Psalm 51:10 "Create in me a pure heart, O God, and renew a stead-fast spirit in me."

What did steadfast mean? Renae searched it. Steadfast means unwavering and firm. So, we are restarting with a firm and committed spirit. This sounds like dedication and hard work, she thought to herself. But in reality, it's where she wanted to be. She wanted to be committed to her family; she wanted to have peace and have a pure heart. She wanted to get rid of all the junk that was causing her anxiety and fear, and embrace the holiness, whatever that meant.

3. Restore the Newness

Psalm 51:12 Restore to me the joy of Your salvation and uphold me by Your generous Spirit.

Somewhere, somehow, she had lost her joy. She was often frustrated, pissy, and angry. Especially in her marriage. But it wasn't limited to just that. People at work didn't want to cross her and without Joshua around, she really wasn't nice to many people. Was she ready to release and renew so she could restore?

The musicians were making their way to the platform. The message would be wrapping up soon and Pastor Reeves would somehow close this out. He was a master at wrapping up his messages and tying everything together. He was also good with words, words that pulled on your heartstrings, causing you to search your heart to determine where you fell in this call to action. Renae looked over her notes and at the Scriptures one last time. She knew she had to work on her inner being in order to have a relationship with Alex, but suddenly it occurred to her...she needed to clear the air with God before she could be content and live a fulfilled life with anyone else.

Renae closed the app on her phone and tossed it in her purse along with her notepad and pen. She sat at attention, listening close to what Pastor Reeves was petitioning. The keyboardist began to play as the other musicians and singers stood by, nodding their heads in agreement with the encouraging and confirming words coming from the pastor. Renae could sense he wasn't moving into a salvation altar call after all. This topic was affecting people who already decided to follow Jesus, too.

"I'm speaking to those of you here who have taken offense with someone in your past or present that you're still holding onto." Pastor Reeves had the attention of everyone under the sound of his voice. "You recognize there are some things weighing on your heart that you need to release. Some of you may be dealing with bitterness or anger; maybe past offenses have created a hardening in your heart that you know beyond a shadow of a doubt you need to let go of. Others may be saying, 'I've released that offense; I'm ready to commit again. I'm ready to dedicate myself to the cause of Christ and to those around me,' and others may be sitting here saying 'I'm ready to have the joy of Christ's salvation cover me again; I need the newness restored in my life.' If any of these apply to you, sir, ma'am, would you please stand? We want to pray with you."

Renae scanned the room in front of her as people stood to their feet. She knew deep in her heart that she belonged standing with these individuals today. All of it applied to her. She just wasn't willing to make the commitment, especially when she was pretty sure people would be coming to pray with her. She was physically tired from her emotional rollercoaster over the last week; another emotional release would shut her down. Ruth looked at Renae and smiled, giving her a pat on the leg. She believed her daughter knew she should be standing, but she also knew her daughter would be called to do so in God's timing, not hers.

"Church body, we won't keep you here for more than a few more minutes, but those have been attending here long enough know we don't walk through these moments alone. I'm going to ask if you're seated next to someone standing, would you go stand with them? We're going to pray together corporately."

Alex rose and quickly made his way to a young man standing two rows away from them. Others around her were quick to join into groups for prayer, some with two to three people surrounding them. As Pastor Reeves prayed, Renae locked her eyes on Alex. His love and compassion for someone he had never met was pouring out from his lips as he spoke words of release and affirmation over this young man. Renae never would have imagined he would be at this place in his faith, where he felt confident and bold enough to pray for other people; people who may even be at a different level of spiritual maturity than him. This is something she witnessed her father do numerous times, and she admired her dad for it. Today, her love for Alex was deepening as she witnessed how transparent he was with his faith.

Ruth whispered in Renae's ear and smiled. She looked to her daughter for a reaction, but Renae was clearly deep in thought. Ruth followed Renae's gaze and her eyes stopped on Alex. She saw her husband in him--a noble, faithful, loving man--and she was delighted her daughter held his heart. She grabbed Renae's hand and tenderly rubbed it with her thumb as she prayed through her breath for God to draw her little girl closer to Him, and to strengthen the relationship of her and Alex.

As the prayer ended, Alex stood next to the man he'd prayed with and gave him a quick hug while Pastor Reeves ended his portion of the service. The music pastor invited the congregation to stand to their feet once more as they closed the time in a song of celebration. Renae recognized the song, another original from the worship team, as her father had added it to his playlist. Alex returned to his seat, and Renae outstretched her arm to welcome him and give a side hug. He returned the hug, squeezing her tight, and sealed it with a kiss on her forehead.

Renae decided in those moments that she needed to make things right with God. She needed to restore the faith she once held onto when she was so young. She needed to embrace this overwhelming, persistent love of God that refused to give up on her, even though she'd turned her back on that love more times than she cared to think of. As the song ended and the music pastor invited the congregation back for evening services, the room quickly emptied of parents eager to gather their kids and go home for lunch.

"Want to go with me to pick up Maddy?" Alex asked.

"Sure. Mom, do you still need to meet with someone?"

"I do. Can you wait for me in the cafe? It shouldn't be longer than twenty, maybe thirty minutes."

"Sure."

"Alex, will I see you later?" Ruth asked.

Renae was quick to answer for him. "We haven't talked about our plans for this afternoon or evening; we'll let you know."

"Okay, well if I don't see you later, it was so good spending the morning with you. Don't be a stranger." She gave him a hug and kiss on the cheek. "Love you, son."

"Love you too, Mom. I'll see you soon."

As Renae and Alex headed toward one door, Ruth walked the opposite direction. Curious as to whom Ruth was meeting with, Renae turned and watched as her mom walked up to the care pastors and was embraced and led away by the wife. Besides Eric and Renae, Ruth didn't have an opportunity to openly discuss her loss with anyone, and she certainly hadn't spoken with anyone concerning her loss from an eternity perspective yet. Renae was once again grateful for an army of supporters surrounding her mother.

"So, do you ladies want to grab some lunch when your mom is done?" Alex offered.

Renae pulled Alex next to a palm tree in the courtyard, away from the sea of foot traffic headed towards the building the children were in.

"Alex, would you mind if we don't do lunch together today? Not that I don't want to spend more time with you,

I just...I need to go get some fresh air and reconnect with...I don't know...I need to clear my head and get in my own space and try to figure some things out."

She could see a look of concern appear on Alex's face. He didn't appear hurt, but somewhat confused.

"Alex, we're solid. I'm not reconsidering anything or backing away from us. I just really need to clean house and today's message hit pretty hard."

His face softened at her words of reassurance. If God was speaking to her and she wanted to take the time to sit in silence and listen to Him, Alex would gladly step aside.

"I'm good with that. Do you want me to take Maddy with me, or do you want to keep her?"

"How about she stays with Mom this afternoon, packs up all the clothes you got her, and she can go over tonight or tomorrow?"

"That works for me."

Tabitha greeted them as they entered the building the children were in, and Maddy made a beeline straight for her daddy. She showed him her paper with the content she learned in kids' church, and after Renae and Tabitha had made arrangements to meet in the courtyard in ten minutes to chat and exchange numbers, the family began the walk to Alex's car.

"Daddy, what's for lunch today?"

"Well, I have to go home and get some things done around the house, so you are going to go have lunch with Mommy and Grammy today."

Maddy's disappointment was written all over her face. That disappointment quickly escalated into sadness as she unsuccessfully tried to fight away tears. Renae halted and knelt to Maddy's height, quickly embracing her little girl. "Hey there, now. What's the matter? Is lunch with Mommy and Grammy so bad?" She kissed her little girl and tried to rock her to comfort her. Alex knelt down and rubbed her back.

"No." Maddy was sobbing and had a hard time getting her words out. After a couple of tries to look at her mom and speak, she kept returning her gentle yet pained face to her mother's shoulder.

"Sweetheart, did you want to have lunch with Daddy instead?"

"It's not that!" she cried out.

"Can you talk to me and tell me how I can help?"

Maddy straightened up and wiped the tears from her eyes, her nose red and her eyes becoming puffy. "Pastor Jonathan asked us if we had a prayer request today and I raised my hand. I prayed that you and Daddy would get along and we could live together and now I don't think Jesus heard me." As Maddy began sobbing again, Renae scooped her into her arms and stood, quickly making her way to Alex's jeep.

"Maddy, listen to me carefully, Jesus heard you. And He loves you and wants what is best for you. Sometimes He answers prayers and we see the results so fast. And sometimes, it takes a little longer and may look different than what we were praying for. But I guarantee you Mommy and Daddy are going to do everything we can to be a family again. We love you so much, baby girl."

Renae was hesitant to make promises to Maddy, especially over something regarding the matters of the heart. But she was also confident there was a future for their family, and she couldn't hold back revealing that truth to her brokenhearted daughter. Her words comforted Maddy, who stopped crying and looked to Alex from behind her mother's shoulder. She made the hand sign for "I love you" to him. He signed it back.

The family arrived at Alex's car and Renae put Maddy down as she got to the driver's door. Alex bent down to Maddy, his little girl squeezing him as tightly as she could. "I'll see you tonight or tomorrow after school, okay?"

"Promise? Pinky promise?"

"Pinky promise."

"I love you, Daddy."

"I love you too, Munchkin."

He kissed Maddy on the cheek and stood to face Renae. Maddy grabbed her mother's hand and stood close to her.

"I hope you don't mind what I just said." Renae was trying to keep outside of Maddy's earshot but she needed affirmation from Alex that he was fine with what she'd told their daughter.

"You handled that well. I know I feel better." He smiled at her and pulled her in for a hug. "Promise you'll call me as soon as you're ready."

"Ready for what?" She knew; she just wanted to hear him say it.

"Ready for lunch, ready for another date, ready to move back home." She knew him so well that she could hear the smile on his face through the sound of his voice.

"Hey, Alex?"

"Hmm?"

She turned her face to his ear and closed her eyes. "I love you. So much."

Alex closed his eyes and tightened his hug around her, Maddy still attached to her mother's hand. "I love you, too." He released his hold on her to face her, both of them beaming. He began giving her random kisses on her face which made her burst into laughter. She grabbed the back of his neck and kept him still to give him a quick peck on the lips. "I'm late to meet with Tabitha! We need to run."

"Ok, but I hate leaving without you two." He gave her another kiss on the cheek. Now they had established this was okay, he couldn't get enough of her.

"I promise I will call you. I'll see you tonight or tomorrow."

"How about you bring Maddy over tonight and you can stay until tomorrow?"

Renae smiled coyly. "Bye, Alex."

"Can't blame me for trying."

"Bye, Daddy!" Renae turned with Maddy and began walking back to the courtyard. Alex fondly watched his two favorite girls until he saw them reach their destination safely, then he pulled out of the parking lot and headed toward his house. As Renae was preparing her heart to let him back in, he would begin preparing their home.

* * *

Tabitha walked out of the double glass doors as Maddy and Renae approached the children's building. She waved at her husband, who'd loaded up their children in his car to head home.

"I'm sorry," Renae began, as she looked to Tabitha's family, "I don't want to keep them."

"Oh, they're fine, we take two cars here since I have to come so early. They're going home; I'll catch up with them in a few."

"Oh, okay."

The weather in the courtyard couldn't have been more beautiful. The sun was brightly shining, and the late morning/early afternoon breeze was cool and refreshing. This kind of weather made the locals feel bad for everyone who lived elsewhere. It had to be experienced.

"How was today's service?" Tabitha asked.

"It was really good. I have some work to do, but uh... yeah. It was really good."

"Okay, and I'm not trying to be nosey, but how are you two doing?" She looked down at Maddy, who was still attached to Renae's hand.

"Me and Maddy?"

"No. Not Maddy."

"Alex?"

"Yes." Tabitha wore a hopeful smile on her face.

Renae cautiously examined her. She had no reason to

believe Tabitha had malicious intentions or reason to gossip. She trusted Tabitha, and she knew that whatever she said would stay between the two of them.

"Hey, Maddy, how about you go sit on the bench over there under the shade and read this book while Mommy talks to Mrs. Benson?" Renae often kept books or a small tablet in her oversized bag so she could entertain Maddy when the occasion arose. Maddy gladly accepted the book and headed to a nearby bench to quietly read.

"So, Alex and I, we're doing really well."

"Yeah? Like reconciliation well? Because the two of you belong together; it's so obvious!"

Renae was becoming a little more comfortable talking to her. "Tabitha, he's been a dream!"

"Ahhhh!!" Tabitha really didn't know the two, but she was more than happy for them.

"It's just so weird because a week ago, well, you heard. I physically injured him! I think that was a result of a wall I was building up because I was afraid of getting hurt by him again. I'm pretty sure all this time I've always loved him, but I refused to address or acknowledge it because I was afraid. Does that make sense?"

"Yes! That makes perfect sense. Renae, I could tell Saturday night how good of a fit you two are. You both have this energy and light that shines from each of you when you're together. I'm just so glad you both realized it and acted on it instead of ignoring it and continuing to push each other away."

Renae caught Tabitha up to speed on her relationship with Joshua and how she and Alex were moving forward. She told Tabitha how he was willing to wait for her to work on her inner core before fully diving back into their relationship. Tabitha was so excited to listen to her that she intentionally ignored multiple calls from her husband. He was probably just checking on her for lunch.

"I'm sorry, your phone keeps going off. You should probably get that, and I need to meet my mom in the cafe;

she'll be-" Renae was interrupted by the sound of a blaring siren from a fire engine passing by. She and Tabitha turned to watch as it passed. It was quickly followed by two fire rescue trucks. They could hear police sirens coming from the opposite direction.

Renae looked at Tabitha, her eyes squinting from the sun. "That doesn't look good."

Tabitha said a quick prayer under her breath for whomever those vehicles were headed toward. "No."

"You better call your husband. Here, what's your number? I'll text you mine."

After the ladies exchanged numbers, they hugged goodbye and Renae retrieved Maddy so they could find her mother. She felt a special friendship was forming in her relationship with Tabitha, which made her happy. She needed someone in her corner--someone who could cheer her on and encourage her. And Renae hoped she could one day become an encouragement in return.

As Tabitha was walking to her car, she received another call from her husband. "Hey, I was just about to call you-"

Greg cut her off. "Tabitha, did Alex Murphy pick up Madeline today after church?" He sounded desperate.

"He did, but she's here with her mom."

"Oh, thank God!" His voice cracked as he tried to remain calm on the other end.

"Greg, what's happening?" Tabitha knew something was terribly wrong.

"Tabitha, Alex has been in a terrible accident about two miles north of the church. He was hit head-on. I was scared Maddy was with him."

"No, she's here still." Tabitha's heart sank. Her chest felt so heavy; her voice was barely audible.

"It doesn't look good. I'll reach out to Pastor Reeves and the care team. Do you have Renae's number? She should get to the hospital as quickly as she can."

Tabitha became nauseous as she turned to see Renae, Ruth, and Maddy walking to their car.

"Yeah, I'll call her." Tabitha hung up with her husband, took a deep breath, and asked for grace and strength as she dialed her new friend's number.

E LEVEN

Renae stared down at her feet, wishing she had remembered to grab her flip-flops from the car. Her shoes were too tight in the toes and she kept wiggling them for relief. Ruth took Maddy home in Renae's car while Tabitha drove Renae to the hospital. She beat Alex there. According to an officer on the scene who spoke with Renae at the hospital, it took a great deal of time and effort getting Alex out of his vehicle. He'd been approaching a sharp curve when a speeding truck passed another truck and hit Alex head-on. Other than the condition of the other driver, Renae didn't care to hear any more details. She didn't know if she was relieved or mad that the driver that caused the accident wasn't badly injured.

The waiting room chairs were uncomfortable. She wondered how often they had been cleaned. She shuddered at the idea of all the germs that she might be sitting on. The hand sanitizer looked like a good idea. After helping herself to some on the wall, Renae walked the room to look at the paintings. All she could focus on were colors, not shapes. Her mind was too frazzled to make out shapes. How long had it been since she talked to the lady at the desk? It had to have been an hour. Surely they must know something by now. They probably forgot about her.

"Excuse me, ma'am, do you have any updates on my husband?"

The kind woman behind the desk looked up at Renae and saw the pained hope in her eyes. "I'm so sorry sweetheart, but we haven't heard anything about Mr. Murphy since you asked fifteen minutes ago. But I assure you, once we hear something, I will personally come find you."

Renae looked confused and lost. "Fifteen minutes? It feels like it's been a lot longer."

Renae's breaths became shorter and more laborious as she tried to fight back tears. The nurse came from around the desk to attend to her. "Here, Mrs. Murphy, why don't you sit down. I'm going to get you some ice water." Renae nodded her head as the tears broke through. "Is there somebody I can call to come sit with you?"

"I don't want anybody sitting with me," Renae said as she shook her head no. She preferred to be alone so she could sink into her own feelings without someone asking her how she was doing. She had tried calling Josh because he was the only one who understood how she coped, but he wasn't answering her calls today.

Another hospital employee came to her side with a Styrofoam cup filled with ice water and placed it in her hands. "Here, sweet girl, take a sip of this. I'm going to go check on your husband and see if we can get you in to see him."

Renae looked at her and nodded. She had been delivered a small dosage of hope with this cup of water. She took a sip as she sank into her chair. The receptionist returned to her desk but kept a close watch on Renae while the coworker disappeared through a set of locked double doors. Renae wanted to escape the sound they made. It was a familiar noise that she recognized from her visit there one week ago. She looked at her phone to check the time. There were numerous missed calls and text messages. She scanned them to see if any were from her mom or Joshua. Not finding any, she put her phone away. She was too numb to read, comprehend, or respond to any of the messages she'd received. She'd look at them later. She took her phone out to look at the time again. She couldn't remember if it said 2:23 or 3:32. It was 3:53. She had been in that room all afternoon. Ms. Deb,

Alex's mother, would arrive in about three hours. She was driving down from Savannah, Georgia. Renae was not looking forward to seeing Ms. Deb. She was a spiteful and judgmental woman who showed up to Alex and Renae's wedding in a navy suit so dark, she appeared to be in mourning. Everyone in attendance received her not-so-subtle message. Ms. Deb disliked Renae and didn't make a secret of it. She tolerated Renae at family gatherings, and although she was brokenhearted for her son when he announced the divorce, she was also relieved. Renae looked at her nails and wished she hadn't bitten them all off. Now she needed a nail file. The fish tank looked inviting. Maybe she could pass the time by counting fish. Just as she stood to head toward the small aquarium, she was approached by the kind woman who offered to check on Alex for her.

"Mrs. Murphy?"

"Yes?"

"Here, I'll take you to go see him."

Renae nodded her head and exhaled as she prepared for the unknown. "Is he awake?" Renae asked as they reached an empty corridor.

"No, he suffered a severe concussion; he's been unconscious. His doctor and nurses will be able to tell you more about his condition, but I just want to warn you he does have some lacerations and bruising accompanied by swelling that may startle you at first."

Renae tried to remember every turn they took so she could find her way back, but it was useless, especially once they boarded the elevator.

"Are we headed to ICU?" Renae recognized the lobby as she walked through the elevator doors.

"We are. It's best that he stays here for the next couple of days until his condition improves." She held her badge up and escorted Renae to the desk. "She's here to visit Alex Murphy. They'll just need your ID, sweetheart." Renae fumbled through her purse to find her wallet. She handed an officer her

ID and after inspecting it, he handed it to the receptionist to scan and print a visitor sticker with.

"Your relationship?"

"Complicated. He's my ex-husband, but we're back together." She was glad she'd procrastinated changing her name on her license. This was a lot easier to do as a Murphy than a Rivera.

"That's really nice, ma'am. I'm rooting for you two." The officer's friendly smile brought a half smile to her own face. He reminded her of the actor from *The Green Mile*. She just couldn't remember his name. But she liked him a lot. He was a gentle giant.

"Thank you. Me too."

As she turned to her escort, another nurse joined them. She was studying Renae's face and offering a kind and sympathetic expression in exchange.

"Mrs. Murphy?" Renae turned to the person addressing her. "I'm Millicent. I'll be taking care of your husband the next eleven hours. We just got him up here, so he's all settled in and ready for you. I need to prepare you; he does have some swelling and bruising on his face and arms along with some lacerations. We have him hooked to an IV. It is critical that he receives antibiotics and we need to keep his pain at a minimum. He does have some pretty severe swelling in his brain, and we haven't ruled out any injury to it as of yet. We'll need to wait for him to wake up for a more proper assessment. The other thing of major concern is his leg. The impact of the collision broke both bones in his lower leg, which protruded through the skin. We cleaned it out as much as we could and have it bandaged right now, but we would like the swelling in his brain to decrease so that we can go in and thoroughly clean the bones and surrounding area to keep it free of infection before re-setting it. I understand your mother-in-law is on her way?"

Renae nodded her head. "She's coming from Savannah, so it will be a couple more hours."

"Okay, we'll let them know downstairs. Let's go see him." The nurse had to nudge Renae to get her walking. She was trying to process what the nurse had said and understand the severity of it all. She didn't want to under- or over-estimate how serious his condition was. The patients in the ICU weren't behind walls, only thick glass, making them visible to the staff. Renae became queasy as they approached a room and she read the name MURPHY, ALEX by the door. This was becoming very real. As Renae and Millicent turned the corner to enter the room, Renae closed her eyes shut and pictured the last image of Alex she saw, standing at his jeep and smiling at her, asking her to move back home. Although Millicent was detailed as to the extent of Alex's injuries, Renae wasn't prepared for the sight when she opened her eyes. She quickly turned around and covered her mouth to quiet any noise coming out as every muscle in her chest and stomach contracted in pain. Tears spilled from her eyes as she looked to Millicent for comfort.

Millicent wrapped her arms around her and rubbed her back. "It's okay, baby, it's okay," she whispered in Renae's ear. "You don't have to go see him, but I know he would love to hear your voice or feel your touch."

Renae pulled back and looked at this kind nurse in the face. She had to trust her. Renae nodded her head in agreement, pulled herself together, and slowly walked to the foot of the bed.

"Which leg is broken?"

"His left one. Here, you can have a seat next to him." Millicent pulled a padded leather chair next to Alex on his right side. Renae sat down and stared at him, her hands clutched tight in her lap. His left side looked much worse than his right side. His eye looked swollen shut. There was a stream of dried blood in his hairline.

"Is his nose broken?"

"It looks like he took a massive hit to his nose, but it isn't broken." Millicent looked at Renae's sad face and felt pity for her. "You can hold his hand on that side; he'd like that. I'm not sure how much he can focus on right now, but I'm pretty sure he knows you're here and he may just respond to your voice."

Renae lifted his arm and slid her hand into his. She leaned her elbows on the side of his bed and brought his hand to her lips. Bringing a part of him close to her brought her comfort and relaxed her.

"Millicent? How serious is it?"

Millicent stood and crossed her arms, looking down at a distraught young woman who was looking to her for hope. She didn't want to break her heart any more than it was already hurting. Then she noticed a small cross hanging from around Renae's neck and felt released to encourage Renae to pray. She believed it wouldn't fall on deaf ears.

"Sweet girl, whose report would you rather believe? A doctor who can't give you assurance, or a Healer who can?"

Renae winced as her chest tightened again. She knew that response meant it was critical enough to pray for a miracle.

"I believe in the power of prayer. Keep your faith strong, Mrs. Murphy. Lift him up. You need to be the one to stand in the gap for him right now." Renae looked to her and smiled as tears rolled down her cheeks and onto Alex's hands. She nodded in agreement and turned her attention to Alex.

"His vitals are good. Can I get you anything before I step away for a couple of minutes and leave you alone?"

Her nerves got the best of her, and Renae sprang to her feet and covered her mouth, running to the nearest trash can. She didn't have much in her stomach, but whatever was there was quickly regurgitated. Millicent walked to her and rubbed her back. "It's okay. Everything is going to be okay." She handed Renae a paper towel as Renae stood up and apologized.

"I'm so sorry."

"Don't be sorry, Renae. I know it's a lot to take in."

"It's just that my dad was here last week, and I lost him. We laid him to rest three days ago and now here Alex is, and I don't know if I'm going to lose him just like I lost my dad. And our daughter...I don't even want to think about what losing him too would do to her. I just keep thinking that if I hadn't been so selfish, then he would have stayed with us after church, and he never would have been in this accident and lying here in this bed."

Although Millicent was shocked as she absorbed this information, she kept a calm composure for Renae's sake. She'd read how hurt Renae was when she first approached her; she just had no idea how much pain and perhaps guilt she was carrying. Millicent wrapped her arms around Renae to embrace her, but the embrace wasn't returned. Renae was broken and too exhausted to even lift her arms. She just sank into the hug as Millicent held her up.

"I don't have the words to express how sorry I am that you are going through all of this. I don't know why it's happening. But I do know that when we're at our lowest, God can do His mightiest. He's walking through this with you, and those times when you're being knocked out and you can't take any more blows, tag Him in. Let Him fight the fights you aren't capable of winning in your own strength. He *will* get you through this."

Renae took a few more moments to gather herself, then graciously thanked Millicent for her encouragement. She felt some of the weight was being lifted in that room as they spoke. She felt released to briefly catch Millicent up to speed on her current relationship status with Alex and their hopes and prayers for a future together. Millicent knew she would be praying for this patient more than usual.

"Do you know what time it is?"

"There's the clock right there; it's 4:35. Do you want a few moments alone with him?"

"If that's okay? I'd like to have him to myself as much as I can before his mom gets here."

"Do you two get along well?"

"Not at all. I don't know what to expect when she sees me. She celebrated our divorce."

"Oh, child. Go spend some time with him. I'll be just outside this door."

"What if I need you? Do I press a button?"

"Oh, believe me, we'll know." She smiled at Renae and left the room.

Renae returned to the seat by Alex's side and grasped his hand again.

"Hey, you." She sat silent and stared at him for a moment, rubbing the back of his hand with her thumb. "So, this day didn't turn out like we thought it would. Looks like we got to see each other this afternoon after all. Mom took Maddy to the house; I can't believe she agreed to drive my car. Tabitha drove me here. I really like her, Alex, and I think you and Greg would get along well, too. Maybe we can all hang out when you come home." Renae struggled with the words to say to him. "I really don't know what to say right now. I'd like to say I wish I could take it all back. I'd like to say that I wish we could go back in time and undo the wrongs. But I don't think I want to say that, either. I'm afraid that if we didn't experience the pain that led to our healing, we never would have known the love that we rediscovered over the past few days. I wish I would have told you that I loved you earlier. I wish I had gone home with you Saturday night after the team party, because that's when I knew I wasn't over you and I was already falling back in love with you. The truth is, I never fell out of love with you; how could anyone that experienced your love possibly fall out of love with you? I was so stupid to walk out on us, and I'm scared to death I'm about to lose you for good." Renae let the big droplets of tears fall wherever they wanted to land. "Alex, you're my rock and I don't want to live in a world without you by my side. I wish I could just close my eyes and when I opened them, we would be right back where we were this morning. Except this time, we would just lie there and stay all day like you'd suggested." Renae's chin quivered as she took deep breaths to calm herself down. She pressed her cheek into his hand again and rested her head against it in silence. "Please stay with us, Alex. Maddy and I need you." Renae laid his hand down and held it with one hand. She stretched out her other arm along the length of his bed and rested her head on it. Her eyes were swollen and tight, and her emotions had taxed her heavily. Closing her eyes, she slowly drifted off into a peaceful nap.

Millicent stood in the doorway with Alex's doctor and they watched for any changes, responses, or signs from Alex while they spoke. To Dr. Robert Mavi's dismay, there were none.

"We'll take another CT in the morning to see if the swelling is decreasing. I really want to get that leg thoroughly cleaned and mended as soon as possible. Feel free to page me if anything changes. And let her stay as long as she needs to. Visiting hours don't apply to her tonight."

Millicent had informed him of what she learned from Renae, and after reviewing Phil Rivera's chart, they didn't want to add to her pain. The sudden death of a loved one could throw a person into depression; the sudden death of two in one week could deliver a blow so severe she might never recover.

❊ ❊ ❊

The stirring movement of Millicent in the room awakened Renae. She stretched her arm and her neck and looked at the clock. She had been asleep for almost two hours. Once again, a sick feeling came over her...Ms. Deb would be there any moment. Renae was hoping she'd get caught in traffic.

"How is he doing?"

"Well, since you've been here, his heart rate and blood

pressure have returned to normal ranges, so I'm pretty sure he knows you're here and he's enjoying your company." Millicent smiled at her and winked. "So, how old is your daughter?"

"Madeline is six."

"Madeline is a beautiful name."

"We call her Maddy for short."

"Well, you can call me Milli for short. Only my closest friends and my coworkers know that nickname. And now you and Mr. Murphy do, too. You can remember that when you invite me to your wedding."

"Okay, Milli. Thank you, and I will." The thought of them reaching the other side of this obstacle and getting remarried made Renae smile. She was glad Milli was working tonight.

"Milli, will you be here tomorrow?"

"Yes ma'am. I'll be back at 3:00 and I'll make sure I'm Mr. Murphy's nurse, if that's what you would like."

"I would love that." Renae looked to Alex and began to touch his face, tracing his cheek and chin with the back of her fingers.

"How long were you married?"

"Sixteen years. We dated for three before we got married--high school and college sweethearts. I swear he gets better looking with age. I'm a lucky girl."

"You're both extremely blessed."

The women heard a loud voice in the hall being encouraged to quiet down. Renae recognized that voice, and it brought a chill down her spine.

"That's her."

"I'll be right back." Milli left to greet Ms. Deb.

Renae stood up and bent over to kiss Alex on the cheek. "I love you," she whispered in his ear. "Never forget that. You're my hero, Alex."

She stood up just in time to see Ms. Deb make her grand entrance into the room, Millicent standing behind her. Ms.

Deb had nearly the same reaction as Renae upon seeing her son in the hospital bed, but she didn't hesitate to run to his side, subtly pushing Renae away from him, crying in agony over the sight. Renae was unsure what the proper reaction to witnessing this would be; she felt sorry for Ms. Deb, but also annoyed and displaced.

"Alex, everything is going to be okay. Mama's here now. You just rest and get better, my sweet boy. I'll take care of everything." Ms. Deb was raised in the south and during emotional outbursts, her southern accent became exaggerated. She was having one of those outbursts now and Renae stopped herself before she rolled her eyes. Yeah, she still didn't like her. Millicent reviewed Alex's condition with Ms. Deb, as well as the doctor's concerns.

After about ten minutes of crying and praying, Ms. Deb turned to Renae and dropped a bombshell Renae should have seen coming.

"You can go now, Renae. Thank you for sitting with him until I got here. I can take things from here."

"Oh, Ms. Deb that's okay, I'd like to stay with him. The doctor said I could stay tonight."

"That's before I got here and told them what a threat you were to him. We don't need you here adding any unnecessary stress and hurting him any more than you already have. Please leave with dignity, Dear, before security escorts you out."

"What?" Renae couldn't believe what she was hearing. But then again, considering the source, she could.

Ms. Deb stood to face Renae, and even though Renae was physically bigger and stronger, Ms. Deb was taller and positioned herself to intimidate Renae. "Dear, come with me outside a minute. I don't want Alex to overhear us needlessly arguing."

Renae looked at Milli in disbelief. Milli stood helpless near her. Once the women reached the hallway, Ms. Deb's voice turned from southern sweet-as-tea to course and threatening. "Look, my precious girl, my son is clinging on for his life in there. Haven't you done enough damage to him? Leaving him wasn't hard enough on him? Now you're here to finish the job and put him in his grave? You've done nothing but slowly destroy him from the moment he met you. You're a mean-spirited, wicked, despicable girl and I will not allow you to hurt him or cast any unnecessary stress upon him. You don't deserve the love of the man he has become without you; the man I raised him to be. So, take your bag and leave now before I have security throw you out. And I do not want to see you around him again, ever."

Renae was standing with her lips pursed and her fists clenched at her sides. She was raised to respect her elders, but she was having a hard time putting it into practice at this very moment. Milli came to her side and grabbed her arm, pulling her towards the desk where the friendly security guard was watching closely.

"Sweetheart, maybe it's a good idea to go home tonight and get some rest. I know she isn't about to leave and sitting around the waiting room won't do you any good if you can't get in to see him."

Renae didn't know if she should be angry or devastated. She felt as if her life was being shattered at this very moment.

"Young lady," the security guard's voice was gentle, "I want you to know I wouldn't make you leave. There's only one mean-spirited person on this floor, and it certainly isn't you. But it's probably best that you go home. She's going to be here a while. Maybe Miss Milli can talk some sense into her."

"I promise I will call you if there is any change whatsoever. I won't leave him, not even after my shift is over, I promise. Not until he is out of the woods or you come back, whichever is first."

Renae nodded and thanked them both, her emotions shutting down as she headed to the elevator. She didn't even get a chance to tell him goodbye. What if that was the last moment she saw him alive? She didn't want to think about that. What she wanted to do was to fall to the floor just to feel the cold hardness of it. It would convince her she was real-- that this moment was real. She'd feel on the outside how she felt on the inside. Hatred and hurt were slowly sneaking their way into her heart.

Taking the visitor route to the exit, Renae stepped off the elevator and noticed a sign on the wall pointing to the chapel. She took several steps past the chapel and stopped. An older gentleman carrying a prescription bag made his way towards her from the other side of the hall. He reminded her of the men she and Alex had treated to dinner at the park the night before. He had thinning grey hair that reached the middle of his neck. As he passed her, their eyes locked and a sense of peace and calm fell over her. He smiled and con- tinued walking. She looked at the floor, her breaths slow and deep. Renae quickly forgot about the encounter with the stranger as the damning words used to describe her surged in her thoughts. She wouldn't believe the things Ms. Deb said about her but they were playing on repeat in her mind. She turned around and slowly walked into the empty chapel.

The space was familiar although she had never been there before. The benches resembled the old wooden pews in the church she went to when she was a little girl. She ran her hand along the back of the long, smooth, wooden seat and walked around it to sit down. She sank far back into the bench, her feet barely touching the floor. She could never touch the floor sitting in them when she was a little girl, ei- ther. She leaned over, propped her feet up, and laid down, curling herself into a ball. She recalled falling asleep in her mother's lap many Sunday mornings, just like this. The wood smelled just like she remembered: musty.

She closed her eyes, wishing her father was there to gently wake her from the nightmare she was living. Feeling dizzy, she quickly reopened her eyes and looked around the room to keep it from spinning. The carpet underneath her was a rich red and there was an old communion table by the pulpit. On the communion table was an open Bible, and on the wall behind it hung a nearly life-sized crucifix. Renae sat back up and glared at the man on the cross. She slowly stood up and made her way to the front. She stopped and looked at the open Bible, curious to the book and passage it was opened to. Isaiah 40 and 41. She read the last verses in chapter 40 and looked to the cross. Her anger was building as she thought of the hell she had endured with the loss of her father and now this. The words on the paper were empty to her. She stepped onto the small platform and walked behind the podium, so there was nothing between her and the crucifix. She knew it was just an object, but she needed a visual to direct her anger at. She knew He'd hear her. Staring Jesus down, Renae paced back and forth. After a couple of minutes of pacing, she stopped in front of the crucifix and faced Him.

Renae was shaking, overcome with too many emotions for one person to carry. "Don't you *dare* take him from me." Her voice cracked as she said it. She felt so small. She was a speck of dust compared to the size of the universe He'd created, and here she was making demands of Him. She changed her tone, her chest breathing heavily. "You *can't* take him from me." She knew better. If it was God's will, He would take Alex. Perhaps taking Alex would save him from another devastating future with Renae. Maybe that was part of God's plan. The damnable words that Ms. Deb spoke over Renae were penetrating her thoughts, as if it were all confirmation from God. She crumbled to the ground in grief and submission and cried, "Please don't take him from me!" Renae was sobbing uncontrollably, seated on the floor of the chapel at the feet of Jesus. She was done. Renae thought of Millicent's advice. She needed to tap out and let God take over. She couldn't manage any more of this in her own strength. And the passage she'd just read in the Bible, Isaiah 40:31, began to echo in her mind.

*'But those who trust in the Lord will
find new strength.
They will soar high on wings like eagles.
They will run and not grow weary.
They will walk and not faint.'*

Her sobs stopped. She gained control of her breathing and stared at the wall as she wiped the tears from her face. The anger had left her, and she began to feel empty again. It was time for her to go home. She needed rest. Slowly, she stood up and returned to the table with the open Bible, taking a picture of the verse that came to her, and made her way to the exit.

* * *

Sundays were long days for pastors. Today just seemed a little longer and a little tougher than some of the others. It started out fine, but it took a turn fast when the news broke of Alex Murphy's accident. Mr. and Mrs. Reeves' hearts were aching for their neighbors and for Alex. They just couldn't imagine what Renae and Ruth were going through. They had been updated occasionally by a young lady from the hospital, but Renae had been out of touch with everyone and didn't want visitors, so they allowed her the space. They knew they would hear of any changes in his condition, for better or worse.

The couple pulled into their driveway, ready to wind down with some hot tea and conversation on the back porch. It was their Sunday ritual to relax together and reflect on the day that had passed.

"Do you smell that? I smell smoke," Mrs. Reeves observed when she exited the car. She had a keen sense of smell and was very aware of changes in her environment.

"I smell it too; it smells like cigarette smoke." Mr.

Reeves looked around for anyone who might be walking around smoking when his eyes landed on the front porch at the Rivera home. "Elaine," Mr. Reeves nodded in the direction of Renae, seated on the porch. Without speaking, they clasped hands and walked to the Rivera home by way of the sidewalk.

Renae had her driver stop at a liquor store on the way home so she could get cigarettes and a bottle of her favorite whiskey. She never was a smoker, but tonight it sounded like a good idea. She sat hunched over in a rocking chair on the porch and stared at the bushes while sipping whiskey from a plastic red cup and chain-smoking her cigarettes. She had yet to go inside to see her mother and Maddy, although Ruth knew she was out there. As she saw her neighbors approach, she extinguished the cigarette out of respect for them.

"Hey kid," Mr. Reeves began, "you don't have to put that out on our account."

"I'm done." By her facial expression and the tone of her voice, that statement encompassed more than one thing tonight.

"Would you mind if we sit with you for a little bit?" Mrs. Reeves asked.

Renae shook her head no. Mrs. Reeves sat in the chair next to Renae and reached for her hand. Renae responded by squeezing her hand tightly. She didn't want to let go of someone who carried such a peaceful presence. "Renae, in times like this we struggle to find the right words to say, but we want you to know that we have been praying for Alex and for you and Maddy. If there's anything you need from us, please don't hesitate to call either one of us, anytime."

Renae nodded her head and gave a quiet "thank you." Her short response hinted that there was no change in Alex's condition, which, given the circumstances, was received as good news.

"How is Maddy holding up? Does she know?"

"No, and I don't know what or how to tell her. Alex

told her about Daddy. I just don't know what to say to this precious little girl, especially when I don't have any answers to give her. She's going to want to know when she can see him or when he can come home, and I can't even tell her if he will be here tomorrow."

"Renae, I know it's late but if you want to go back or if you want someone to go to the hospital with you tomorrow-"

"I'm not allowed to go back." Renae didn't like cutting off Mrs. Reeves mid-sentence, but she also didn't want her to speak of the impossible. Without going into details, she told them that Ms. Deb was there now, and she'd made it very clear that Renae was not welcome near her son. Mr. and Mrs. Reeves' hearts broke for her.

"Elaine, we need to pray with her," Mr. Reeves broke his silence.

Renae nodded her head. "Will you please? I haven't prayed at all today. I just don't have the words to say and to be honest, I don't know if I have the faith to stand on. I did get mad at God at the hospital. So, He gave me Isaiah 40:31 in return."

"That's a great scripture to stand on," Mr. Reeves assured her.

Renae's phone started to vibrate next to her. Joshua was calling. She let it go to voicemail. "I should have stood at church today. My heart is trying to release all this junk; I am committed to rededicating my life to God, and I really want to renew the joy in my life. Alex and I went our separate ways today knowing I would work on my heart issues and he would be standing by waiting for when I was ready. I hate myself for not standing in church for prayer today."

"Do you want us to pray with you right now? Are you ready to recommit your life to Jesus Christ?"

Renae nodded her head as she was surrounded by her pastors. First, Mr. Reeves led her through The Sinner's Prayer. Her past was being erased, and no person or being would have the power to undo the redemption freely given to her that Jesus bought and paid for when He laid down His life for hers. No person or being would ever possess the power to separate her from the love of God. She would begin walking in a renewed spirit, one that overflowed from the love of God that was within her. Mrs. Reeves then began to pray over Alex, for his supernatural healing, that the Holy Spirit would step in and intervene on Alex's behalf. She prayed for strength for Renae and Ms. Deb as they walked through this with Alex, and she prayed for restoration in their relationship. Renae felt as if chains were being released from her as Elaine spoke, and her spirit felt alive and strong. Weakness left her body and confidence moved in. She was ready to fight fear and intimidation, yet, she knew she didn't have to; there was Someone she could call on to dispel those demons in an instant. As Mrs. Reeves ended her prayer, Renae felt an overwhelming sense of peace; she had sensed it before, but this time she didn't feel forces attempting to stifle it. As she opened her eyes, the familiar scent of her mother's gardenias filled her senses and a light breeze brushed across her face.

"That aroma is incredible!" Mrs. Reeves exclaimed as she came closer to embrace Renae. The trio briefly spoke some more and Mr. Reeves continued to encourage Renae, assuring her that they would be available should she need them. He gave her a few Scriptures to reference and encouraged her to stand firm in her faith. She graciously thanked them for their insight and kindness and for taking their time to deposit wisdom and pray with her.

"Want me to throw these in the trash can for you?" Mr. Reeves offered to take the cigarettes for Renae.

"Oh, yes, please. I don't need that crutch in my life," she smiled.

"What about?" he pointed to the whiskey.

"Oh yeah, no; I'm keeping that one," she laughed.

"Just checking! You never know!" He winked at her as he took his wife's hand and headed down the driveway.

Renae stood on the porch and watched them leave. She was so grateful and felt so lucky to have neighbors like them. Just as she turned to head indoors, she saw lights from an oncoming car light up her front door. She recognized the sound of the car. It was Joshua. Renae met him in the driveway, tackling him in an embrace before he could shut the door to his car.

"I didn't see him; I left when the nurse told me what Ms. Deb did to you."

"Well, if she kicked me out, she may have had you shot."

"That woman is a nightmare."

"I'd probably be the same way if he were my son, knowing how awful I was to him back then."

"She was never nice."

"Mmmm. I don't want to talk about her. Did you get my messages?" She released her hug and snuggled against his chest, a cue that told him she just needed him to hold her tight.

"I did. I'm so sorry, we had an event after church that I'd volunteered to help out with and then we decided to go see a movie. I finally checked my messages before it started and that's when I went to the hospital. How are you holding up? And have you been to a bar?" He could smell the smoke from the cigarettes in her hair.

"I haven't even been inside yet." She pulled from his embrace to talk to him face-to-face. "I haven't talked to Mom at all since I left for the hospital and Maddy knows nothing. Josh, I have so much to catch you up on."

The two friends chatted for a few more minutes in the driveway so Renae could explain to him where she and Alex now stood. Genuinely happy for her, Joshua decided to stay and support her in any capacity she would allow. Tonight she needed him by her side as she explained to her mother the events that had taken place at the hospital. She needed Joshua there to calm Ruth down, because once she heard how her daughter was treated by her former mother-in-law, Ruth would need some divine intervention.

Deciding it would be best to wait to tell Maddy once they knew more about Alex, Renae peeked in on her as she slept to kiss her goodnight. Joshua offered to stay the night, but Renae reassured him she would be okay. She told him of her revelation and the work she was allowing God to do in her heart. As they approached his car, he stopped to turn and look at her. He could see her face looked lighter and brighter than it had in the past, as if her inward change was being exposed on the outside. Grabbing one hand, he took a deep breath and sighed.

"Alex Murphy is a very lucky man to have you, Renae Dawn." She gave her friend a half smile. "When he pulls through this--and he will--God is going to have this incredibly huge gift in the form of you for him."

Renae didn't know what to say. All she could do was hug her friend before they exchanged kisses on the cheek goodnight. "I want to see you tomorrow, Josh, so please drive safely."

"I will drive extra-safe just for you."

"Thank you."

And as she always did, Renae watched Joshua's tail lights until they were no longer in sight. She walked back into the house feeling lonely. As she entered the kitchen to put away tonight's whiskey, the bouquet of flowers Alex had brought her the night before caught her attention. He told her he wanted her to look up the meaning of each of them, knowing it was how he and Maddy felt about her. Now seemed like a good time to do it. She pulled out her phone for reference as she tried to identify the plants she'd received. There were various colors of dahlias, several daisies, sunflowers, pink roses, a single red rose, and eucalyptus. She pulled each stem from the vase and examined the meaning behind their beauty.

Dahlia: elegance and dignity; one who stands strong in

her sacred values.

Sunflower: adoration and loyalty.

Gerbera daisy, each color holding a different meaning: cheerfulness, admiration, fully immersed in love.

Pink rose: joy and grace.

Red rose: passion and love.

Eucalyptus: protection.

There was a small ribbon tied around the vase with a pin of a Star of Bethlehem flower. It stood for atonement and reconciliation. Renae nodded in confidence and thanksgiving as she swept away tonight's final tears from her cheeks and smiled. In the midst of all the darkness, Alex had unveiled the light he saw in her. The timing was perfect. These beautiful flowers symbolized his perfect love letter to her.

Her eyes were heavy, and her body needed rest, so Renae turned off the lights in the house and covered her mother, who was once again sleeping on the sofa. As she crawled into bed, Renae grabbed the pillow Alex had slept on the night before and laid her head on it, hoping it would make her feel closer to him. Before she could sense anything, she drifted off into the most peaceful sleep she'd experienced in the past two years.

✳ ✳ ✳

Millicent had more than her fair share of Ms. Deborah Murphy tonight, so she sent her to get some rest in one of the family rooms nearby. Both Alex's heart rate and blood pressure had risen since Renae left, which Milli didn't believe was a coincidence. She debated calling Renae to have her come in, but didn't want to face the 'Dragon Lady' when she learned Renae was there.

As Milli started to check the fluids in Alex's IV bag, she heard movement on the bed. Alex lifted his arm to his face as he was trying to open his eyes.

"Oh God, why do I feel like I've been beaten with a truck?"

Millicent came to his side, "Well, because technically you were, Mr. Murphy. But you're going to be just fine."

T WELVE

Renae rolled over and hit snooze on her phone. She hadn't been to work in a week and wasn't looking forward to returning today. As she rolled back under her covers, she remembered the events of yesterday and sat up, grabbing her phone to check for messages. She still had over a dozen to listen to, so she looked through the call log for unknown numbers. She discovered one from 1:23 this morning. Please God, let it be good news. She hesitated to listen, but knowing doubt wasn't faith in action, she selected the message and brought the phone to her ear. It was Milli.

Hi Renae, this is Milli, Mr. Murphy's nurse. Just wanted to let you know Mr. Murphy woke up for about five minutes an hour ago. He asked about you. He's sleeping again, but the doctor is very pleased about this progress. I'll keep you posted when anything else arises. Hope you're getting a good night's rest. Bye, now.

Renae fell back into her pillow. She was relieved and so grateful. "Thank you," she whispered as she closed her eyes, wishing she could have been there when he woke up. Although she didn't know or understand the significance of this progress, she felt confident that this small step was just the beginning of many miracles along his journey to recovery. Hearing the tv from downstairs, she hopped out of bed and headed down to tell her mother the good news.

Ruth was already seated on the sofa with her first cup of morning coffee, watching the local news. "Mom. Listen to this voicemail. Alex woke up last night." Renae was trying to keep her voice low so Maddy wouldn't hear her, but she had a difficult time containing her excitement. Ruth's eyes widened as she listened to Milli's message. She smiled at her daughter as she handed the phone back.

"Sweetheart! That's great news! Alex will make it through this, and I think God is doing something bigger in your lives than you two may be aware of." Renae smiled and nodded her head in agreement as she was texting her neighbors, Joshua, and Tabitha. "Are you planning on going to work today?"

"Well, I have nothing else to do and it's not like I can go visit Alex, so, yeah."

"Would you like for me to take Maddy to school?"

"That would be nice, Mom. You feel like getting out today?" Ruth hadn't been out much. Church was the only place she'd gone, other than the one trip to the grocery store she'd taken with Eric and Andy when they were visiting.

"I figure it's about time to start living life again. Sitting in my house won't bring your father back, nor bring him any closer to me. So, I should get some errands done."

"No one expects you to just return to life as normal right now, Mom. I'm proud of you, though."

"Thank you, baby." They leaned in and gave one another a kiss on the cheek, then Renae bounced off the sofa and headed to the kitchen to make some coffee. "Do you want to call your brother, or do you want me to?"

"Eric? Why? What does he want?"

"He and Andy were worried sick last night. Andy was calling and texting non-stop. I called him after we were done talking, but I know he would like to hear about Alex's progress."

"Ok, I'll give him a call then. Should I wait an hour or so?"

"I imagine he won't mind you waking him."

Renae headed to the kitchen to make some coffee and call her brother and Andy. She appreciated knowing they had been calling to check on Alex. The conversation advanced backwards chronologically, from Alex's progress, to his injuries, to church, and then breakfast and the date. Andy wanted to hear every detail, as he was hoping for an Alex-and-Renae reunion. Renae wanted to tell him everything, but she realized time was not on her side and she had to get ready for work. Just as she was headed to the stairs, a sleepy Maddy was making her way down, carrying Mr. Snuggles by his arm. Renae met her at the bottom of the staircase, sat on a stair, and pulled her little girl into her lap. She was happy Maddy still enjoyed being cradled. She absorbed as much of this love as she could, for she knew her baby girl wouldn't fit in her lap forever. Holding Maddy usually made Renae feel vulnerable, mostly due to Renae's fear of hurting or losing her. Today, holding Maddy brought her tranquility and strength. However, she still wasn't ready to tell Maddy about her father.

"Grammy is going to pick you up after school today. What do you feel like having for dinner tonight? Meatloaf?"

Maddy shrugged her shoulders and played with Mr. Snuggles' ear. "Is Daddy coming for dinner?"

"No, baby," Renae kissed her forehead and squeezed her a little tighter as she proceeded, "Daddy had something come up. And you know he really must be stuck where he is if he couldn't come see his number-one girl."

Maddy was clearly disappointed. "I guess." She slipped out of her mother's lap and sat on the sofa with her grandmother. Ruth put her arm around her and cuddled her, signaling to Renae that she could take care of Maddy from there. Reluctantly, Renae went upstairs to get ready for work.

* * *

Ruth Rivera was a woman strong in her faith. She loved God; she loved her husband, and she loved her children. She made an effort to read her Bible every morning and often bought devotional books for herself, although she rarely ever finished them. She tried hard to be the perfect wife and mother, taking guidance from Proverbs 31. She often discovered she wasn't perfect. The one thing that she knew was perfect was her love for her children. She was a mother lion who protected her cubs at all costs. Well, almost all. She'd nearly left her husband over his refusal to attend her son's wedding, which hurt her son more than could be expressed in words. But after much prayer, she extended grace to her husband and loved him regardless of his choice, whether she felt it was wrong or right was something she kept to herself.

Her daughter had rushed out of the house to get to work, so Ruth was left getting Maddy ready for school. She didn't mind, as she'd expected she would be taking on further responsibilities with her granddaughter when Renae moved back in. Renae was a single working mother, and since Ruth was home most of the time, she gladly stepped in when Renae was absent. She understood sometimes it took a village to raise a child, and Ruth was glad to be a part of Madeline Murphy's tribe. As Maddy finished getting dressed for school, Ruth flipped through her own wardrobe for an appropriate outfit to wear. She wanted to make a statement, one with authority and confidence. She chose a pair of slim-leg black pants and a charcoal long-sleeve tunic layered over a cream camisole. She opened her jewelry armoire and reflected on the moments she'd received some of the beautiful pieces from her late husband. She wished she could take the time to reminisce, but she was pressed for time. She grabbed a beautiful oval pendant adorned in various shades of blue crystals hung on a long chain. After locating the bracelet and earrings to match, she quickly checked her hair and makeup in the bathroom mirror. All she needed was a little lipstick and she would be ready to go.

In hopes of seeing her dad today, Maddy was wearing one of the outfits they'd picked out on her shopping spree. Her grandmother walked into the room and helped her get her shoes on. "Let me see you now," Ruth examined Maddy as she posed for her grandmother. "I would say you look just like your mommy did at your age, but a little bit more like a royal princess. That's because your daddy raised you to be one, you know."

Maddy smiled and giggled at her grandmother's remark.

"Let's get you off to school now." Madeline grabbed her grandmother's hand and her backpack and headed downstairs. Ruth shut off the lights and prayed for guidance, restraint, and safety on her way out the door.

* * *

Renae sat at her desk going back and forth between postal mail and emails, trying to figure out which to tackle first. She had missed over a dozen meetings, had cancelled speaking at a monthly conference, and she had no idea what marketing plans were scheduled for the next month. As much as she loved working on the marketing and merchandising side of this women's clothing company, today she was feeling quite unmotivated and overwhelmed. Most of her mail included cards of sympathy or advertisements from companies asking for her business. The emails were just information overload for a mind that was focused miles away. She pulled out her phone and looked for new messages, but there were none. She put her phone back in her bag and stared at the computer screen. There were several invitations to conferences out of state sitting on her calendar. She couldn't leave town right now, that just wasn't an option. Upon opening the invitations, she realized she was scheduled to present at ninety percent of them. There were six scheduled over the next two months. Why on earth did they need to have so many conferences? She looked at the locations and dates and realized she would be gone between three and five days each week. What about Alex? She didn't want to leave him for that amount of time in his current condition, even if Ms. Deb never allowed her to see him again. How would her mother handle Maddy on her own? She was committed to putting her family first, but it was clear she was needed and wanted at her job too. She had to walk away from her desk and think. Grabbing her phone, she headed to the bathroom where she could get some privacy.

As she walked down the hall to the bathroom, most of the people she ran into didn't return her smile. Instead, they kept their heads low and avoided eye contact. She knew why; she was mean. People didn't cross her, and she belittled them when they questioned her. Maybe she should treat the office to lunch today, she thought. She could do a simple act of kindness to show her appreciation. Lunch seemed so far away. She wondered if Alex had woken up again. She wanted to go see him.

Upon entering the bathroom, she sat down on a small sofa in the waiting area and unlocked her phone. Still no messages. She figured now would be a good time to go through the ones she'd received but ignored yesterday. As she read through each message, her heart began to swell. She never realized she was surrounded by so many people who genuinely cared about her and Alex. So many prayers had been said and so many Scriptures and words of encouragement were passed along to her. She opened her Bible app to read some of the verses that were sent. Occasionally someone would enter the bathroom, but Renae was so focused on what she was reading, she didn't notice them. When she finished, she stood and headed for a stall. She needed some time with God without any outside distractions. She needed His wisdom and guidance to help her with an important decision she needed to make.

* * *

"Renae, it is so good to see you back." Richard, a co-worker who was also an admirer of hers, was standing over Renae's desk as she was replying to her emails. "How's the family?"

"Hey, Richard, thanks. We're doing fine." She nodded her head without offering more information.

"Well, we missed you around here last week. I missed you...bulldozing around here," he let out a brief chuckle that Renae tried hard to ignore. "How about I treat you to a long overdue lunch today? Just you and me?"

"Oh, wow, thanks for the offer, Richard, but I just asked Cheyenne to cater lunch for the team today."

"Wow, you got a budget for that?"

"No," Renae was getting tired of her conversation with him already, "I'm paying for it. I just want to show my appreciation to the team for holding down the fort last week. I have a lot of emails to get through, though, can we catch up later?"

Richard looked confused and almost disappointed as he started to turn away from Renae. "Uh, yeah, maybe we can go to lunch later this week." Renae smiled without replying and returned to declining the conference invitations. As she was responding to the last one, she received a notification from Robert, her manager. They had an excellent relationship and he had mentored her over the past couple of years. She credited him with helping her get to the level she was at now.

Welcome back, Firestarter, what's going on?

Renae closed her eyes and took a deep breath. Then she typed out

Hey Coach, we really need to talk.

* * *

Ruth pulled down the sun visor in her car and opened the mirror to take one last look at her makeup. She pulled out her lipstick and applied a fresh coat before grabbing her purse and exiting her car. One could clearly tell by the clanking of her heels that she was a woman on a mission. As she approached the entrance to the hospital, she stopped and sighed. Her last trip here was the worst day of her life. She prayed things would go much better for her today, even if this wasn't intended to be a friendly visit. She approached the visitor desk and took off her oversized sunglasses to look the receptionist square in the eyes. "Good morning, I'm here to visit Alex Murphy in the ICU."

"Good morning. Yes, ma'am. Let me look him up for you." The receptionist tried to make small talk while being stared down by Mrs. Rivera. "How is your day going so far?"

"Well, I'm here to see my son-in-law who is knocking on death's door in your ICU, so I can say I've had better days," Ruth replied.

"I'm so sorry, ma'am. Um, what is your name?"

"Ruth Mable Rivera. Here is my identification."

The receptionist thanked Ruth as she took her ID and called over a volunteer to accompany her to the ICU. "Victor will take you to the ICU floor. I hope your son-in law gets better, ma'am," she said as she handed Ruth her ID back.

"Thank you, and I'm confident he will." Ruth walked alongside an older gentleman who clearly enjoyed his time serving at the hospital. Not only did he escort her to where she needed to go, but he also informed her of the services available to the public at the hospital and invited her back to try one of the classes at the adjoining wellness center. The sight of the Intensive Care Unit brought back a dreadful memory Ruth wasn't ready to re-live. However, she had her mind set on something, and once Ruth Mable Rivera's mind was made up, there was no stopping her. She approached the desk and decided she would offer a different tactic than that of the vile woman who sat in the room with her son-in-law.

"Hello, I'm here to see Alex Murphy, please." Ruth spoke in a pleasant tone and offered a friendly smile to the staff, whose heads quickly turned to see who it was.

"They'll just need your ID again, Mrs. Rivera," Victor told her.

"Of course." She was happy to give them her identification and attempted some small talk with them. "If you all get a chance in your day, you should step outside and enjoy some of the nice coastal breeze that's made its way up here."

"Oh, believe me, we try to get outside as much as possible on our breaks," the security officer replied.

"And your relationship to Mr. Murphy?" asked the nurse at the desk.

"His mother-in-law. Well, former mother-in-law, but soon to be mother-in-law again. We'll just say I'm his mother-in-love. Once you've had a son be a part of your life for over half of his, you just can't stop being his mom."

Another woman approached them. She looked tired but delighted to see Mrs. Rivera.

"You must be Renae's mom."

Ruth turned to the sweet voice and knew instantly she was looking at Renae's Millicent.

"And are you Millicent?"

"I am."

Ruth wrapped her arms around her wholeheartedly. "Thank you so much for embracing my daughter and taking such good care of her and Alex. She was over the moon thanks to your message this morning."

"Mrs. Rivera, I wish there were more I could do for her. Everyone can see how much she loves him, and to learn of your loss just last week, I'm so sorry."

"Thank you. Are you still working?"

"No, ma'am, I've been off a few hours, I just promised Renae I wouldn't leave until she came back. Hannah is with him now. So is Mrs. Murphy. I can take you to his room, though."

"You are so kind and thoughtful to do that. Thank you for going above and beyond for our family. It is so appreciated."

Millicent watched for a reaction from Mrs. Rivera at the drop of Mrs. Murphy's name, but Mrs. Rivera didn't flinch. Perhaps she was being cautious and trying not to react. Nevertheless, Millicent felt it was safe to take her to see Alex. It would be good for Renae to know her mother was there, and Alex as well.

"I assume Renae told you what you could expect when you saw him."

Ruth nodded her head as they approached Alex's room. The lights were dim and the first person she saw was Ms. Deb in the corner doing a word search. Ruth's eyes quickly shifted to Alex, and the sight of him pulled on her heart. "Oh, son," she whispered. She approached his bed as Milli introduced her to Hannah. Ms. Deb stood from her chair as a slight fear came over her. Renae had called in the Big Dog. Suddenly, Ms. Deb regretted all the times she'd been unpleasant to her daughter-in-law.

Hannah filled Ruth in about Alex's injuries and told her places she could feel free to touch. Ruth made her way to Alex's right side as Hannah suggested. As she did, she nodded at Ms. Deb to acknowledge her. "Deb, how are you holding up, dear?"

Ms. Deb couldn't speak.

"That's okay, I understand." Ruth turned her focus back to Alex as she began to rub his arm. "Has he moved or been awake since earlier?"

"There's been movement and he feels pain, which are both excellent signs. They'll be coming to take him for another CT scan soon to see how far the swelling in his brain has gone down. His doctors really want to get his leg thoroughly cleaned and mended so an infection doesn't set in and it can heal properly."

Ruth sat next to him and grabbed his hand. "Alex, it's me, Ruth, your other mom. Not sure if you can hear me, but I just want to let you know your girls miss you very much. Maddy's been asking about you, but Renae assured her you would be with her if you could. You have a lot of people in your corner praying for you. Renae has some great news to share, but I will let her tell you when you see her. I will say that she spent quite a lot of time with Mr. and Mrs. Reeves last night. All good things." She began to rub his arm as she struggled with her next words. "Alex, hon, I don't know if I ever properly thanked you for everything you did for us last week. The funeral service was absolutely beautiful. I especially want to thank you for taking the initiative to talk to Eric about his father. He has been so hurt through all of this, and I think--I hope--that what you said to him helped bring some understanding and closure. Most of all, I want to thank you for loving Renae like you do. Your actions and whom you have become have already ignited a change in my daughter I never expected to see. You've extended so much grace and love to her that now, instead of walking in fear, she is walking in confidence and hope. I know God has big plans for the two of you. He'll get you through this. You just get some much-deserved rest and heal so the three of you can start your new life together. When you get home, I'll make you some more of that bacon you like so much." She stood to her feet and kissed his cheek. "I love you, son."

Millicent and Hannah watched Alex closely while Ms. Deb watched Ruth, distress written all over her face. All of this was news to her. She didn't know there was a reconciliation between Alex and Renae. She didn't know her son had helped the family out so much at the funeral. Maybe he had told her some of it and she'd heard only what she wanted to hear. Guilt was sinking in as she realized how distanced she was from her own son's life. She also felt terrible for not checking in on her own granddaughter yet. Ruth certainly did a good job destroying the feeling of contentment Deb had felt when she ordered Renae out of her son's life.

"Millicent, Hannah, thank you. I trust you'll let us know if anything changes during the day, as well as the results of his CT scan when you find out?"

"Yes ma'am," Hannah replied. The women stared in awe at Mrs. Rivera's boldness and tenacity. They wanted to be like her when they grew up.

"My daughter, Renae, will be back tonight after work. I trust there won't be any problems." She turned and looked directly at Ms. Deb, who couldn't maintain eye contact.

Millicent smiled as she replied, "I look forward to seeing her again."

"I hate to cut this visit short, but I must get going. First, Deb, a word outside, please."

Deborah Murphy was not a woman easily intimidated, but at this very moment she was. She followed Ruth out of Alex's room and into the waiting room, which was more private. The nurses were disappointed to miss the show. They couldn't wait to see the Dragon Lady's fire extinguished.

"Deb," Ruth began, "I am so sorry for what you are going through. No mother wants to see their child in pain. I can't imagine how helpless you must feel right now." Ms. Deb nodded her head as tears began to emerge. "Alex has been around every day since Phil passed and there are no words to express how grateful we all are for everything he has done to help our family. Deb, I'm not sure if you know or not but your son and Renae have decided to work things out." Deb began to roll her eyes and Ruth began to sharpen her voice, "You know, for a woman who claims to be walking with the Lord, you must do an awful lot of the talking and none of the listening. As a mother who knows what it's like to see their child in pain, you will understand how I felt when my daughter returned home crushed last night from the unjust harm you pitched on her. Deborah Murphy, I've sat silent and bitten my tongue over all these years of your unapproving remarks and actions towards her. But I will not sit by and allow you to push her away from him when they need each other most. She will be back tonight and yes, I am threatening you. If you *dare* push her away one more time, I promise you Alex will find out who is responsible for her absence. I'm praying for you, Deb. Praying you can find peace with my daughter and peace with yourself. Most of all, I'm praying for your boy. He is precious and I think we can agree we both just want to see him healed and living a long and happy life."

Deb stared forward as Ruth touched her arm and headed to the elevator. She wasn't happy about the threats. She wasn't happy to learn Alex was back with Renae. And she was embarrassed with the way she'd treated Renae in the past. As she headed back to the double doors to get back to Alex, she was greeted by Millicent.

"He's awake again."

* * *

Alex Murphy first fell in love with Renae Rivera when they were in high school. He loved her adventurous spirit and her spontaneity. If she wanted something, she pursued it. At times she was completely reckless and irresponsible, but that kept life interesting in his conservative upbringing. She kept him on his toes, and he needed that excitement in his life. He then provided the stability she needed. Today, she proved she possessed those same qualities he'd originally loved about her.

As Renae drove home, she reviewed the day's events in her head. Lunch went well, she thought. It gave an opportunity to open lines of communication between coworkers who never had the chance to relax and get to know one another. It gave her a chance to get to know a few of them a little better. Robert even joined them for a bit as he processed how he would move on indefinitely without his right-hand girl.

Renae looked to her passenger seat, filled with books and personal items from her desk that she might need at home. She and Robert had negotiated to allow her to work part-time from home the next couple of weeks so she could focus on her family. After that, he would release her with no return date set in stone. He just assured Renae there would be a position waiting for her when she was ready to come back. Unbeknownst to her, he was already in contact with human resources to work out a generous package for her leave of absence. He loved her like a daughter and wanted to ensure she and her family were well taken care of as they navigated through the storm they were in.

She quickly dismissed the thoughts crossing her mind that perhaps she was being irresponsible and making an emotional decision. She was aware she needed to put her family first, and living with her parents had given her some financial security she could fall back on. She never took vacations, so at least she had a few weeks' worth of paychecks to keep her going. She was so grateful for Robert, and she hated leaving him. However, she felt at peace with her decision, as it wasn't made recklessly, but through much thought and prayer.

Joshua was also supportive of her decision, and he arrived at her house before she did after stopping by his house to pick up Milo. Mrs. Rivera enjoyed their company, but she held the news of Alex's progress until Renae arrived home. Joshua promised Renae he wouldn't tell her mother she was temporarily leaving her job.

Renae opened the front door, empty handed, and was greeted by an overzealous Milo at her feet. "Mom, we need one of these." She picked up the wiggly beagle and he greeted her with a dozen kisses. Ruth shook her head "no" as she stood to set the table for dinner now that Renae was home. "Where's Miss Maddy?"

"She's in the kitchen finishing her homework."

Renae set Milo down and walked by Josh, who was seated on the sofa. She tousled his hair as she walked past him to go see Maddy. "Want a cocktail? I have whiskey."

"Renae, I need to talk to you two before you decide to get hammered tonight," Ruth called out from the kitchen. Intrigued, they both went to the kitchen, Renae first giving her princess a big squeeze and kiss. Joshua started to clean the table off and Ruth directed Maddy to tidy up for dinner.

"Why don't you take your things upstairs and wash your hands in your bathroom, sweetie," Ruth suggested to her granddaughter.

"Why don't you change into your pjs too, Punkin. You don't want to get ketchup on your new outfit."

"I don't want to sleep with ketchup on me either, Mommy."

"Smart girl, just go change into something you won't mind getting dirty, okay?"

Maddy nodded her head in agreement, her facial expression sad. Joshua knelt down to her height to check on her. "How's my little superstar doing?"

Maddy shook her head as tears began to show. Joshua opened his arms and she wrapped her tiny arms around him. Joshua looked to Renae as he stood with an upset Maddy in his arms. "I miss my grampy. I want my daddy." Maddy clung tight to Joshua as she longed for the men who brought her so much security in her life. He tried to comfort her as best as he knew how. It was apparent to Renae that in that moment, Joshua was able to fill a void Maddy felt missing in her life, and she was so thankful for him. Maddy needed the comfort and protection she received from her father and grandfather. How fortunate Maddy and Renae were to have so many caring and considerate men in their lives, she thought. Joshua took Maddy to the sofa and cradled her until she calmed down. After Renae finished helping her mother set the table, she sat with Joshua and Maddy until Maddy felt better and was ready to get cleaned up for dinner.

"Could you two come in here while Maddy is upstairs? I still need to talk to you," Ruth called from the kitchen.

Renae and Joshua entered the kitchen, welcomed by the aroma of meatloaf and mashed potatoes with homemade gravy. "This looks delicious," commented a hungry Joshua, who always rushed over at an invitation to have one of Mrs. Rivera's home-cooked meals.

Ruth didn't know exactly how much information she should tell Renae about her visit with Alex today, so she decided to keep it short and to the point. "I met Millicent at the hospital when I visited Alex today," she started.

Renae was shocked her mother was just now telling her this. "What?! You went to the hospital today? How is he?"

"The Beast let you see him?"

"Yes, I went, and quite frankly I went on my own accord. I told Millicent she could expect to see you tonight.

"What?! Mom, I can't go up there, I told you Ms. Deb won't let me in."

"And I told Deborah Murphy you would be there, and she won't try to stop you from seeing him anymore." Renae stood in disbelief at her mother. She had no idea what had happened at the hospital, but she knew her mother was a force to be reckoned with. "Also, his CT scan came back, and the swelling has decreased drastically. He's been awake on-and-off throughout the day, and he's looking forward to your visit tonight."

"Mom!" Renae wasn't sure if she should be happy about the news or mad that her mother didn't tell her earlier.

Joshua grabbed Renae by the hand and pulled his keys from his pocket. "Let's go; I'll drive."

"Wait, how do I look?"

"Beautiful, did you wash your hair, though?"

"No, do I still smell like a bar?"

Joshua sniffed her head and rocked his head side to side. "Nah, you're good. You may want to spritz a little Chanel on it for good measure, though."

Ruth watched, amused. She loved their friendship and was happy they could remain close friends even with Alex back in the picture.

As Joshua pulled Renae to the front door, she thought of Maddy. "Wait! We need to tell Maddy we may not be back before bedtime. Mom, can you talk to her about Alex?"

Ruth waved at her as the two ran upstairs to kiss Maddy and ask her to take care of Milo until Joshua got back. She was delighted to get Milo to herself for the rest of the evening. Renae ran into her own room, checked her hair and makeup, and spritzed herself with perfume as Joshua had suggested. Then the pair dashed down the stairs to the car and made their way to the hospital.

* * *

Alex had a hard time staying awake during the day. His pain level was excruciating, so the doctors tried to reduce it with morphine. In the moments he was awake, he was agitated, mostly due to the pain and not being able to leave. Ms. Deb tried her best to calm him down in those moments, but his restlessness continued until he was able to go back to sleep. He only asked about Renae once, when his mother wasn't in the room and Millicent was attending to him. Millicent informed him that Renae had been there for hours the night before and that she would return tonight. He rested better after that.

Ms. Deb had returned to her word search in the corner of the room when her son called out to her. "Yes, sweetheart, I'm here." She went to his side and put her hand on his arm. He reached with his other hand to place it on top of hers. His head hurt too much to open his eyes, so he kept them closed so he could focus on his words.

"Mom, I need to tell you something, and you probably won't be happy."

Ms. Deb had a feeling she knew what he was going to say.

"Mom, I know you've never been a fan of Renae's; it has always been pretty obvious. You were always pretty shitty to her."

"Alex." She didn't like it when he cussed; it was obviously a side effect from spending too much time with Renae.

"No, Mom, it's true. You've always been shitty to her, and I can't say there weren't times I didn't enjoy it, because sometimes she could be pretty shitty to me too and I thought she deserved it." He paused for a minute to gather his thoughts before he spoke again. He really just wanted to go back to sleep.

"It's okay, sweetheart; you don't have to talk." She rubbed his head at his hairline.

"Mrs. Ruth came by today and she briefly told me what you and Renae have been up to lately."

"Mrs. Ruth was here? Did she bring me anything to eat?"

His mom chuckled. She was secretly jealous of how her son always raved about Mrs. Ruth's cooking but never about hers. Today, she was thankful he had another mother in his life whom he could appreciate and that loved him in return. "No, she was here pretty early, just before you woke up this morning. If you feel like eating, I can see about getting you something."

Just as she spoke, Millicent walked into the room with the meal tray that had just been delivered from the cafeteria.

"Look at that. Ask and ye shall receive," Ms. Deb said.

"Here you go, Mr. Murphy, we brought you some dinner." Alex opened his eyes, skeptical of the food set before him. He closed his eyes in hopes that it would go away. "I know," Millicent started, "it isn't the most appetizing; liquid diets never are. But it's what the doctor wants you on today. Maybe after tomorrow's surgery you can start looking at more solid foods."

Alex looked at the beef broth, Jell-O, unsweet tea, and

juice in front of him. His mother handed him the remote to his bed so he could sit up and eat. He winced in pain as the bed shifted his body, most of the discomfort shooting through his leg. He leaned back in his bed and took a couple long, deep breaths until the pain subsided. Reluctantly, he reached for the Jell-O after his mom opened it for him.

"Hey handsome, mind if I join you for dinner?" Renae entered the room, her heart skipping a beat when she saw the miracle sitting in front of her. Her warm and loving smile was therapeutic for Alex. He put the Jell-O down and rested his head back on his pillow, studying the beautiful sight in front of him. Ms. Deb stepped to the side as she made room for Renae to join Alex. The lovers clutched hands and shared a long, soft kiss. Tears of relief streamed down Renae's cheeks as she broke away and kissed his forehead and cheeks.

Alex raised his left arm to her cheek and wiped away her tears. "Hey, no crying. I'm here; I'm going to be okay." Renae nodded her head as she gently rested her forehead on his.

Millicent stood by them, smiling and wiping tears away. She was so happy to see Alex return the deep love she knew Renae felt for him. She was witnessing a miracle before her eyes and couldn't hide her emotions.

Ms. Deb lightly nodded her head, admitting to herself that this was best for her son. With that, she resolved to stay out of his relationship and hoped that one day she and Renae could become friendly. She had to keep the peace for her son's sake.

Renae stared into Alex's eyes. "You *are* going to be okay. I'll be standing beside you every step of the way to see to it." Alex showed his relief to have her with him by the expression on his face. "You should get back to eating." She gave him another kiss before pulling away and bringing his food-tray table closer to him. Renae really wanted to say more to him, but seeing as she had an audience, she decided to hold back and keep the more intimate conversations to themselves, when they could find time alone. She looked around, noticing she was missing Joshua. "Hey, Milli, did you see a tall guy with dark hair come in behind me?"

"Josh is here?" Alex questioned, as he lifted a spoonful of gelatin to his mouth.

"Yeah, he was with me at Mom's for dinner, so when Mom said I could come up here and you were awake, he grabbed me and drove us here."

Alex looked confused. "Why would you need your mom's permission to come up here? Didn't they let you in here last night?"

Renae shifted in her seat. She didn't want to rat out Ms. Deb and make Alex mad at his mother. She also didn't want Alex to think she didn't care about being with him. It did sound like a jerk move that while he was up here suffering, she and Joshua were having dinner with her mom. "I was here last night, but when your mom got here, it was a little crowded. And she hadn't seen you in so long, it was best that I went home."

A knock at the door interrupted their conversation. It was Joshua, who was grinning from ear to ear. Alex motioned for him to come closer, giving him a fist bump when he approached.

"Dude, you look rough."

"I've seen better days."

"Well, yesterday definitely wasn't one of them."

"Thanks for driving her up here."

"Yeah, I should be thanking you for landing up here. Turns out I kind of know one of the nurses on this floor. Hey, Ms. Deb. Anyways, we had a class together in college but I was married and never paid attention to her. But we remember each other. And now I have her number and we're going on a date Friday night."

"Nice!" Alex had been waiting for news like this from Joshua since Renae had left him. Joshua hadn't dated at all since Angie had passed away.

"Wait. What?! Who?" Joshua began to go into details but Renae didn't hear him. All she knew was that she hadn't vetted this girl whom her best friend was beaming over. Ms. Deb figured now would be a good time to excuse herself to get some dinner. She didn't care to hear about this love triangle, or to be in the same room as the young man she'd always thought her son's wife was really in love with.

"Where does she go to church? You said you weren't interested in missionary dating." Renae was skeptical. Her best friend was a catch; he had a house, a good job, a nice car; he was established. But there really wasn't a way for this nurse to know that from their short conversation in the hall.

"Funny you should ask. She goes to yours."

"Wait, what is missionary dating?" Alex questioned.

"It's where a Christian dates a non-Christian and thinks they can help them become right with the Lord," Renae informed Alex.

"Kind of like you and Renae," Joshua joked.

"Exactly." Renae replied with a wink.

"Wait a minute, are you talking about Mandy?" Milli felt she was welcome well enough to join in on the conversation.

"Yes! Hi, I'm Josh, by the way. Are you Millicent?" He extended his hand to Millicent and she accepted his greeting.

"I am, and Renae, you have nothing to worry about with that one. However, I'm going to keep an eye on this guy. Mandy isn't someone we would want to see get hurt. She's a special young lady."

"Well, if things go well, she's very lucky, because he's quite a catch."

"I'm right here," said Josh, slightly perturbed.

Renae then directed her attention back to Alex. He was exhausted and it showed. "Do you want your tea or broth?" Alex closed his eyes and put his hand up to decline both. He rested his head back to recline in his bed. Renae pushed his tray away and Millicent took it out of the room. Upon her return, she informed Renae and Joshua that visiting hours were up in 15 minutes but would resume in two hours for another hour-long session. Since his condition was improving, Alex's doctors had resumed normal ICU visiting restrictions for him.

Joshua excused himself and left Renae alone with him for their remaining time. Renae once again took a seat beside Alex and grasped his hand. She rubbed her free hand through his hair, noticing it had been washed free of the dried blood and glass that was there last night. Contentment swept across Alex's face at the sense of her touch. Millicent dimmed the lights over his bed and left the two alone.

"How's your heart?" he asked.

"Pretty healthy, if I do say so myself. How's yours?"

"I think it's the only thing functioning like it should."

He brought her hand up to his mouth and kissed it. He peeked at her and caught her looking at him. He shut his eye and slowly opened it again. He loved to make her laugh. The third time he opened his eyes, she was in his face, ready to give him a kiss, but instead of kissing him, she whispered in his ear, "I love you, Alex Murphy."

"I don't think I heard you. Say it again."

"I love you, Alex Murphy." Renae kissed his cheek and held his hand close to her chest.

"I love you more."

Renae wanted to tell him about the night before with Mr. and Mrs. Reeves. She wanted to let him know she no longer walked in fear but was starting a new walk with God. She had so much to tell him. But he needed rest. She decided it could wait.

"Get some sleep, Alex. I'll stay with you until it's time to go."

"Will you come back tonight?"

"I will."

"Renae?"

"Yeah?"

"When I get out of here, will you move back home? You and Maddy. Life hurts without you two in it."

Renae's heart was pounding. Not because she was afraid, but because she was ready to make a leap of faith that she would have thought was crazy two days ago. "We will. When you walk through that door, I'll be right beside you. For good."

Her assurance was all Alex needed to slip back into a peaceful sleep. Renae recognized that her faith in his healing needed to become bigger than her fear of losing him. She watched him until it was time for her to leave, praying for him as the words came to her. She joined Joshua in the waiting room, and they left to head back to Renae's for two things: her car and some of Ruth Rivera's meatloaf.

T HIRTEEN

Renae sat in the corner of the hospital room and opened her work email from her laptop. Alex had been moved from ICU into a private room three days after the accident. Today was day nine. He had already had two debridement surgeries to remove some dead and infected tissue in his leg. Since he had multiple compound fractures, he was at risk for infection. Tomorrow he was scheduled for the last surgery before they attached an external fixator to hold his bones together so they could heal. Renae looked over to Alex to watch his breathing. On day five, after his second surgery, he nearly died in post-op. When he woke, he couldn't breath and began to suffocate. The doctor said a fatty embolism had passed into his lungs and tried to shut down his respiratory system. Millicent sat with him for twenty-three hours as air was being forced into his lungs. Renae needed to see his chest move when he was asleep to give her peace of mind.

She had a difficult time focusing on work. She searched articles about Alex's condition, about the device they would put on his leg, and about the at-home care she would need to provide once he left the hospital. She realized she would have to wear a hat she wasn't trained or qualified to wear: the hat of a nurse. However, Renae was willing to do what it took to help Alex heal, and if the surgeons and nurses believed she could do it, then she knew she would find the strength to do so.

During Alex's surgeries, Joshua helped Renae and Maddy moved their clothes and personal belongings back into the house Renae once shared with Alex. It was strange for her to walk through her old home for the first time since she'd left. The house was tidy, but it looked lonely. Besides the things she took with her, not much had changed. He had left some of the pictures of the two of them on shelves. A broken mirror, broken blinds, and a small hole in a wall-- all casualties of their anger towards each other--had been re- paired. She wasn't prepared to see the small sofa that her dad bought for the two of them in their bedroom. It brought back so many memories of happiness, followed by memories of rejection. She swept those negative memories aside and told them they would be replaced with new memories of unre- lenting love. Upon Alex's request, Joshua had retrieved some items from the safe and taken them to the hospital. Renae wasn't sure what he needed, but she trusted Alex and Joshua, so she didn't question it.

Ruth wasn't too happy about the thought of being alone in the house, but she knew Renae and Maddy needed to go. Renae sometimes wondered if her mother would sell the house or if Eric and Andy ever thought about moving in. She really would like to have them closer. Then again, she wasn't sure what would happen with the house she and Alex shared. He would take disability leave, but he wouldn't be bring- ing home his entire salary. Renae had some money set aside, but it wouldn't last more than a couple of months. Her head began to hurt as she thought about all of that. She recognized she wasn't placing her faith in God as her provider, so she opened her Bible and began to read.

"Good morning." Renae's reading was cut short by her favorite voice in the world.

"Good morning," she replied as she went to Alex's side. She touched his face, which was becoming more recognizable by the day, and leaned down to give him a sweet kiss hello. After the events of the past few days, she vowed to start and end her days with a kiss for him. She wanted to be the first thing on his mind when he woke and the last before he closed his eyes at night. "How are you feeling?" she asked.

"Still pretty tired. Is Maddy at school already?"

"She is. Mom is going to bring her up again today after she gets home."

Alex nodded his head. "Is it just us this morning?"

"As far as I know it is." Alex had his fair share of visitors over the past couple of days: pastors from his church and from the Rivera's church, Tabitha and Greg, Joshua, Maddy, and even Carrie stopped by with some flowers. Carrie didn't get the memo about Alex's reconciliation with Renae, but her embarrassment was quickly put to rest by Renae's kind and hospitable treatment toward her. When Alex didn't think he could love Renae any more than he already did, she did something surprising and remarkable to prove him wrong. Even Ms. Deb was thrown for a loop when Renae reached out to embrace her and told Ms. Deb to 'keep in touch' when she left to go back home.

"Can I get you anything?" Renae offered.

"No." He had trouble reaching his water, so Renae helped him with that and then fluffed and rearranged his pillow. "What have you been up to this morning?"

"Oh just checking emails and reading."

"Oh yeah? What are you reading?"

Renae sat next to his bed and grabbed her Bible and phone. "About the Proverbs 31 Woman. Check it out, it says here she makes her own bedspreads. Ha! Well, I don't know about that; it just doesn't seem realistic. Let me look up a different translation."

"I could see quilting in your future," Alex remarked.

Renae searched her phone for different translations of what she'd just read. "'*She makes tapestry for herself.*' Who is this woman? Oh, here we go, I like this one... '*her clothing is beautifully knit together, a purple gown of exquisite linen.*' that's my kind of girl. '*Her husband is famous and admired by all*'... that's you, Alex Murphy. I like this Passion Translation."

Alex and Renae hadn't talked much about their future, getting remarried, or how they would handle the finances through this process. Alex figured since they were alone and she'd just referred to him as 'her husband', now would be a good time to start that conversation.

"Renae? Are you sure about this?"

"About the Passion Translation?"

"No, about us. About moving back in, taking on my caretaking, staying with me? It was easier to say 'yes' on Sunday before any of this happened, but tomorrow we're looking at another surgery and then what? Eight more weeks of recovery? Then there's the financial burden --I don't know if we'll be able to make the house note on my salary decrease. Who knows what all this is going to cost. Are you sure you really want to sign up for that?"

"Alex, where is all this doubt coming from? Hey, look at me." She pulled his face to look at her. "For better or for worse, right? Sickness and in health? I think the divorce was the worse. Now we just have to get through the sickness, which is such a small amount of time compared to our past and future together. The finances? Let God take care of them. I am more than positive about us. This is just another part of our story, Mr. Murphy. I love you more now than ever, and you're not about to go through this without me."

Alex's eyes began to turn slightly pink as tears began to form. Renae's facial expression brought him reassurance and comfort. While he was feeling somewhat lost and vulnerable, she was helping him find his strength.

"Renae, how is your heart?" This was the second time he'd asked her. She finally caught on to what he meant.

"I would say it's in a really good place right now."

"You think it's ready?"

"Do you doubt that it is?"

Alex had witnessed an incredible transformation in the love of his life during the short nine days since his accident. He knew this was just the beginning, and he knew without a shadow of a doubt that he wanted to walk by her side through every moment for the rest of their lives together.

"Would you mind grabbing my backpack? Josh put it in the cabinet."

Renae retrieved Alex's backpack and handed it to him. "You getting hungry? I can go grab some fruit for you if you don't want any more hospital food."

"Maybe in a few minutes. Come, sit with me for a minute." Renae sat at his bedside as he pulled his backpack closer. He grabbed her hand and soaked in her beauty. Never could he recall her smiling so much when she looked at him. He had zero doubts about what he was about to do.

"Renae, you're my best friend and the love of my life. We've lived our best days together and suffered through our worst together. We've made some really stupid decisions over the past few years, and we've made some pretty incredible ones, too. I'm so proud of the daughter we're raising, and I know that's mostly because she is a reflection of you. You're such an amazing mom. I am more than ready to move forward into a future with you. When I'm with you, I feel complete and at peace, like a part of me that has been missing without you in my life has been perfectly placed back where it belongs."

Renae held back tears as she knew where this was going. So did the nurse who walked in and quickly called an audience to the door.

"I wish I could do this the right way and ask for your dad's permission for your hand in marriage, but when I think about it, I believe he opened the door for this to happen." Renae let out a small laugh through her tears as she nodded her head in agreement. "I hate doing this laying down, but I can't really get down on one knee right now." Alex pulled a small box from under his bag and opened it; inside was a stunning diamond engagement ring. "Renae Dawn Rivera, will you do me the honor of being my wife?"

Renae didn't take a moment to look at the ring or think before she spoke. She wrapped her arms tightly around Alex's neck and said "Yes! Alexander Murphy, yes!!" As the couple embraced and kissed, cheers were heard from the door as the surrounding staff members congratulated them and celebrated. When the cheering subsided and the couple no longer had an audience, Renae pulled away and Alex showed her the ring.

"I had your old ring redesigned about three years ago when you stopped wearing it. All the original diamonds are there, plus I had some added." Alex didn't feel the need to go into any more detail as to when he'd originally planned on giving it to her and why he didn't. Bringing up hurts of the past wasn't necessary and wouldn't edify them in any way. He just absorbed the delight on Renae's face as she admired the ring that he knew she had been dreaming of.

"Alex, it's breathtaking."

He took it out of the box and placed it on her finger. "How about we keep this on here for good this time."

Renae nodded her head as she again teared up and pressed her face against his. He could have given Renae a plastic soda cap ring and she would have been happy. Her heart was pounding. This was all happening so fast, but when she thought about it, they'd never really separated in their hearts. "Where's your ring? Did you keep it?"

"It's actually right here in the bottom of the box. I kept everything together." He pulled out his ring along with Renae's original wedding band.

Renae took the wedding bands from him and examined them, deep in thought. "Alex, I don't need another ceremony, do you? I just want to be your wife, to be by your side through the good and the bad and to know I will always have you in my corner; you know I'll always be in yours."

Alex lifted his hand to a strand of hair falling near her face and began to twist it in his fingers. "So, let's do it. We put these rings on right here and right now and we're married again. God can be our witness and when I get out of here, we can run up to the court and make it legal."

Renae sat up and nodded her head. "I would love that.

Alex, I love you so much."

Alex pulled her close to him. He tried fighting back tears as he thanked God for this second chance, even through all the pain and suffering.

Her father had insisted on communion during their first ceremony; partaking of it again at this one was a non-negotiable for the two. "I'll go see if I can get some crackers and grape juice." They quickly kissed before Renae left the room to find some communion elements for their small ceremony and to make a quick phone call. Alex lay in his bed feeling helpless in his immobility. He called the nurse to help him freshen up. Millicent came in with her.

"What is this I hear about you two getting engaged in my hospital and you didn't even call me?"

"Well, after all the time we've been spending together, I was afraid I might get cold feet and change my mind when I saw you."

Millicent chuckled and brought him a shirt from the closet to change into. She helped him with his hair and brought him a toothbrush. She took so much delight in taking care of him. Nine days ago, he could have slipped into eternity. His bride was cast away by his own mother and for hours Millicent sat in the room with him when the situation looked dark and hopeless. Three days ago, she again sat with Alex for hours as they pressed to keep him alive. But God stepped in and made a way for physical, emotional, and spiritual healing. She expected great things to come out of this family, and she felt blessed to watch a small part of their restoration take place.

Renae returned to the room with a package of broken saltine crackers a nurse had found in a breakroom drawer and a cup of Cran-Grape juice. She was thrilled when she saw Milli sitting by Alex's bed, flipping through Phil's Bible with him. Joshua had retrieved it when he went to look at the Jeep to see if there were any personal belongings he could find from the wreckage.

They invited Milli to join them as Alex read the story of the Last Supper, and the trio took the communion elements. He led them in prayer and as he concluded, Milli finished by praying over the two of them. She prayed for healing, health, favor, and provision. She prayed over the good times and the hard times. She spoke grace into their lives and blessings over their children.

After she finished, she left them alone so they could have privacy as they issued their personal vows to one another. Alex went first, and Renae was overcome with so much love and affection towards him. Her heart pounded as he slipped the wedding band on her finger. She shook as she made vows in front of God to her spouse, not out of fear, but because she felt freedom and a release as she spoke words of affirmation, admiration, and eternal love for Alex, something she held back for far too long. As she slipped Alex's ring on his finger, their sentimental moment was interrupted by their own laughter.

"It won't go on."

"Here, let me try." Alex tried to put the ring on, but it wouldn't move over his knuckle.

"You're too swollen," Renae teased him.

"Yeah, I don't think that is going on," Alex conceded.

"Want to try the other hand for now?" Renae took the ring and placed it on his right hand. It was a much better fit.

There was an awkward silence for a minute, as they weren't sure what came next.

"Now what?"

"Well, I think it's time for me to kiss my bride, Mrs. Murphy."

"Sounds like a plan Mr. Murphy." Renae leaned over to Alex as they grasped hands and kissed, both savoring the moment and permanently placing it in their memories. Renae lay her head on his chest as Alex closed his eyes and earnestly thanked God for another chance to love and be loved unconditionally.

* * *

"You know what I want for my first meal when I get home?"

"Steak and potatoes?" Renae replied.

"Sausage and peppers. And homemade fries."

"Really?"

"Yeah, I think I'm just over this bland comfort food they serve every night. Can you honestly tell me you would like another iceberg-and-cheese salad after eating them every night since you've been here with me?"

"I haven't been eating the salads. I've been sneaking out every night when you go to sleep and getting hot roast beef and cheddar sandwiches with curly fries across the street."

"Seriously?"

"No," Renae laughed and grinned mischievously at her husband. He wasn't sure if she was kidding or not.

"Oh, you think you're funny, don't you?"

"Mm-hmm." Renae leaned over for a kiss. "Mr. Murphy, you can have whatever you want when you get home."

"Whatever I want?" The couple grinned at one another.

"Yes, sir. But tonight, you should try to eat some of this yummy meatloaf, mashed potatoes, and peas they brought you."

"It's so bland."

"Well, I shouldn't have to tell you if you don't eat your dinner, you don't get your dessert."

"And what's for dessert, Mrs. Murphy?" Alex was having fun playing this game with his wife.

"Well, seeing as it is our wedding night, I thought the two of us could, you know, celebrate."

"How do you propose we do that?" With impeccable timing, there was a knock at the door.

"With cake!" Renae replied.

The door swung open and Maddy rushed into the room, Ruth and Joshua behind her.

"Daddy!" Maddy ran to her father's bedside, bouncing up and down, ready for her mom to lift her onto his bed. Alex was happy to see his little girl, mother-in-law, and best friend. Ruth was carrying a store-bought sheet cake, and Joshua balloons, flowers, and champagne.

"So, Renae called us up here to celebrate, but she didn't say why," Joshua said, after everyone greeted one another with hugs and kisses.

Renae approached Joshua and reached for the champagne bottle with her left hand, trying to expose her ring to him and Ruth. "Oh, is this champagne chilled or do we need ice?"

"Oh my gosh!" Ruth exclaimed, covering her mouth with her hands.

Joshua looked around himself and jumped. "What?! What is it?"

"Should I open this now?" Renae was grasping the neck of the bottle, holding it in front of Joshua so he would see her ring.

"I don't know, should we? Is there something near me? Ruth, what is it?"

Amused, Alex whispered into his baby girl's ear, "Guess what?"

"What, Daddy?" she whispered back.

"Mommy and I got married today." Maddy's eyes grew, her mouth turning into a perfect letter "o" as she gasped in excitement. "Tell Uncle Josh; he's not getting Mommy's hints."

"Mommy and Daddy are married, Uncle Josh!" Maddy giggled and leaned back to lay down by her father. She wrapped her small arms around him as best as she could. "I love you, Daddy." Alex closed his eyes and squeezed his munchkin tight. He was grateful for this second chance with his family, knowing they wouldn't be spending long weeks from each other ever again.

Joshua had known an engagement was coming. He'd retrieved the rings from the safe for Alex when he was at the house with Renae. He just wasn't expecting "marriage" so soon. Although he was thrilled for Renae and Alex, he also felt a twinge of disappointment. He wasn't sure if it was stemming from the fact that she was married, or if it was because she went through something so big without him. He could see her happiness begin to fade as she studied his reaction. He looked past Renae and walked over to Alex to congratulate him. Renae tried to keep the smile on her face as she walked to her mother, placing the bottle of champagne by the cake.

"Give him a minute," her mother whispered in her ear. "It's just a little shocking. It has all happened so fast, but I know he's thrilled for you. We all are." Ruth grabbed ahold of her daughter and held her in a close embrace. Renae sank into her arms. "I am so happy for you two."

"Me too, Mom--so happy."

Ruth let go of her daughter and took a step back to look at her. "Oh, I wish your father were here for this." Renae smiled and lightly nodded in agreement. She felt, in a small way, he was there. Not by spirit, but in reflections she saw of him through Alex, Maddy, and herself.

"You're a blessed man, Alex Murphy."

"Thanks, Josh. We've gone through hell the past two weeks--the past few years is more like it--but despite everything we've been through, I know we're going to be okay."

"You will be, isn't that right, Miss Maddy?" Madeline was still cuddling beside her daddy.

"Daddy, we brought you and Mommy a cake. Is it time for cake, Uncle Josh?"

"Oh, you want a piece of cake? That isn't just for the grown-ups?"

"No, Uncle Josh, we all get cake!"

"We do? I don't remember agreeing to that. Ms. Ruth,

Miss Maddy says she would like cake, what do you think?"

"I think that is a fabulous idea! Maddy would you like to help me slice the cake and serve...Joshua, we forgot plates. We have plastic champagne flutes but no plates."

"That's okay; I'll go see if I can track some down somewhere really quick." Joshua headed towards the door.

"I'll go with you," Renae chimed in. He still hadn't acknowledged her since the announcement, and it bothered Renae. Joshua held the door open for her and followed her out.

Ruth could read the troubled look on Alex's face as he watched the two walk out the door. She stood by him and reached for his hand. "Three weeks ago, he was the only man in her life. Give him a little time to digest it. They'll be okay. He's so supportive of you two."

"Thanks, Mom, you're right. Want to hand me the champagne? The least I can do is open it so we can get some glasses poured while we wait for them."

Joshua and Renae headed down a long corridor toward the visitor lounge, Renae trying to keep up with Joshua's quick pace. Neither said a word to the other until they reached the lounge. "I bet someone left some plates they didn't use in one of these cabinets," Joshua said, as he began to open doors and drawers. Renae didn't look; she just stared at her friend.

"Josh." She waited for a response. "Josh." Ignoring her, Joshua opened more doors, pretending he was too occupied to notice her calling his name. "Joshua Matthew Levingston, will you please look at me?" Joshua closed the door to the cabinet he was rummaging through and turned to Renae. She looked ready to fight.

"What's up?" he said as he leaned against the counter.

"What's up? Seriously?! Alex and I got married today and I can't even get a 'wow, Renae, I'm so happy for you' or 'that's great, Renae, hoping it works out for you this time.' Instead I get the silent treatment and 'what's up?' You haven't even looked at me until now. Pardon me if I go a little bridezilla here, but the least I would love to hear from my best friend is a 'congratulations'--especially since you of all people know how far we've come and what we've been through to get here."

"Well, that's just it, Renae, I do know how far you've come and what you've been through to get here. I've been there for every moment and I don't know, maybe I'm just feeling a little left out for not being there for this moment. Maybe because I spilled my heart out to you two weeks ago... to hear this so soon...I'm just a little bit speechless. Maybe I just need some time to process it all before I can give you the reaction you really want from me."

Renae's frustration began to escalate. "Well, do whatever the hell it is you need to do to process this, because I'm really freaking happy. This is a joyful day for me, and what I really don't want is the friend who's been by my side almost my entire life to try to guilt me for making an insanely awesome decision and not waiting to ask him to be a part of that moment. What I would like is for him to pull his shit together and celebrate with us, because he's been our biggest freaking cheerleader and I don't want to celebrate without him."

Joshua matched her sarcastic tone. "Well, fine, I've processed it. Oh Renae, I'm happy for you. Better? Now let's just get some plates--and we should probably get some forks as well, because I forgot those too--and we'll go celebrate. Will that make you happy, Bridezilla?"

"*Very*, thank you."

Joshua turned to the last cabinet, opened the door, and found a small pile of paper plates. He grabbed five from the pile and slammed the cabinet door shut. The force of the impact caused a shelf inside the cabinet to break, sending heavy plates to the bottom of the shelving unit. Renae and Josh froze, awaiting a loud crash. To their relief, the door held the contents behind it. Renae grabbed Josh's hand and they slowly crept away from the counter. Hearing several cracks coming from the wall behind them, Renae squeezed Joshua's hand tight and he turned to look at her.

"Renae, run!"

The best friends ran away from the crime scene together as the cabinet partially fell off the wall, sending the contents to the counter and floor below. They burst through Alex's door and quickly entered the room, slamming the door behind them. Once inside the safety of the room, they turned to each other and laughed hysterically.

As always, Ruth dismissed their peculiar behavior and asked politely, "you two didn't happen to grab any forks, did you?"

* * *

Renae couldn't push off work any longer. A day had passed since they'd remarried, and Alex had just returned from his final surgery. She had time to answer some emails before he woke up. She knew he wouldn't like the sight of the fixator attached to his leg, and she was sure it was painful. He had a cage surrounding his shin, attached to the bone with metal rods, and it extended from just below his knee to his ankle. The nurses told her they would show her how to clean it and give her a couple of chances to do it before they released him into her care at home. She wasn't afraid to admit that it intimidated her.

She had prioritized which messages she needed to respond to first and was preparing to read through new emails when she received a message from Robert.

Hey kid-important-can we talk

Renae grabbed her phone and left the room to call her boss.

"Hey, Coach, what's up?" Renae was happy to hear his voice. She really liked working with him. He was one of the few people at her job that liked her.

"How's Alex doing?"

"Good! He just got back from the last surgery to get him back to normal. They attached an external fixator to his leg, so now he just needs everything to mend and get back in place. We're hopeful he can get this off quick."

"What's the average healing time for that?"

"The doctors said about eight weeks, and then there's some physical therapy that he'll have to go through afterwards. Maybe three months of that."

"So, we're looking at about five months or so?"

"Yeah, but if you need me back before then, I'd be happy to talk to Alex. I have my mom here to help out and maybe his mom can come down some."

"Well, I wanted to reach out to you before you saw the email Human Resources sent to you. I approved it and they just told me they were sending the digital copy to you today and that you'd get a hard copy to return and sign in the mail."

Renae was getting a little nervous, but not too much. She did trust this man.

"Renae, I want to talk to you really quickly about compensation during your leave of absence. Seeing as you held what I would consider a higher-level position, since I relied so heavily on you, Human Resources and I agreed on an indefinite leave of absence paid out at one hundred percent for the duration of the absence, plus you can hold on to existing medical benefits. This is much better than your taking vacation time, and I can always bring you back on staff once you're ready. I'd even be willing to create a new position to get you back if I have to hire someone to fill your existing position. But for now, with the passing of your dad and the added undertaking of Alex's at-home care, I thought it would be best to make sure you two were financially secure. It is one less thing you two need to worry about."

Renae was speechless. She wasn't sure if she was making up the words that were coming out of his mouth. It was all too good to believe.

"Renae, did I lose you?"

"No, I'm here. Robert, what are you saying?"

Knowing her well, he let out a chuckle before giving her the shortened version. "Renae, you'll receive one hundred percent of your salary during the duration of your leave of absence, however long you may need. I just want you back stress- and worry-free."

"Robert, I don't know what to say." She had been refusing to think about the financial burden they could face with Alex being out of work, and now she realized she wouldn't have to.

"Well, it's my way of saying thank you for all the dedication you've put into the company. You're an invaluable asset, and I just want to make sure we give you a reason to come back. I have to jump on a call. You should be getting the email anytime now, just let me know if you have any questions. Take care, kid, and keep in touch."

"Robert, you're the best. Thanks so much." She hung up the phone and held it close to her chest. Her thoughts immediately went to the countless times in church during prayer when praise reports of miracles of healing, financial breakthrough, and restoration had been spoken of. At times, she had doubted their validity. This week, she was experiencing them, and her wavering faith was stabilizing.

Alex was still asleep when she walked back into the room. She checked his chest for movement. Watching it expand brought her relief. She sat down in her chair and finished replying to emails. She felt she was in a good place. Her husband was going to recover and financially, they were secure. God had been faithful in seeing them through this trial, keeping true to his promises. She felt the storm they were in was passing and they would soon experience the refreshing serenity that came after it.

She opened a journal she'd decided to start writing in again. She read through some notes she had jotted down sporadically from years prior. One entry in particular caught her attention. It was dated seven years earlier, almost to the day. It was from a message of Mrs. Reeves.

'You don't wait until you're in a crisis to build your faith. You have to have strong faith in preparation for whatever crisis may come.'

Renae looked to Alex. She kept telling herself she wouldn't speak her fear, although it was trying its hardest to pierce her faith. Not knowing what else to do, she closed her eyes and softly prayed. As she spoke, God began to move, for they were nowhere near the other side of their storm, but in the eye of the hurricane.

FOURTEEN

Joshua Levingston was in high spirits. He and Mandy had hit it off pretty well, and tomorrow night would be the three-month anniversary of their first date. To celebrate, she was introducing him to her five-year-old daughter Emily at dinner. Like Joshua, Mandy was widowed. The pain of her husband's passing had caused her to close off any thought or opportunity of ever dating again. Then she ran into Joshua, her perfect prince. Joshua treated her like royalty: with respect, love, and affection. He adored Mandy and looked forward to every precious moment he could spend with her. Tonight, however, he was going to spend some quality time with his favorite little girl and take her out for ice cream. Outside of going to school, Madeline didn't get out of the house much, so Joshua picked her up once a week and treated her to her choice of a movie, ice cream, or dinner. It was also a good time for him to drill her about what the likes and interests were of a five-year-old girl. He wanted to relate as much as possible to Emily and to make a great impression. As he pulled into the driveway, he looked at the overgrown grass and made a mental note to hire someone to take care of the Murphy's usually perfectly landscaped lawn.

Maddy was watching out the front window of her house, waiting for her ice cream date to pick her up and holding on tightly to her favorite stuffed lamb that Josh had given her for her birthday. She opened the door and ecstatically jumped up and down in the doorway as she waited for him to approach the house. She'd dressed herself in one of the fanciest outfits and matching shoes that that her daddy had bought for her. Her hair was set in perfect curls, pulled back in a giant ponytail, and Joshua couldn't adore her any more than if she were his own little girl.

"Hey, pretty girl! You excited about our ice cream date, or what?!"

"Yes, Uncle Josh!!" She stood still, squeezing her hands and shaking from the excitement that she had a hard time containing. "I can't wait!"

"Well, I have been looking forward to it all day. I have something for your daddy; mind if I come in and give it to him before we go?" Maddy led Joshua inside as Renae came to greet him in the hall. "Oh my, the 80s called and they want their style back." Renae's wardrobe lately consisted of over-sized sweatshirts and jeans. Her hair was easy to maintain in a ponytail and she just kept it straight, since it was lower maintenance. She was too tired to respond; she just walked up to him and gave him a hug.

"Thanks for taking her out tonight. I know she looks forward to your little dates."

"Thanks for trusting me with her. Is it okay if I take her to get something to eat before ice cream? I was thinking about some Jesus chicken."

Renae nodded her head and kissed him on the cheek. "You're the best; you know that?"

"I do; it's why you keep me around. Is the man busy?"

"He's in the office on the computer, but you can go see him."

"How's the leg? Were you able to get him in to see the doctor?"

"Yeah. Hey, Maddy, can you tell Daddy Uncle Josh is here and wants to see him, please?"

"Okay!" Maddy loved helping wherever and whenever she could. It made her feel like an important part of her father's healing process, which it actually was. She was help-ing her mother keep the stress level down, therefore Renae was able to provide higher-quality care for Alex. Every act of service on Maddy's account was definitely noticed.

"So, we went to the doctor today, and he's going in on Friday for another surgery."

"What?"

"Yeah, well, Mandy was right. Apparently these antibiotics aren't strong enough. This is the third one they've had him on, and they just keep getting more aggressive. So now the doctors want to run a PICC line, and we'll be here administering antibiotics through that every couple of hours. Joshua, I can see bone. The tissue and I guess muscle around the break are deteriorating. The doctors aren't positive the bones are sealing like they should and now they're talking about him developing an infection in the bone."

"And you trust them?"

"We're just doing what they tell us needs to be done. Alex keeps telling me that we have to walk in faith through this, so I'm not about to let any doubt wreck his faith. Really the only thing I know to do is trust they know what they're doing and pray and trust that God is in this every step of the way."

"I'm here if you guys need anything." He gave his friend a side hug.

"I know." She smiled back and gave him a tight squeeze as Maddy escorted Alex around the corner.

"Josh, hey!" Alex greeted Joshua as he approached the two in his wheelchair.

"Hey, man," Joshua walked to Alex and shook his hand. "Good to see you moving around. Looks like you're mastering that chair."

"Yeah, well, I'm determined not to get too attached to it."

"Oh, here," Joshua handed Alex a small paper bag that Renae could only assume was a bottle of wine. "I found the one you wanted."

"Thanks; I appreciate it. So, I assume you're here to

take one of my girls out tonight?"

"He is, Daddy! We're going to go out for ice cream! Uncle Josh, did you say we're getting Jesus chicken, too?"

"Miss Maddy, if you want Jesus chicken and waffle fries and ice cream, you've got it."

"No soda, though; she'll be up all night and she has school tomorrow," Renae instructed.

"Your mommy is fun-sucker, you know that?" Joshua picked up Maddy and had her give her parents kisses good-bye. "You two have fun while we're gone! We'll be back in two hours at the latest."

"Thanks, Josh. Take care of our princess. Here, take Renae's car since Maddy's seat is in there." Alex tossed him Renae's keys and followed them to the door, watching as Joshua put Maddy in her booster seat and left.

"So, we're kid-free for two hours," Renae began. "What are you up for, Mr. Murphy? Scary movie?" Alex reached for her waist and brought her close to him, wrapping his arms around her. "A nap?"

"Neither."

"I hate that you're looking at me from this angle. I feel like you're getting my Jabba the Hutt face."

"You're beautiful," he replied, admiring his wife.

The sound of the doorbell interrupted their moment, and Renae pulled away to answer.

"Maddy must have forgotten something," she said, as she opened the door to a meal delivery driver. Alex joined her at the door and handed the driver a tip as Renae grabbed the bags.

"Was this you?" She gave her husband a mischievous smile, and he winked at her in return. The family didn't need meals since family, friends, and their churches had made sure they had more than they needed, and their freezer was full of options. However, since Alex couldn't surprise his wife by driving to a secret destination for dinner, he occasionally surprised her by having the dinner come to them. Whether he had a chef come to the house to prepare and serve a romantic five-course meal for two, or ordered lobster rolls from her favorite food truck, Renae was always overwhelmed by his thoughtfulness and enthusiasm to keep the romance alive in their relationship, even in his current condition.

"I love you." Renae bent down to give her husband a kiss.

"Maybe you should wait to see what's for dinner before you show your gratitude," Alex joked.

Renae took the heavy paper bags filled with food to the kitchen, the aroma suggesting they might be eating a very early Thanksgiving dinner tonight. Alex selected a playlist from the Echo and 90s pop music began to sound through the house. Renae looked to her husband, confused, because he knew how much she detested this genre of music.

Alex joined Renae in the kitchen and placed the paper bag Joshua had given him on the table as Renae began to pull out plates and utensils. "Oh, can we use the paper plates tonight?" he asked Renae.

"Uh, okay," replied a still-confused Renae. "Red solo cups to drink from?"

"Don't be silly. I'd never serve your favorite white wine to you in a plastic cup."

Renae joined her husband at the table as she placed paper plates, wine glasses, napkins, and forks in front of them. Alex began to unpack the contents of the bag, closely watching his date for a reaction. Each item was packaged in a black disposable container with a clear lid, revealing the contents held inside. He brought out the cranberry sauce first, stalling to see if she could get the meaning behind the music and choice of food yet.

"Thanksgiving theme?" she asked.

"Nope." Alex pulled out the next two containers, one with mashed potatoes and gravy, the other holding cornbread stuffing. "Still nothing?"

Renae shook her head 'no.'

"Alright, it's going to be a complete failure on my part if this doesn't give it away." Alex pulled out the last large container to reveal sliced turkey with gravy.

"Oh my God, Alex!" Renae held her hands to her mouth. "Prom!" She laughed and wrapped her arms around her husband's neck. "You're recreating our prom date!"

"Were you thinking I'd completely lost my mind for playing shitty 90s music?"

"Kind of! I was thinking it might be time for another MRI or something."

"Well, since I really can't dance with you right now, and we didn't dance at prom because you hated all the music they played, I thought this playlist would be perfect."

"Alex, it is perfect! This meal is perfect. Everyone else went out for a fancy dinner and who knows what other debauchery, and we ditched prom and went to my house and made frozen dinners. I love it!"

"Well, I hope this is a step or two above the three-dollar frozen dinners we ate that night," Alex remarked as he began to serve his wife. After Alex blessed the food, the couple indulged in wine, comfort food, and meaningful conversation, reminiscing on the moment they knew they were meant for each other.

"So, how much trouble did you really get into for staying out past 2:00 a.m. that night?" Renae asked.

"Dad was mad, but he was too sick to punish me. And Mom blamed it all on you, so I really didn't get in any trouble."

"I was doomed from the beginning with her, wasn't I?"

"Pretty much. She told my dad I was out doing 'only God knows what with that little vixen on the soccer team.'"

"Didn't you tell her we were just talking on my back porch all night eating frozen dinners and laughing at old Carol Burnett reruns on Daddy's black-and-white TV set?"

"She wouldn't hear it. She thought you were trouble and I was the apple of her eye."

"Well, you still are, I'm sure."

"And you're the apple of mine," he replied, with a flirtatious wink.

When they had finished dinner and the table was cleared, Renae joined Alex on the sofa. She cuddled next to him as he adjusted his leg on the cushions to keep his leg elevated. "Joshua should be home with Maddy in about twenty minutes," she told Alex.

"I have one more prom-night memory for you," Alex said as he forwarded through songs on the playlist until he reached the only song he and Renae had danced to on their first date.

"The Ramones." Renae instantly recognized a song she loved, and a smile grew across her face.

"I knew how much you liked them because you had them all over your notebooks at school, so I figured you might get out on the dance floor if the DJ played something you knew. It took three trips to the DJ stand to get him play anything by the Ramones. I bribed him fifty bucks to do it. That's why I kept asking you about dinner that night and where you wanted to go. I spent half my money on getting a chance to dance with you."

"I didn't know that. I'm so glad you did." Renae released her hold around her husband and stretched to give him another kiss. "Thank you," she said as she rested her head on his chest. Alex ran his hand through her hair as he softly hummed along to 'Baby I Love You,' the song they called their own. The couple sat together in complete serenity until it was time for their daughter to arrive back home.

* * *

Soon after the PICC line was inserted, Alex gained a new hope that this would be a major turning point in his recovery. At Joshua's suggestion, Renae and Alex started their days by taking communion together. Often, Maddy would join them. Ruth even joined in whenever she stopped by from time to time to prepare breakfast. She wondered why she and Phil had never thought of doing that together when they were going through tough times. She watched Alex and Renae grow together on a new spiritual maturity level each visit. Ruth could not have been prouder of her daughter and son-in-law. Their house had transitioned from a place of hostility and resentment to a place of peace and happiness. Even in their sleep deprivation, they maintained a positive attitude. They spent many days on the couch together renting comedies and binge-watching their favorite shows. They were determined to keep their sense of humor to help them maintain their sanity.

Renae faithfully administered antibiotics to Alex, interchanging prescriptions every two hours. They reached a new level of intimacy as she dedicated her life to his care and wellness. She looked to him and couldn't imagine what he was silently enduring. She let him sleep when he could, even when she wasn't able to herself. She spent many nights in his office, listening to worship music and reading her Bible or other inspiring books she found on his bookshelf. Over the past couple of years, his reading choices had transitioned from science fiction and hunting to books on the Holy Spirit and theology. Curious and longing for answers as well as a deeper relationship with God and her family, Renae scoured through the books. She didn't understand why Alex wasn't getting better, but she also didn't dare question it. She recognized this was part of their journey and anticipated healing in God's timing.

As things became increasingly challenging, Alex learned to lean on the same Scripture God had given Renae in the hospital the night of his accident. When the lights would go out, voices would start to taunt him with words of doubt and fear. He embraced Isaiah 40:31 and repeated it until those voices were silenced.

'But those who trust in the Lord will
find new strength.
They will soar high on wings like eagles.
They will run and not grow weary.
They will walk and not faint.'

He *would* run again with his daughter. He *would* walk her down the aisle. And he *would* dance with his wife once again.

* * *

Joshua and Mandy were preparing the final touches on dinner when the doorbell rang. Milo was already at the door, his tail wagging exuberantly. Joshua knew Milo sensed who was on the other side of the door, and he opened it eagerly.

"Uncle Josh!" Maddy exclaimed, jumping up and down. "Is she here?"

"You wouldn't be talking about Emily, would you?" Maddy's excitement was written all over her face. "She may be, but I won't tell you until I get my hug." Maddy reached her arms toward Joshua as he picked her up and squeezed her tight. "Oh, sweet girl, I'm not going to be able to do this much longer. Either Uncle Josh is getting weaker or you're getting heavier."

"Mommy says I'm growing, but not to tell Daddy," Maddy whispered in his ear.

"Okay, we won't tell him. And Emily is upstairs in the bonus room. You can go see her; she brought her ponies, just like you asked."

"Ok, Uncle Josh. I have my ponies in my bag. I'll show her." Maddy trotted towards the familiar stairs, her bag over-flowing with assorted colorful ponies and unicorns. She had spent quite a lot of time at this house, and his home was a place of comfort to her.

"Thanks for having us for dinner," Renae said as she kissed her friend on the cheek, entering the house with an appetizer in one hand and a dessert in the other.

"Hey, Josh, good to see you, man," Alex greeted his long-time friend and followed his wife inside. Joshua had made the house wheelchair-friendly in order to make Alex as comfortable as possible.

"Hey, Mandy; it smells great in here." Renae walked into the kitchen and looked around at the gourmet meal Mandy must have been slaving all evening to prepare.

"Oh, thank you. I never get the opportunity to cook extravagant meals, but I really enjoy doing it. Here, let me get those dishes out of your hands for you."

"No, that's okay, I've got it." Making herself at home, Renae placed the appetizer on the counter, grabbed a spoon for it from the first drawer she opened, and headed to the refrigerator with the dessert and a small bag containing Alex's medications. She knew her way around Joshua's kitchen better than her own. Out of habit, she checked the expiration date on the milk. Joshua wasted more milk than he drank, and Renae could almost always guarantee whatever was in the refrigerator would be spoiled. She was right. Instinctively, she grabbed the milk jug, took it to the sink, and began to empty it. "Josh, how old is the pizza in the fridge? Can I toss it?"

Mandy turned to see what Renae was doing, feeling slightly inadequate and intimidated. "I'm sorry, I meant to toss all of that out that earlier." Renae froze as her eyes met her husband's. He'd cautioned her about 'pissing all over Josh's house tonight and becoming territorial.' It was beginning. There was another woman in the kitchen she and Joshua used to bond in, and she was pounding her chest and showing dominance.

"Oh, Mandy, no worries. I just have a bad habit of

checking milk expiration dates and tossing old milk every-where I go. I'm mental." She released a forced laugh. "We brought some wine and bourbon, would y'all care for some?"

"I'd love a glass of wine." Mandy needed something to calm her. She was so nervous about hosting Joshua's friends tonight, especially the one who had been the woman of his house and his life for the past couple of years.

Not wanting to overstep her boundaries, Renae sat on a stool next to Alex, allowing Mandy to get the glasses and serve her guests. Nervously, Mandy began to open cabinets and look for the wine glasses and tumblers. Renae knew they were on the other side of the kitchen, but she feared retriev-ing them would make Mandy more uncomfortable. Joshua furrowed his brow, questioning Renae's odd behavior in his house.

"Here, sweetheart, I'll get them," Joshua said as he opened the cabinet and pulled out two wine glasses and a tumbler. "Alex, you drinking?" Alex held his hand up, imply-ing he was not. Renae stood, taking the bottles to Joshua.

"I can pour. Do you have something I can open the wine with?"

Joshua stared directly at Renae as he opened the drawer next to her and pulled out the wine-bottle opener she had used at least a hundred times. "Can you figure out how to use it?" he questioned her suspiciously.

Renae smiled affectionately at Joshua. "Yes, I think I can manage. So, Mandy, did Joshua help you cook all this?"

"No, he said he is a disaster in the kitchen. I let him make the chicken nuggets and macaroni and cheese for the girls, though."

"I'm sure it will all turn out great," Renae replied as she handed Mandy a glass of pinot grigio. Mandy graciously accepted the wine and took two nervous sips while Renae stood a foot away from her and stared, trying to come up with something to say. Unbeknownst to Renae, the stare was more of a glare, and Mandy was on the brink of tears in her presence. Seeing her distress, Joshua came to Mandy's rescue, wrapping his arm around her waist and positioning himself between the two women. Renae backed away. Joshua turned his head and gave her a look she never would have expected to come from him.

'What is wrong with you?' he mouthed towards her. Her face full of surprise, she shook her head to tell him she was unaware what he was referring to.

"Alex, could you help me in the bathroom? I need help with the zipper on my outfit."

"Gladly." Alex followed his wife to the bathroom and closed the door behind him. "What is your problem with her?"

"I don't have a problem with her! This is your fault. If you hadn't mentioned me pissing on my territory while I was here, I wouldn't be so freaking nervous to do anything."

"Oh, so staring her down and looking like you're going to chew her up and spit her out is my fault?"

"I wasn't looking at her like that. Don't be ridiculous."

"Why else do you think Joshua went to her rescue? You looked like you were planning how to get rid of her. She's a nervous wreck right now. And watching her suffer while she tried to find the glasses? That wasn't cool. She knew you knew where they were; you looked like you were trying to prove a point."

"What point?"

"I don't know; maybe that you'll always be around to make her uncomfortable or that you'll always be watching her every move around him?"

"Alex, that is so not fair! That is not what I was trying to do! Making her uncomfortable is the last thing I wanted to do tonight." Renae leaned against the bathroom wall, troubled. She was unsure what was troubling her more, the perception Alex and Joshua had of her behavior tonight, or the fact she and Alex were having their first quarrel since they'd reunited.

Back in the kitchen, Mandy was pouring out her own troubles. "I don't know if I can do this, Josh. She hates me."

"She doesn't hate you. She's acting weird, true, but I know her. She doesn't hate you."

"I just want tonight to go right, and I'm so nervous around her. I know her opinion of me matters most to you."

"You're wrong, Mandy. My opinion of you matters most to me. And I think you are an incredible, strong, caring, and sensitive woman. And I am so honored and thankful that you would open your heart and push aside your insecurities to host this meal tonight for some people who are really important to me."

"I want them to be important to me, too. And me to them," she said, tears running down her face. She quickly wiped them away when she heard the door to the bathroom open. Joshua embraced her, giving her a quick kiss before Renae and Alex entered the kitchen. Determined to set things right, Renae walked to Mandy, looked her in the face, and embraced her tightly. Relieved, Mandy squeezed her back.

"Like I said, I'm mental. I'm sorry if I've been coming across weird tonight. I just want you to feel comfortable here and around us."

"Thank you," Mandy said as she pulled away from Renae. "That means so much. I want us to become good friends."

Joshua sat next to Alex and took a drink, sighing with relief as the ladies put the finishing touches on dinner. Alex explained what had transpired between him and Renae before they'd arrived, as well as what had been discussed in the bathroom. Renae's reactive behavior now made complete sense.

When it was time for dinner, Renae served the giddy little girls at the counter while the adults gathered around the table. Her spirit felt heavy and sad; she had not spoken to her husband since their argument in the bathroom. As she laid the plates down for the girls and kissed them on the cheeks, she lifted her eyes to look at her husband. He was staring at her, his expression revealing he felt the same heaviness she did. Renae approached the chair next to her husband, but before taking her seat, she leaned over to him and whispered in his ear. "I don't want to fight with you. I'm so sorry."

"I'm sorry, too."

"I love you."

"I love you more."

As she watched her parents kiss, Maddy exclaimed to Emily, "they're going to make a baby sister!" The girls erupted in laughter.

"She goes to public school," Renae remarked to Mandy, with a smirk on her face.

The evening progressed with tales of many fond memories and plans for the future. Renae and Mandy moved past their awkwardness and found common interests in clothes, tv shows, movies, and food. Mandy delighted in the stories Renae and Alex had of times they'd punked Joshua: some intentional, most completely unintentional.

"Ok, so you know how Queen is his all-time favorite band?" Renae began. "Well, I was in Atlanta for a conference and I saw a Creative Loafing ad for The Ultimate Queen Karaoke Annual Event at this huge club there. So, I'm thinking this will be a great twenty-fifth birthday present for him, and we all could go and have a night out in Atlanta."

"Great, do we really have to relive this one?" Joshua sighed, grinning as he said it.

"Yes," Renae continued as Alex buried his head in his hands laughing. "So, the four of us fly into Atlanta, get situated in the hotel, have drinks, and then head out to this club for Queen Karaoke. Mandy, the ad made it sound epic and Josh was so freaking excited to go! We get to the club, and Josh and Angie head in first. He's got this huge smile on his face; he can't wait to get up there and sing. Funny thing is, the kid doesn't even sing." Mandy was taking much delight in Joshua's embarrassment. "And as Alex and I walk in, we notice the people who are there. They're all freaking drag queens! It was a *drag queen* karaoke night. We're talking to the guy at the door, dying because we thought it was Queen the band, and now Joshua and Angie, who are both completely conservative and completely naive and so freaking sweet, are in the middle of a homophobic nightmare. But it's all so darling, because as this guy is showing us to where he'd seated them so we can retrieve them, Josh is sitting around just smiling at everyone, excited for the karaoke to begin."

"He'd been practicing the entire plane trip there," Alex chimed in.

"The staff and entertainers found him so endearing and pure, they just fell in love with him. They *changed the entire night* to be Queen-themed, sung by drag queens,"

"And Alex and I," Joshua continued. "We were treated to free drinks and appetizers all night because it was my birthday."

"And Joshua had the biggest, most flamboyant audience as his overhyped, drunk self dove into 'Don't Stop Me Now,'" Renae reflected. Mandy reached across the table and grabbed Joshua's hand, completely amused.

"After which Alex jumped on stage with me and led us all in 'Fat Bottomed Girls.'"

"Yes, and he dedicated it to me." Mandy exploded in laughter at this. "The queens around me were like 'oh no girl, you better leave him.' Which I didn't-"

"But I did sleep on the sofa bed in the hotel room that night."

"More like morning. Renae took us to some pretty questionable places that night at after we left the drag club. She wasn't living for Jesus then, and I vowed to God as I pulled myself off the bathroom floor after puking my insides out that if I lived through the morning, I would cast her aside and follow Him all the days of my life."

"The plane ride home was miserable and very quiet, and we didn't speak for--what, four months?"

"Yup, not until your birthday."

Renae's alarm went off on her phone, signaling it was time for Alex's antibiotics. Forever placing her passion for people and nursing first, Mandy offered to administer his antibiotics and clean the wound for Renae. Seeing that Alex was comfortable with Mandy doing it, Renae allowed it. Not only would if give the two a chance to bond a little, but it would also open an opportunity for Mandy to freely ask questions and evaluate Alex's condition. From Renae's prospective, Alex was not getting any better, and she asked Mandy if she wouldn't mind looking at his leg. Mandy was more than happy and honored that Renae would trust her enough to ask her.

As the friends ended their evening together, Mandy pulled Renae to the side, discreetly advising her to get Alex back to the doctor as soon as possible. She was worried about his lack of progress and also concerned about his health. "Renae, you don't see it because you're with him every day, but his color isn't good and he's looking slightly frail. I have a nutritionist I can refer you to; she goes to your church. It wouldn't hurt to see if there was some way she could help."

"Yeah, I'd love to give her a call, if you think he needs one. I'll call his doctor in the morning. Thanks, Mandy, not just for the advice but for everything tonight. Dinner was great and we had a great time. He really needed to get out and spend time with some other people besides me." She gave Mandy a hug, then said her goodbyes to Emily and finally Joshua. Mandy packed her daughter's things and headed out behind the Murphys. Instead of walking Renae to her car door like he usually did, Joshua joined Mandy at hers. Renae and Alex waved at the couple as they backed out of Joshua's driveway, thankful for their friendship and delighted that God had brought Joshua and Mandy together.

* * *

Two days later, the Murphys found themselves back at the doctor's office, as Mandy had suggested. Renae knew the antibiotics weren't doing what they needed to. They were approaching six months after the accident. Her husband was looking thinner and weaker, but maintained a positive outlook despite those factors. As they waited for the doctor, Renae decided to order some sandwiches and salads from their favorite lunch spot to pick up after they were done. "Do you want a cookie?" she asked Alex, before placing the order.

Alex's head shot up, somewhat excited, and he began to look around the office. "What, here?" he replied with a grin.

"What?" Renae was confused.

Alex looked at the page Renae was showing him on her phone and saw an assortment of cookies on the page. He burst into laughter. "That is NOT what I heard you say." Renae quickly caught on to what he thought he'd heard and turned two shades redder as she laughed with him. "I was thinking you were getting a little adventurous, making a proposition right here in the doctor's office."

"Well, there is a bathroom right there..." Renae thought about it for a second before they both exploded in laughter again. Dr. Mavi walked into the room and noticed the pair was having a difficult time keeping a straight face. He was glad to see they still had joy in the midst of their suffering.

Dr. Mavi confirmed that the antibiotics from the PICC line were not working and that they'd be contacted to schedule surgery for an antibiotic bead treatment. Both left the office feeling defeated, although neither of them would admit it. Renae got in the car, which she noted was way overdue for a wash, and took a deep breath before putting it in reverse. She grabbed her water bottle and gave it a vigorous shake to ensure her first sip would be cold. She gasped as the water shot all over her face and chest.

Alex turned to her, compressing his lips to keep from

chuckling, as he didn't know what to expect from her. He had loosened the cap to the bottle when she wasn't looking, unaware she would shake the contents all over herself. Renae turned to her husband, water dripping down her nose and chin, and snorted as she dissolved into laughter with him. He grabbed the extra sweatshirt she always kept in the back seat and patted her face dry. Wholly amused, they found a re-newed feeling of hope and the feelings of defeat quickly dis-appeared.

"Well, I was just thinking how freaking hot it is out-side, but, hey, you took care of that! Thanks for always look-ing out for me, Murphy," Renae said, as she pulled out of the parking lot and they headed to get their lunch...and possibly a cookie.

✷ ✷ ✷

"Mr. and Mrs. Murphy, I think it's time we discuss the possibility of the loss of limb." There was a new doctor at the office, and he was asked to join Dr. Mavi to assess Alex Murphy's condition. Alex had been diagnosed with osteomy-elitis, an infection of the bone. The tissue surrounding the bone was dead. The antibiotic bead treatment had given him a serious allergic reaction; now this stranger was standing in front of them and trying to rob them of the hope they had held on to for the past six months. However, their faith was stronger than his foolishness. His voice and opinion were si-lenced quickly; he found himself unable to find any words to further say to the Murphys. Alex's doctor was also in the room, and knew the couple believed in healing and wouldn't accept anything less.

"Renae, please don't cuss out the doctor when he comes back in," Alex pleaded with his wife.

Renae had already utilized a colorful assortment of words after both doctors left the room to discuss further treatment. Alex's doctor, Dr. Mavi, returned alone. "Sorry about earlier. I won't be asking him back to consult on your case again. I do have another option we can talk about, if you're willing to give it a shot." Dr. Mavi explained that there was an experimental surgery they could try, but it didn't sit well with the Murphys. After several days of seeking answers in prayer and fasting, they made a critical decision. They were standing on God's Word and the Word told them "let the peace of God rule your heart." Neither one of them had peace about this surgery. They decided to see Mandy's nutritionist first to address Alex's health.

❋ ❋ ❋

Mandy's nutritionist, Linda, was more than happy to make a house call to meet with Alex. Renae greeted her at the door, freely giving her a hug, something she used to think was awkward. "Hey, Linda, thanks so much for coming and seeing him."

"It's my pleasure! I'm so glad you two decided to seek this route and give it a try, and thanks for calling on me."

"Alex is in his office; I'll take you back there."

"Okay. So, remind me, how long ago was his accident?"

"Six months."

"And he's been taking the antibiotics for how long?"

"The entire six months. First they were the ones he got in the hospital through the IV, then oral, then the PICC line, then the bead treatment."

Linda's eyes widened as she absorbed the information and turned the corner to see Alex. His coloring was grey. He was visibly malnourished. Today, Linda would play the role of a rocket scientist and create a plan to counterattack the damage done to Alex's gut. She knew he wasn't absorbing any nutrients and one more surgery could place him in physical jeopardy.

Alex and Renae stared at the green concoction Linda set before Alex. It was made of Aloe vera and a mix of leafy green veggies. The sight of it turned Renae's stomach. It reminded her of the split pea soup her mother used to make from a can when she was little. Renae hated everything green and slimy because of that. Her husband, however, took it like a champ. His wellness was his priority, and, eager for healing, he submitted to wisdom from people he believed God had partnered him with during this taxing season.

Renae's afternoons involved searching social media for meal ideas that limited their meat intake but were rich in nutritious fruits and veggies. Fortunately, Maddy was also enjoying all the new foods they tried, and they were able to find renewed nutritional health and well-being as a family. They were determined to walk this through united to see Alex healed. Within a week of his diet change, his body began to heal, and he was finding a renewed sense of strength.

* * *

The following few months included three more surgeries: one to have the external fixator removed, one to remove a portion of his bone, and the last and final reconstructive surgery. As Renae sat in the waiting room during that final surgery, she opened her journal to reflect on the better part of the past year. She and Alex had been sent numerous blows and setbacks over the past nine months. There were moments of disappointment, but the ability to laugh together kept them from feeling overwhelmed by the tasks and obstacles they faced. She was glad and extremely thankful they had reconciled before this happened to him. Not that she felt like she was his savior, but she couldn't imagine him having to endure this on his own with Ms. Deb. She was also grateful for the opportunity to grow stronger as husband and wife. Choosing to walk side by side with him through this trying time strengthened their love for each other and for the friends and family around them.

She flipped through the pages of her journal and saw an entry written during a visit from Mr. and Mrs. Reeves.

'Do everything in the natural you know to do, and trust God for the unseen and in the supernatural.'

She wasn't sure if she and Alex would be here right now, at this final stage, without their trust in God. Their faith was strong, and in this case, it needed to be long. The week prior to the accident showed her how fast God could radically move in the hearts of people who were willing. The first ten days after his accident were a lesson of building her faith and gave her an opportunity to lean on God and trust Him with the little and big things in her life. She believed He had a supernatural influence on their financial provision, and she honored Him where it was due. Those nine months were a battle, but neither one of them spoke their fear. They endured each obstacle together, and their faith and relationship with God and each other grew stronger for it. Getting to this point was the biggest struggle she never thought she would have to live through, but here they were looking at the end of this part of the journey, and all she knew to do was to thank God for all of it.

She looked at the clock and realized he had only been in surgery for an hour. She was becoming restless. She didn't want to read, watch tv, or write. She wished she had someone to sit with and talk to. As she picked up her phone, she realized she had a missed call from Joshua.

"Hey love, I need to talk to you. Can you give me a call when you get a chance? Crap, I forgot Alex is in surgery. Call me when you can. It's not an emergency but pretty important."

Renae quickly dialed his number, begging him to answer.

"Hey!" Joshua picked up. "I wasn't expecting to hear from you so soon."

"He's in surgery and I am super restless. What are you doing?"

"Well, I'm taking the rest of the day off work to run an errand. Mind if I join you at the hospital?"

"That would be fantastic."

"Want coffee?"

"That would be great. Iced, please."

"You've got it. I'll see you in a few; I'm about twenty minutes out."

"See you then. Drive safe." Renae hung up the phone and went to the bathroom to freshen up. Since Joshua's comment about looking like she'd rolled out of the 1980s, she had been dressing better and making an effort to look nice every day. Although she knew Alex didn't mind her relaxed look, she wanted him to know he was important enough for her to look her best.

She sat back down in the waiting room and watched the door. She knew Joshua would be in a suit and tie, and she always thought he wore it well. He walked through the door and spotted her, and a welcoming grin grew on both their faces. She quickly sprang to her feet to greet him.

"I miss you; you know that, right?" Renae gave him a quick kiss on the cheek.

"Not as much as I miss you." He handed her the coffee and the two took a seat.

"How's the soccer season going so far?"

"Pretty good, I guess. Our team got off to a slow start. I know one player doesn't make a team, but she sure can make a heck of a difference."

"Well, I'm looking forward to the next season, but if Alex coaches, I may have to switch teams. Who knows though, we may be coaching Maddy's team by then."

"Oh yeah? Is she showing some interest?"

"Not really, but you know we have to at least let her try."

"I'm sure she'll love it. Does Alex have dreams of playing again?"

"Right now he's just focusing on being able to walk again." She caught him up with Alex's progress and plans for physical therapy after this final surgery. He gave her the name of a place nearby that Mandy had recommended. "Josh, she really is precious. Alex and I absolutely adore her. I'm so glad you two found one another."

"Yeah, I didn't think I would be able to love again after...well, you know. But she's incredible. And Emily--I loved her the moment I met her."

"So, is she the one?"

"Well, that's what I'm here to talk to you about." He grabbed Renae's hand and stared into her eyes for a moment. He pulled out a small box from his suit pocket and Renae gasped. Those who hadn't been watching them already were now invested in what they were up to, all eyes locked on what they thought was a proposal. Renae wrapped her arms around Josh, and the room erupted in applause and cheers.

The two stopped hugging and looked to their audience, confused. "Oh my gosh." Renae realized what it looked like and she held up her left hand with her wedding ring on it. "No, it's not that! I'm already married."

The faces on the people cheering for them changed from joy to puzzlement. One older woman stood to her feet and walked out of the room, hitting Renae's leg with her cane, calling her a 'tramp' before she left.

"He's just showing me a ring!" Renae exclaimed as Joshua laughed next to her. No one seemed to care. They'd already passed their judgement. "Ugh. Whatever. Show me the ring! When is this happening?"

Joshua opened the box and Renae had to contain her jealousy. It was the dream ring she had shown to Joshua many times when they were younger. Either he had forgotten, or he knew he would nail it with this choice.

"I know it's something you picked out, and that's what makes it special to me. I really want this marriage. I want to spend the rest of my life with her and with Emily. Hopefully she and I can have more kids, which we both want. But I just really need your blessing before I talk to her father. I need you to tell me I'm making the right decision. I need your seal of approval before I can move forward."

"Josh, I don't think you need it, but I know you want it. And I'm going to tell you to go for it! Go for it, and go all in. I haven't seen you this happy in so long. She's made such a positive impact on your life and I can see how much you two love each other already. You have my blessing one thousand times!"

"I have to admit, I'm a little nervous about messing this up."

"Don't be. Just love her, honor her, respect her. Show her she is the number one person in your life. Take her flowers for no reason at all. Encourage her and let her know how valuable and worthy she is to you."

"Are you telling me this because it's how Alex has been treating you?"

"It is, and you know, I fall in love with him a little more every day."

Joshua closed the box and put it back in his pocket. He sat back in his chair and contemplated how to surprise Mandy. Renae leaned back and propped her legs over his lap, sipping on her coffee. "The ring is beautiful, you know. If you've been half as wonderful to her as you have been to me over the past hundred decades, she's going to say yes."

"I know. I don't doubt she'll say yes. She's the one."

"I'm so happy for you. I really am." Renae felt a small loss as she realized that Joshua was moving on for good. She sat up in her chair and rested her head on his shoulder as he put his arm around her.

"And I'm so happy for you," he replied as he kissed her

head. He sat with her until the doctor came to tell her Alex's surgery was finished and it went very well. Renae felt a sense of relief fall over her, followed by nausea. She covered her mouth and quickly headed for the trash can. Joshua rubbed her back as she heaved.

"Hey, you okay? Can I get you something?"

"No," she shook her head as she stood and wiped her mouth with a napkin someone offered her. "I think it's just my nerves after all of this. It's like I'm releasing all this stress or something."

"How long has this been happening?"

"I don't know, like a couple of weeks. It comes in waves." She took a sip of water another person close by handed her. She appreciated the generosity of the same people who'd judged her several hours earlier.

"You haven't missed, you know, your monthly girlie friend or anything, have you?"

Renae thought about it for a minute. She didn't have time to track that. She thought harder and then looked at her grinning and suspecting friend.

"Oh, God."

* * *

A couple of hours had passed since Alex had been brought to his room. While he was in post-op, Renae found some friends she had made at the hospital, and they were more than happy to run tests on her. She sent Joshua away before she received the results. Out of respect for her husband, if they were expecting another baby, she wanted him to be the first to know. Sitting next to his bed, Renae grasped Alex's hand and held it next to her cheek as he opened his eyes.

"Hey, you," she greeted him as she kissed his hand.

"Hey." Alex smiled, relieved to see her. His least favorite part of surgery was saying goodbye to her. Seeing her on the other side was his favorite.

"How are you feeling?"

"Still pretty good. Can't feel much of anything right now."

"Your nurse just brought in some fresh ice. Want some?"

"Please."

Renae filled a small cup and brought it to Alex.

"So, this is it, your last surgery. How do you feel?"

Alex thought about it before answering. "Grateful. I know that may sound weird but…I don't know if I have ever felt so loved and cared for as I have the past nine months." He rubbed his tired eyes and face to help wake himself up so he could carry a lucid conversation. "Our relationship has reached heights I never thought could have been achieved. God, Renae, a year ago we couldn't speak to each other, and here we've been given this second chance, and even through all this I have to say it's been our best year yet. So, I'm grateful, I'm blessed, and I'm so content. Thank you for sticking with me these past nine months. I promise I'll make it up to you."

He kissed her hand as she wiped away one of her tears.

"You are an incredible man, Alex Murphy. I can't get over how lucky we are to have a second chance, and even though it's been brutal, I wouldn't change a thing. And, hey, you can make it up to me by taking care of us over the next nine months," she said this cheerfully, as she handed him a folded piece of paper.

Alex opened the paper containing the lab work performed on Renae that day, the results revealing a positive pregnancy.

"Looks like we made another itty-bitty human, Mr. Murphy."

With tears beginning to stream out the sides of his eyes, Alex grabbed the back of his wife's neck and pulled her close for a kiss. He wrapped his arms around her as she lay her head on his chest. New life sprang out of something that once seemed so dead. Through all the emotional and physical pain, God had remained faithful and His promises true. Alex and Renae Murphy had passed the road to restoration and were looking forward to living their lives renewed.

FIFTEEN

Eric and Andy pulled into the driveway of Ruth Rivera's home, their car loaded with personal belongings and their tiny Chihuahua. The movers would be there soon; they would be calling Ruth's house 'home' for now. Andy had secured a position at the children's hospital downtown, and as an artist, Eric was able to move pretty much anywhere he pleased. Eric stepped out of the passenger seat and looked to his neighbor's house. He wasn't sure how they would feel having a gay couple move in next door, but if their reception at Phil's funeral indicated anything, they would love Eric and Andy regardless. At least he hoped they would.

Ruth stepped out of the house, rollers in her hair, overjoyed to see them both. She gave them both huge hugs and then met her granddog. She had been looking forward to this moment for four months and the day was finally here. It was a big day for everyone in the family.

"Renae and Alex should be here around eleven, so I'll have some light refreshments for brunch. They probably will only stay an hour or so, but they wanted to see you both before they leave for their trip."

"Is Maddy staying with us, then?" Andy asked, hopeful.

"Yeah, she'll be here while they're gone. What was it, eight days? Anyways, with the wedding happening tonight, I wasn't sure if you two would want to eat here while I'm gone or go out for dinner. I don't mind making something if you want to get settled in."

"Don't worry about it, Mom. We'll figure it out."

"Okay, well, you know where everything is, so make

yourselves at home. Welcome home!"

Andy stepped indoors and looked around the house, recalling the events that had happened when he walked through the door to the Rivera's for the first time. "We can do this. This will be good," he reassured himself.

❊ ❊ ❊

The morning light was shining through Renae's bedroom window, awakening her as she rolled over in bed. She reached for her phone and, seeing how late she'd slept in, quickly kissed her husband and hopped out of bed, making her way downstairs to get coffee and breakfast going. On her way to the kitchen, she lightly shook the lump occupying the sofa. "Wake up, Princess, today's your big day."

Joshua moaned from the couch, feeling the effects of too much wine and whiskey from the night before.

"Do you want coffee or orange juice? I can make you a bloody mary if you think it will make you feel better," she teased him. "Mimosa? Whiskey sour?" A pillow flew across the room, barely missing her. She chuckled. She didn't feel sorry for him or Alex, who was still in bed recovering. They'd decided to go out and celebrate a little too much last night after Joshua and Mandy's rehearsal dinner, leaving Renae as their designated driver.

She brought a bottle of water over to him. "Hey, lightweight, I need to get Maddy from Mandy's house. Can I get you something before I leave? You have to get up!" She pulled on his arm, dragging the top part of his body onto the floor.

"Leave me alone," Joshua moaned. It was evident he wasn't ready for Renae's shenanigans this morning.

"No. Here, you need to drink some water and go out for some fresh air. I'll get the coffee going. You, my dear, have to feel better fast. I'm not taking the blame for you getting hammered and not being able to function on your wedding day. Drink the water; I'll grab something for your head."

"It is your fault. You're the one who introduced me to the demon whiskey."

"But you didn't have to drink it, my friend."

Joshua drank the water and took the pain killers. He looked at the clock. He was getting married in nine hours. He wasn't sure if he had nervous butterflies in his stomach or if he needed to vomit from trying to drink Alex under the table, something in which neither of them succeeded as Renae had cut them both off. The last thing she wanted was another karaoke night with the two, and that's where she saw it was headed.

"Renae?"

"Yeah?"

"Come sit with me for a minute." Renae and Joshua propped themselves on her sofa and sat next to each other. "This could be our last time alone together and I just want to sit with you for a couple of minutes and enjoy the moment." Renae tilted her head on his shoulder. She had morning breath and he had morning alcohol-breath, so they tried to avoid breathing on each other completely. "You've been my best friend for as long as I can remember. You've been with me through all the ups and downs of my life, and I've been there through yours. Meeting you helped me adjust to an awkward time in my life, and I honestly think you may have saved it. If it weren't for you, I wouldn't have had your mother to help walk me through the single most devastating season of my life, losing Angie. You've always been there for me; you fit me like a glove, and you're my security blanket. I'm so glad you and Alex trusted me to be Maddy's godfather; you know I love that kid like she's my own. I just, I want you to know, that no matter where our paths may lead us in the future, you're always in my heart. I will always love you, unconditionally, and I'm always just a phone call away."

Renae was tearing up. She knew this wasn't "goodbye,"

but it was leading to a separation between the two of them. She knew it was best for the two of them focus on their relationships with their spouses, and it was best they didn't give their spouses a reason to be suspicious, even if it meant limiting contact. She would always hold a special place in her heart for him as well. But that place could never take up the space filled by Alex, and she knew he needed to feel the same about Mandy.

"We've had a great ride, friend." She grabbed his hand and held it. "You're going to make an incredible husband and father. And you know Alex and I will always be here for you. All of you. We love you so much." She turned and hugged him, assuring him her feelings towards him would never change.

Alex hesitated before making his way down the stairs. He wasn't sure if they were finished, but he wanted to make sure they were before he interrupted their moment. He knew they held a special bond, and it didn't threaten him in the least. Renae had more than proved her love for him, and he was confident in their relationship and her faithfulness to him. He also knew Mandy may not understand this dynamic, so he'd cautioned them to exercise wisdom.

Renae hopped off the sofa the moment she saw Alex making his way downstairs. After three months of physical therapy and prayer, he was mobile, although still in pain and discomfort. The doctors had fitted him with a prosthetic and prescribed a cane. The cane sat unused in the corner of the foyer, and they never used the prosthetic. She went to his side to walk with him to the kitchen. She knew he had to be feeling some pain this morning, since he'd decided to go without pain meds the evening before so he could enjoy partaking in some adult beverages.

"Morning, Joshua, and don't think you're getting rid of us. You're going to have two more godbabies of ours in a few months. You have to stick around." Renae smiled at Alex's revelation to Josh. They had been holding on to this secret for too long, and she was happy he felt led to share with their friend.

"Two? Wait! What? You're having twins?" Joshua jumped up and joined his friends in the kitchen. His headache and nausea quickly passed, being replaced with enthusiastic joy. Renae laughed and nodded her head as Josh hugged her again and high-fived Alex. "No wonder you're so much bigger than last time!" He grabbed her stomach and lightly rubbed it. "Do we know the sexes yet?"

"Actually, that's your job." Renae grabbed a sealed manila envelope from a nearby drawer and handed it to him. "I don't want a party; I just want a photo shoot with us and Maddy. And I want you to do something fun and creative to reveal what we're having. Is that dumb?" Alex stood behind Renae and wrapped his arms around her, kissing her cheek. Renae pressed her head against him.

"That's amazing. And yes, I would be honored to do that for you. Wow." He looked at his friends. "You two are couples goals, you know that?"

"Yes, we are, and yes, we do," replied Alex. "And today is your day. I didn't mean to spring this on you today, because it's supposed to be all about you. I figured with all the sentimental feelings you two were having down here, you needed something to lighten the mood."

"Ok," Renae broke away, "coffee is ready. I put out some fruit; we can have poached eggs and bacon. Alex, can you handle the bacon while I grab Maddy? We have an hour and a half before we have to be at Mom's, and Maddy needs to come home and get a bath first. I can do the eggs when I get back."

"Can I handle the bacon? You have two bacon masters here. We've got this."

* * *

Andy sat next to Renae during brunch at Ruth's and couldn't help but rub Renae's belly. She knew there was a reason why he went into the business of saving babies; he genuinely loved them.

Joshua joined them at Ruth's house since he was Alex's responsibility for the day. Ruth took Joshua outside to talk. He had questions about love and loss and moving on after Angie. He knew Ruth couldn't directly relate, as she hadn't moved on yet herself, but he knew she could give him sound advice. He truly valued their time together.

Inside, Eric's Chihuahua was under the table trying to get acquainted with Renae's leg. She kept kicking him away, but he kept coming back for more. "Eric, what's your rat's name?"

"My dog's name is Maximus, and you can stop kicking him now, thank you."

"I have turned over a new leaf, Eric, and I won't make fun of you for having a rat dog named Maximus. But I think he needs a girlfriend or something. He's getting fresh with my leg."

"How do you know he doesn't need a boyfriend, Renae? He just may like boys too, you never know."

"Well, he needs something before I kick him into next week."

"Ok, the last time you two saw each other, things were a lot more pleasant. Can we please not fight today?" Alex wasn't feeling up to separating the siblings today. His pain killers hadn't taken their full effect yet, and he was determined today was going to be a good day.

Renae apologized and went to the kitchen to grab more strawberry lemonade for everyone. Eric excused himself and met her before she came back to the dining room.

"So, are you and Alex excited about your trip?" After the accident, Renae had told Andy and Eric that she and Alex were dreaming about taking a Mediterranean cruise this year. The boys made it happen.

"Oh my gosh, Eric! We are! We really can't thank you and Andy enough for treating us to it. The two of us haven't taken a vacation alone since before we had Maddy. This will be like a second honeymoon for us."

"Except you're huge."

"Except I'm huge. Can I tell you a secret, but you have to promise not to tell Mom." Eric nodded. "We're having twins."

"No way! Wow! That's...that's incredible. I'm so happy for the two of you--soon to be five of you! I bet Maddy's thrilled!"

"Well, we've known for weeks but haven't said anything to anyone but Josh and now you. We were thinking about waiting for a baby reveal party, but we decided not to do one of those." She could tell from the look on her brother's face that he was deep in thought and not hearing much of what she had to say "Is something bothering you? You look troubled."

He hesitated before he spoke, and he chose his words carefully. "Renae, I'm really glad that Alex is sitting here with us today, that you two worked out your differences and found a way to make your relationship work, and that you two are more in love than I've ever seen you before. I'm honestly a little astonished he's walking again, let alone here, given everything he went through. I just...how did you do it?"

Renae looked at her brother, confused and almost embarrassed. "How did I get pregnant?'

"Oh my God, no! Renae!"

"Oh, thank God," she laughed out loud. "Because I really don't feel comfortable explaining that to my older brother."

"Oh my God, now I have a visual in my brain, and that's disgusting. No! What I meant is how did you, you know, change. How did you make it through the toughest trial of your lives together? Get to this point?"

Renae didn't have an easy answer for him. She knew what they'd done and the underlying reason she sat with Alex, who was healed, at her mother's table. She knew through surrendering to God that she was able to find re-demption and restoration, and that led to her transform-ation on the inside and out. But she didn't know how to elo-quently express it.

"I guess you could sum it all up by saying I surrendered everything to God and had faith He would get us through it. And He did; He moved in more ways than we would have ever imagined, and we owe Him everything," she stated, matter-of-factly.

Eric studied her for a moment. This sounded nothing like the Renae he knew. "You really believe that?"

"I do," she assured him. "Do you think I could have gotten through the past year on my own strength? He's my anchor."

Eric took another moment before he began to release matters weighing on his heart. "You know, I've been doing some soul-searching myself, and I've come to the conclusion that I think our animosity toward each other is probably an indirect result of the way our parents treated us: the way Dad treated you and the way Mom did me. They may not have realized it, but I think they unknowingly created a bitter jealousy between the two of us. Sis, I don't want to fight with you anymore."

Renae gave careful thought to what he was saying. She'd always longed to have a strong relationship with her brother. What he said made complete sense to her. "That sounds about right. Eric, I don't want to fight with you, ei-ther. The night before you and Andy left, when you came to tell me Alex was waiting for me, I've held on to that moment as what defined our relationship since then. I want to forget about all the bad and only hold on to what is good. I'm so sorry if I keep reverting to being a jerk to you."

Eric studied her for a minute. The answer to his next question could likely define their relationship for the rest of their lives. He normally didn't feel well-received by most self-professed Christians, and here he stood in front of his biggest critic. He was nervous about her response. "So, can I ask you something?"

Renae put down the heavy pitcher of lemonade and asked God under her breath for the right words to say.

"How then, as a Christian, do you feel about me and Andy?"

Renae had to process the question, her feelings, and her response carefully. She wasn't sure if she was being challenged, or if perhaps Eric was looking for acceptance. It may have been neither. "Eric, I'm not sure if you're asking me to engage in a theological debate. If you are, we can sit down and scour Scripture and find answers together. But the straight answer to your question about my feelings for you and Andy, as a Christian...I love you. I love you both." Renae's throat began to once again tighten and the tears were welling in her eyes, her voice trembling. "The past few months I have grown so much spiritually. My relationship with God is the most important thing in my life, and I ask the Holy Spirit daily to help outpour the love of Jesus Christ that's in me. That isn't limited to people who believe like me. It's to everyone. Especially my brother."

Eric tried his best to hold back his tears. "Aren't you afraid people will say you're loving me to hell?"

"Nope, because I'm at peace with it. And besides, those same people have told me I'm on my way because I have a tattoo and drink a little." Renae smiled at her big brother. "I do pray for you, Eric. My prayer for you is the same prayer Dad had for you: that one day you would love God as much or even more than he did. Everything just falls in place where God sees fit after that, but not without work on our part. And believe me, sometimes it isn't easy. But it's worth it. I'm so glad you're my brother. Bet you never thought you would hear me say that."

Eric gave her a long-overdue hug. "I'm so glad you're my sister. But you need to lay off the donuts; your belly is getting in the way. I'm afraid you're going to knock *me* into next week with that thing."

"Shut up; it isn't that big!" she laughed.

Eric kissed her belly and told his nieces or nephews or niece and nephew that he couldn't wait to meet them. To his delight, one of the babies fluttered under his hand. After squeezing his sister one more time, he grabbed the lemonade and they joined Alex, Andy, and Maddy at the formal dining table to finish their brunch. Andy returned his hand to Renae's belly.

"You'll call if you have any problems while you're on your trip, right?"

"I will, but everything is going to be fine."

"I know, but if something happens, promise you'll call. I'll drop everything for this baby and be there in a flash."

"Ok," Renae agreed. "Thank you, Andy." She laid her hand on top of the one he had resting on her belly. She felt so lucky to have such a caring and skilled person in her life during what she already knew was a high-risk pregnancy. With Andy advocating for her and her babies, she knew they were in safe hands.

* * *

"Mommy, I'm nervous. I can't remember if I lead with my right foot or my left."

"Well, I like to remember that right is right, so start with your right. And if it's wrong, by the time you take your second step, no one will notice which one you started with and it won't matter anyways."

Renae and Maddy sat in the back seat of Renae's car while Alex drove them and Joshua down the long gravel driveway to a vintage and beautifully-decorated white barn seated on endless acres of open fields filled with ancient, grand oak trees. An outdoor seating area was covered by strands of yellow lights, and luscious white hydrangeas wrapped in greenery blanketed the wooden arches and trellises. The wedding ceremony would take place there, and the open doors to the barn revealed tables set for the reception. Alex drove the girls to a small cottage designated for the bridal party. He and Joshua would join the groomsmen in a ready-room in the back of the barn.

The men got out of the car and opened the doors for their ladies; Alex helped Maddy out while Renae grabbed their dresses and was helped out by Joshua. She gave him one last hug and congratulated him again before he became a married man.

"You are about to make Mandy one happy woman," she assured him.

"I hope so." Alex and Maddy walked around the car to join them.

"You ladies have everything?"

"We do." Renae smiled at Alex. They had two and a half hours before the wedding to get dressed, fix makeup, and take pictures. Aside from the hospital, Alex and Renae hadn't been away from each other that long since his accident. Joshua appreciated the way his two friends looked at each other. He hoped one day his bride would look at him the way Renae looked at Alex. He vowed he would give her every reason to do so.

After exchanging hugs and kisses, Renae and Maddy headed to the cottage to join the rest of the bridal party. Alex and Joshua got back into the car to park it behind the barn.

"If you have any doubts, speak now and we'll cruise out of here, no questions asked," Alex offered.

"No doubts. I'm ready to do this. I love her, Alex."

"Good." Alex pulled to the back of the barn and parked the car. "Josh, I need to thank you. Thank you for always believing in Renae and me, especially when we didn't believe in ourselves. And thank you for always throwing your support behind us. I'm sure there were times when you could have swept in and charmed her into being with you, but you didn't. And I appreciate the fact that you honored my marriage and relationship with her enough to not interfere, but to encourage. That means a lot to me. I really hope you and Mandy have an incredible life together. I'm sure Angie is looking down and cheering for the same thing. Love your wife, above all else. You two were created to complement each other and from what I've seen of the two of you so far, you're a perfect fit. I'm here for you, just like you've been there for me."

"Thanks, Alex. You and Renae are my family and I don't think I could have taken this step without your support. There's no one else I would rather have stand next to me tonight."

* * *

Renae let out a sigh of relief as another bridesmaid zipped her gown for her. After three alterations, she was scared her belly had further grown and she wouldn't be able to breathe in her dress. On the day it mattered most, it fit perfectly. She thought it was risky of Mandy to ask a pregnant woman to be in her wedding, but since Josh and Mandy felt so strongly about having Alex and Renae stand with them, she conceded. She walked over to Mandy, who was staring out the window, watching her future husband and his groomsmen joke around as they posed for the photographer. Renae followed her gaze and enjoyed the view with her.

"He's one in a million," Renae broke the silence.

"I agree. I can't believe I get to marry him."

"Oh, I was talking about Alex, but yeah, Joshua is great too," Renae smiled.

Mandy turned to her and smiled back.

"He's going to do his best to make you the happiest woman you could ever be, Mandy. Love him. Be patient with him. Show him kindness; he has such a kind spirit. I promise you he's going to show you fierce love in your best moments, and you'll see an even fiercer love in your worst. You're marrying a really good man, Mandy, and I'm so happy for you both."

"Thank you, Renae. That means so much coming from you." She turned her attention back to the scene outside her window and closed the curtain before her groom spotted his bride.

Within minutes, the photographers gathered the women and flower girls and led them outside. Although Renae did her best to be engaged with the bridal party, her attention was diverted to her husband, who was standing by a fence in the open field.

Alex needed a moment to himself to connect with God and to just be. He looked to the magnificent oak trees, whose limbs outstretched across the fields. He appreciated their beauty and admired their strength. Their roots dug deep and wide, enabling them to withstand the greatest storms. They provided shelter and familiarity to the creatures that depended on them. Between two of the massive oaks lay a large body of water, large enough for surrounding wildlife to visit or call home. As the sun began to shift, he felt the comfort of its warmth on his face, its rays creating a sparkling sea of diamonds in the gently-rippling water. He felt good to be alive. He felt at complete peace and immeasurably blessed. He closed his eyes as a familiar hand slid down his arm and grasped his fingers. Neither he nor Renae felt the need to speak. They just stood together and soaked in the view, recognizing how far they had come. They took a moment to appreciate creation in awe of their Creator.

"Hey, handsome," she finally spoke, "they're getting ready. We should get going."

Alex pulled her close for a hug. "You look absolutely amazing."

"I feel amazing," she replied.

That was music to Alex Murphy's ears.

* * *

Maddy lay in her grandmother's lap as the night progressed. Dinner had been served and Ruth was thinking about leaving early to get her little one to bed. Alex and Renae had their bags packed and were flying out on the red-eye, so they planned on staying until the end of the reception. Joshua asked Ruth to stay for just a few more minutes.

The bride and groom had a separate table to themselves, releasing the wedding party to sit with whomever they wanted. The Murphys sat with Ruth, Maddy, and Tabitha and Greg. Each time the server would bring a glass of champagne, he would serve Renae. And every time he served Renae, she slid it over to Tabitha, who gladly accepted it. She was so happy to see Renae and Alex together; tonight she was a little happier than usual.

"I like you. You make me laugh," Renae told her friend.

"We have to spend more time together!" Tabitha exclaimed.

"Promise me we will!"

Tabitha wrapped her arms around Renae and squeezed tight. Renae wasn't sure if she wasn't letting go because she loved her or because she'd passed out. It was because she loved her. She soon let go.

"I love your wife!" Renae shouted to Greg over the music.

"I'm pretty sure she loves you too, along with whatever champagne this is."

"I think it's prosecco, but I'm not one hundred percent sure."

"So, do you have names picked out for your baby?" Greg asked.

"Well," Alex answered, "if it's a girl, I was thinking

Cookie."

Renae choked on her water and drool dripped down her chin.

"Cookie? Is that because it's a thing?" Greg asked.

"Yeah, Renae can't get enough of them during this pregnancy."

Renae was laughing in her hands and tears were squeezing from the corners of her eyes.

"Like chocolate chip cookies? Oatmeal raisin cookies?"

"Sugar. She wants a sugar cookie all the time."

Renae looked at Alex and exhaled deeply. "Stop! I can't breathe." She turned and whispered to Tabitha the story of the cookie in the doctor's office. Tabitha screamed in delight and told her husband, who in turn laughed. "You know, I'll be really disappointed now if you have a boy or even if you have a girl and don't name her Cookie."

The couple's attention was diverted to Joshua, who was standing on the stage with a mic in hand. The guests took a moment to return to their seats and grab some more food or beverages. Millicent and some of the other nurses Mandy worked with took their seats at the table next to the Murphys.

"Hey, friends and family, I just want to take another moment and thank everyone for coming out tonight to celebrate what I like to recognize as the single best night of my life; the night I married the woman of my dreams. Mandy, I am so honored and humbled you agreed to spend the rest of your precious life with me. Thank you for saying yes, and I promise to make you one happy woman, for you deserve nothing less." The room erupted with sounds of "cheers!" "here, here!" and applause. Joshua continued.

"One year ago, a dear friend of mine, whom most of you here know, suffered a life-threatening accident. Prior to that accident, his family had suffered the huge loss of one of the greatest men I've ever known. But through his family's loss, he guided them through their suffering. In doing so, I witnessed love burst wide open. That loved carried him and his beloved wife, my best friend, through the hardest season of their lives together. They thought their hardest would be their divorce, but sometimes it's harder to work on something you really want than it is to give up on something you fear is getting in your way. Some of you know that over the course of nine months he faced nine surgeries, one he almost didn't make it through. After months of physical therapy, he was able to stand at my side today as my best man, something the doctors said wouldn't happen again." Alex leaned close to Renae and put his arms around her. She leaned her head back to kiss him. "Alex and Renae Murphy are a breathing, living testimony of how beautiful marriage was intended to be when you put the needs of others before your own, and when you decide to put God first. These two love each other fiercely. It's evident by the way they look at each other, by the little pouch Renae has in her lap, and by the sweet girl lying in her grandma's lap next to them. Mandy and I really wanted to recognize these two and their love for each other, because we found each other thanks to them. I want to thank you two for your endless support and love and for not only making me the godfather of sweet Miss Maddy, but also of the two Murphy babies coming soon!!"

Ruth looked at her daughter, shocked. "Twins?" Renae and Alex were showered with many hugs and kisses from nearby friends and family.

"In talking with Alex," Joshua continued, "he told me that one of the first things he wanted to do after his therapy was over was to dance with his wife. So, Mr. and Mrs. Murphy, I know your dad dedicated this song to you at your wedding, and it was also the last song you danced to. Please, will you both come to the dance floor and lead us in the next dance?"

This moment would go down as one of Renae's top five happiest moments of her life. Alex took her arm and escorted her to the dance floor as the DJ broke out into "Forever in Blue Jeans." Renae pressed her face against Alex's as she cried happy tears. She was overwhelmed with so much emotion; she didn't know if she wanted to drop to her knees and thank God or if she should just hold onto the love of her life and pray the moment never ended. They were soon joined by more friends and family, including the bride and groom.

"Hey guys, I'm sorry if I ruined the surprise about the twins. I was just really caught up in the moment," Joshua said as he held his smiling bride.

"It's all good,' Alex replied. "You can just make it up to us by paying their way through college."

"Deal."

"I'm gonna hold you to that, Joshua," replied Renae. She leaned her head on her husband's shoulder and watched the bride and groom dance together, gazing into each other's eyes, fully in love.

Renae realized her father had been right. She knew in her heart that men and women weren't created for all the conflict, but for companionship. She was abundantly blessed to have a second chance with the man fashioned for her. She looked forward to the future together, knowing God had a purpose for them, for He saw them through the unimaginable and now they were willing to be used by Him.

"I can't wait for tomorrow, and the next day, and the next day, and every day after that," Alex whispered in her ear.

"Me too, as long as it includes you."

They stopped dancing and stood on the dance floor in an embrace as the song came to an end and another one began. Joined heart and soul with her love, Renae was reminded of the Scripture given by Mr. Reeves the night she'd surrendered her life to God. It was from Ephesians 6:13.

 ' .... And having done all...stand.'

Reconciled and reunited with one another in an unbreakable love, they did exactly that. Stand.